THE DECISIONS WE MAKE

TARA MARLOW

To those who have shown me the way through.

"No one ever told me that grief
felt so much like fear."
- C.S Lewis

SAM. CHAOS.

JULY.

In the muted morning light, Sam Taylor stood at her lounge room window, shivering as the cold air seeped through gaps around the back door. Outside, Mother Nature hurled her fury at the world. The Antarctic blast ripped through the house. She'd been awake most of the night because of the storm, her emotions seesawing between worry, fear, and anger. The damn flapping of metal on the roof hadn't helped, either.

Sam ignored her mobile phone, ringing in the kitchen. Between the wind and the rain battering their tin roof, it was like standing in front of a cluster of speakers at a Bon Jovi concert, like the one she'd attended in her twenties. Conversation on the phone would be impossible. Besides, who the hell would call her this early on a Saturday morning?

Beyond the wood-framed window, the surf churned angrily. Sam could relate. How in hell did she end up with such a rundown house, one that was barely habitable on a clear day? She was so tired of always patching. What she wouldn't give for a house that didn't leak, howl or rattle. But she didn't have time to consider that. She needed to work out how to keep the rest of the house from flying away. The storm was forecast to continue for the rest of the day. Maybe even into tomorrow. Shit. She needed to secure the roof, then get to work. She just hoped the house was standing when she got home.

She thought of Marty, three doors down. Maybe it had been Marty calling? She looked back toward her phone. Sam constantly worried about her ninety-eight-year-old neighbour, but when she checked on her earlier, Marty assured her she was just fine. When she'd stopped in earlier, the woman was already curled up on her red velour couch with her knitting, her record player turning with some nostalgic tunes. Yes, she was just fine. As long as the power held. But how long would that be? It was always sketchy along their row of beach houses, especially in weather like this. But Marty was tough, and she reminded Sam she'd been through a lot worse than this.

Sam heard flapping again on the roof. Damn it. She wished she remembered to secure it before the storm. She couldn't afford to replace the roof. It would, once again, mean more patching. Her anger returned.

"Mum," yelled Bee amidst the pounding rain. Sam turned to see her seventeen-year-old daughter standing in the hall doorway, already dressed for work. Her black pants sat low on her slim hips. Her crisp white work shirt was pressed and tucked in, and her curly auburn hair was pulled back into a high ponytail, making her look closer to fourteen. Why was Bee always neater for work than she ever was for school? Crap. Bee being ready meant Sam was running late. She looked at her watch. It was almost eight-thirty. They were scheduled for work at nine at Georgina's café, and Sam still needed to get dressed. So much for repairs.

She ran her hand through her knotted hair, ravaged from the wind, and walked over the worn wooden floors toward Bee. Something struck the fence outside, grabbing her attention. Ned, their blue cattle dog, woke from his nap and yipped out a warning bark.

"Gee, thanks for the warning, Ned," she grumbled, wondering how he could sleep at all in weather like this. She walked to the kitchen's picture window. The twenty metres to the fence were littered with leaves and small branches. But further down, a large branch from the nearby gum tree lay across the fence. It wasn't a huge branch, thank goodness. But the tree it came from swayed in the wind like it was made of rubber.

"Geezus. This storm is a doozy. I hate to think what else may fly around in it. Getting to work is going to be a challenge," she said, but the words floated away.

"Mum!" Bee called again.

"Sorry. Yes?" Sam faced Bee. But hearing her daughter from where she stood was impossible. She picked up her phone from the kitchen counter and walked toward her. Bee's face mirrored her turmoil. They both hated storms. Storms changed lives.

"Georgina called." Bee was a metre away, and still she had to yell to be heard. "They're not opening the café today. The power is out in Orford."

"That means it'll be going out here soon," Sam muttered, looking down at her phone, seeing the missed call was from Georgina. No power. If it had already gone out in Orford, ten kilometres away, it was guaranteed to go out where they were in Fergus Bay. It made sense for the café to be closed. Business would be scarce. But she needed every penny she could earn right now. She couldn't think about the lost wages. She needed to focus on their safety first.

Focus, she reminded herself. No power in Orford. She needed to check on Jackson. Her grandfather-in-law lived alone ever since his wife, Beverlee, had passed away three years before. He was a cranky old goat, especially now he could no longer drive. Sam always made sure he had everything he needed. If Georgina said there was no power at the café, Jackson wouldn't have power either.

"Okay, so no work today," she yelled. Bee nodded, but Bee was scratching her left arm, her go-to when she was anxious. "I need to call…"

"I checked with Granddad. He's okay," Bee said, reading her mind. Oh good. One less thing to worry about.

"Thanks for doing that," Sam responded, her mind roiling in a million directions. She imagined Jackson getting up to make breakfast at his usual pre-dawn time and falling over a piece of furniture in the dark.

"Mrs Austin went over to check on him. He wasn't happy about that, but I asked if he has everything he needs. He said he did. Georgina said she'd call in to check on him herself later today. She knew you'd be worried." Sam placed her hand on her chest and smiled at Bee. Bee with her freckled face, already with eyeliner tracing her gorgeous blue eyes, returned the smile. But there was hesitancy there. Bee kept scratching. Sam reached over to soothe her before her arm started bleeding.

"Georgina also said old Mr. Collins is forecasting the storm to get worse. He reckons it's one of the worst he's seen, and not to get out in it if possible." Old Mr. Collins was the retired Parks and Wildlife ranger and knew weather like the back of his hand. If he said it was bad, everyone took note. Bee's scratching continued.

"It'll be okay, Bee," she said, hoping to reassure herself as much as her daughter. She took Bee into her arms, held her for a minute, hoping the stillness would calm them both. While she held Bee, she made a mental note to thank Georgina. She was grateful for her help. And Mrs. Austin's too. The Orford community looked out for each other. Sam stayed after her husband Zayden's death because of it. Sam pulled away from Bee, smoothed her hand over her irritated skin and smiled at her daughter, trying to appear like she had things together.

"I'm going to run down to Marty's... make sure she's okay," Bee shouted over the noise.

"Take Ned with you. Convince Marty that we should ride this out together. She didn't want to listen to me this morning, but she'll listen to you. Make sure she knows about the power outage in Orford, too."

There were eight beach houses, or shacks, as Tasmanians called them, on their stretch in Fergus Bay. She and Bee lived in the first house on the row for the last sixteen years. Marty, at number five, had lived in Fergus Bay for well over fifty. The rest were holiday houses, half of them owned by people from Hobart, the rest from the Australian mainland.

She knew Bee would convince Marty, but not without a fight.

Marty was as stubborn and independent as Jackson. Sam grabbed Bee's arm as she walked past.

"Pack a bag before you go. I'll bring it with me," she yelled to Bee. When her daughter nodded and turned, Sam headed toward her own bedroom to pack a small duffle bag, placing her phone on the battered red chest of drawers by the bedroom door.

She sorted through the mess of clothes piled on her bedroom chair, trying to find something clean to throw into a bag, her mind back to the potential damage on the house. The roof was only the start. There was a new leak in the laundry and the fence would need repairing now too. She knew the house needed renovations when they bought it, but now that time had run out. The house was falling apart around them. It was an older shack and while they tried to fix the main issues, Zayden's dreams for the house had been lofty, so the practical projects like the roof remained on the to do list. But Zayden, or Zed as he was known to most people, was no longer with them. This weather reminded her of that horrible day four years ago. While Bee scratched, Sam went into auto mode. It was better than facing reality. Sam threw her clothes forcibly into her duffle bag. It was better than punching a wall or screaming. Although both were damn tempting right now.

Storms were her nemesis. Storms swept your husband off their work boat and swallowed them into raging waters, only to release the body four days later. Storms, with howling winds and ten-foot waves, prevented rescue boats from searching for lost souls. Storms made communication impossible for distraught wives and children, holding on to any hope that their beloved would be found quickly. Storms created widows and left children without fathers.

When her tennis shoe missed the bag, she picked it up and through it hard against the wall, missing the window by mere millimetres. Great. That's all she needed. A broken window to add to the damn list.

Sam was terrified of storms, at least for the first dozen after Zed was killed. But now? Now, the fear was replaced by anger. She knew being angry was stupid. It did nothing to help the situation, or Bee's anxiety. As long as they knew the whereabouts of their loved ones, they were okay. The house could be repaired. Lives could not. She walked over and picked up the shoe and stuffed it back into her bag.

Her phone buzzed.

Hey. Got an alert about the weather. U okay?

Brooke, her best friend and Marty's granddaughter, was vigilant about keeping an eye on them. She knew storms were a trigger for both Bee and her.

Checked on Marty. She seems okay. Brooke added.

Sam shot off a quick response.

We're fine. Heading to Marty's to ride it out together. Checked on her earlier and yep, she's okay. We'll text you later. x

"I'm off to Marmy's," Bee yelled, poking her head into her mother's bedroom, using the nickname she used their friend down the track. Sam looked up from her phone.

"Aunty Brooke?" Bee asked. Sam nodded. "She texted me too. Anyway, I'm going. My bag is by the back door. I'll text you when I get over there. Ned's sitting at the back door ready to go."

"Marty won't be happy with us staying. She's too independent for her own good. Be prepared," Sam said.

"I know. But she won't deny me." Sam laughed. Wasn't that the truth? Marty and Bee were close, like two peas in a pod, just born seventy years apart. Bee learned how to knit, sew, crochet, and cook from Marty's patient teaching. In exchange, Bee taught Marty how to use an iPad. Now the older woman hosted her own online book club. If Sam had suggested they ride the storm out, Marty would take them in and act like she was doing them a favour. But if Bee asked, she'd be laying out the towels and guest soap, and Sam would not be surprised if a cake would be cooling by the time she made it over there.

"Be careful. Stuff is flying everywhere. And bundle up. It's freezing. I wouldn't be surprised if we get sleet with all of this, too. I'll be there soon," she yelled. Bee waved and turned toward the back door.

Sam would still worry about their house, but she'd be able to keep an eye on the roof from down the track. And they'd be safer at Marty's. Her house was a million times more comfortable and worthy of a feature in Home Beautiful. And if she was honest, she worried more about Marty than she ever did about Jackson, despite the woman's need for independence. Marty hated people treating her like she was a frail old thing. She was far from that. The woman was more agile than

Sam most days. Maybe she would be okay with them staying with her? Sam was probably anticipating pushback when there would be none. And really, it would almost be like a mini vacation being at Marty's. She needed to stop worrying, but the constant flapping on the roof was a reminder that this was far from a vacation.

She shot a quick text to Lachie, Zed's best friend and Bee's godfather, letting him know they were heading to Marty's. She didn't need him to worry. He was most likely out in it, rescuing someone from a flooded or damaged house. He was a hero to many in the area, she and Bee included. She'd ask him later to put them on his work list for when the weather eased off. But knowing Lachie was in demand as a custom builder, the timing sucked. And yet, the roof needed to be tackled. She couldn't put it off any longer. Especially if rain got under the metal sheeting. Then, the roof would be well and truly toast. She hated to ask him. She always felt like she was taking advantage of his generosity and skill, but Lachie promised he was there for them whenever they needed him. Now they needed him more than ever. The thought of dipping into her savings made her heart race, but she didn't have a choice. God, if Lachie hadn't been there for them, she didn't know where she'd be.

She knew the shack needed some serious love, but it was love she couldn't afford. Orford was their nearest opportunity for work, and it was only a small fishing village at that. Any hope of finding a well-paying job in the area was equivalent to buying a lottery ticket every week and expecting to win every time. She needed a consistent income. The two jobs she had paid okay, but the hours were sporadic. If she was honest with herself, she had very little chance of finding something nearby that paid enough for the renovations she so desperately needed.

When large hail stones began pinging against her window, she screamed out, hoping to expel some of the frustration. She was not going to let this storm get the best of her. She'd been the victim of a 'once in a lifetime' storm before. No way, Mother Nature. Not this time.

2

BROOKE. ORDER.

JULY.

Brooke Choi-Scott sat at her ex-husband's dining room table, eating what could only be described as a five-star gourmet meal. She would have been fine with just the wild mushroom soup, but the braised lamb shanks, sauteed Brussels sprouts, and mash potato, flavoured tenderly with garlic, could not be missed. Dinner with Dae and his husband, Jase, had become a standing fortnightly date, and it was something Brooke was thankful for. Not just for the food, since she mainly existed on salads and protein bars, but also for the company. But this meal that Jase had slaved over, would have her in a food coma for days. Add in the three bottles of wine between them, and it was unlikely her early morning surf was going to happen. Neither was going home.

Luckily, the granny flat out the back was hers whenever she needed it. She always said she wouldn't stay, but their dinners usually involved copious amounts of wine, and Dae and Jase lived closer to the beach than she did. Since she always went surfing on Sunday morning at Mona Vale, one of the less busy beaches of the north side of Sydney, she often caved.

"Why don't you want to take on another doctor?" grilled Dae. His eyes were dark and boring into hers, his cheekbones protruding sharply in the soft light. He'd been called Will Yun Lee's doppelgänger more than once in both looks and charm. But right now, that charm was lost on her.

She'd been married to Dae for five years, divorced for ten, so she knew all of Dae's forms of manipulation. Theirs was a marriage of convenience, intending to steer his very conservative Korean parent's focus away from his love life. When they divorced, he'd told his parents he was simply unlucky in love rather than being honest and telling them he was gay. His parents were heartbroken when he and Brooke divorced, but even now, Dae had yet to introduce them to Jase. He wasn't in any rush to expose his truth to them. Instead, he lived his life in Australia as he wanted, while his parents remained in distant South Korea.

Tonight, however, Dae had been hounding her about decisions with her medical practice. *Her* practice. Dae was her employee, one of the three doctors on staff. Brooke tried to change the subject, but Dae kept at it like a dog with a bone. She was getting impatient with his persistence. When Jase re-entered the room, he scolded Dae for his rudeness.

She loved Jase as much as she loved Dae. He was a lovely match for her ex-husband. And he wasn't bad to look at either. She could see what had first attracted Dae, given Jase was the poster boy for Australian tourism, right down to the Hemsworth 'just back from the beach' look. Now he was like a brother to her, and a good balance for her ex-husband. Somehow he kept Dae calm. Most of the time, anyway.

"Ignore him, Brooke. You know what he's like," Jase said, pouring more wine into her glass before returning to the kitchen. God, she needed the wine to deal with Dae tonight.

"So? What's your hesitation in adding another doctor?" Dae pushed. She really didn't want to keep talking about this. While she had consulted Dae many times about business decisions with her Epping practice, this was one decision she was firm on. The why was fuzzy, even for her, but something told her it was not the right time to bring on more staff. Even if Dae's argument about the practice being overwhelmed was valid.

"I'm just not comfortable with it right now," she said.

"But why?" he argued. She looked to Jase when he walked back into the room, carrying a tray. It was laden with a small plate of Yaksik, Korean sweet rice cakes, three coffee cups and a French press she knew would be filled with freshly roasted decaf coffee.

"Help, Jase," she begged, feeling bad for him putting up with shop talk all night. Usually they'd move on to more interesting, more inclusive topics like books or music, but tonight, Dae was determined to get his way.

"Dae, honey, you need to let it go. It's Brooke's decision. If you want to be a control freak, maybe you should open your own practice?" Jase advised, placing the tray on the very end of the dining table. Brooke held back a laugh at Jase's words.

"Thank you, Jase," she said primly. "He's right, Dae. If you want things your way, maybe it's time to open your own practice. We've talked about this. You wanted to be fluid in your professional life. I wanted my own practice. What's changed?" She knew she was taunting him and also knew he wouldn't take the bait. The difference was Jase. After buying a house together three years ago, then marrying last year, Dae was happy with his stable life. He just wanted more control. But Dae would never admit that out loud. He was just as stubborn as she was. Brooke knew she'd be lost without Dae in her practice, but she agreed with Jase. When Dae didn't answer her question straight away, she took it as a sign to move away from the subject.

Her phone pinged beside her.

"A text from Bee. They're dealing with a massive storm down there," she said quickly, picking up her phone.

"Is Marty okay?" Dae asked worriedly.

"What do you think? She's probably curled up on the couch with her knitting, distracting Bee with stories about her world travels," she laughed, then read Bee's message out loud.

Just checking in. Staying at Marmy's. She 'threw together' a roast dinner in the old stove while Mum has been running around like a chicken without a head. But we're all okay. Power is out, but fires are roaring, and we have blan-kets galore. Marmy says it's like an old-fashioned sleepover and she's moved on to telling us ghost stories.

Brooke smiled. Even though Bee wasn't Marty's biological great-granddaughter, she was treated as such, right down to their pet names. Bee struggled early on to call her Marty, so Marmy stuck. In return, she went from Beverlee, her biological great-grandmother's name, to simply Bee.

"How's Sam dealing?" Jase asked, standing at the end of the table pouring coffee, his expression matching Dae's worried look. They knew how Sam reacted to storms.

"The usual. She has been in go-mode. Marty will settle her soon enough." She felt better getting the text from Bee. She'd been texting Sam all day, but Sam's responses were quick and to the point. Normal for Sam. Bee gave her the behind-the-scenes story. The storm was nasty, but they were all at least together and safe. Brooke sent a quick response to Bee, then placed her phone back on the table.

"How about you, Jase? Is my mother driving you crazy?" Brooke teased, relieved to know Sam, Bee and Marty were settled for the night.

"Nope. Your mother adores me, and I adore her," he said, smiling over at her before taking his seat. Jase was her mother's right-hand man in her very successful catering company. Her mother played matchmaker between her ex-son-in-law and new chef, then boasted about her matchmaking skills. Thankfully, she'd never tried those matchmaking skills on Brooke. Brooke's mother knew about their marriage of convenience, and given her own Korean upbringing, Brooke's mother helped them navigate Dae's parent's strict beliefs. But through it all, she loved Dae as if he were her own son. And now Jase was an extension of that.

Jase passed her the plate of Yaksik, knowing it was Brooke's favourite. He made it whenever they had dinner, using her mother's recipe.

"It's a love fest of epic proportions," said Dae, his argumentative demeanour finally shelved. "If I didn't know better, I think she loves Jase more than she ever loved me." Brooke found that hard to believe.

Brooke had met Dae at Orientation Week at the University of New South Wales. He'd arrived from South Korea only the week before. While he spoke enough English to get by, Brooke caught him looking dazed and confused at the Korean Club table. Brooke, who spoke fluent Korean, courtesy of her mother, helped Dae navigate uni, and before long, Sydney life. After a year of dorm living, they became roommates. Brooke loved living with Dae because he cooked for them every night. They ate like kings with the allowance his parents provided, but he was frugal, too. They scoured farmers' markets and only bought meat when it was deeply discounted. Her mother gave them whatever left over ingredients she wasn't using in her catering business, which helped too. Dae's cooking every night allowed her to overlook his messy habits. But they were good days, living together. Now, despite everyone's best efforts to teach her, she still hated cooking.

"You're staying tonight. Right?" Jase asked her later, after they'd cleaned up the kitchen. Dae stood at the counter, finishing his coffee, as Jase packed up the leftovers.

"If that's okay? I don't think I should drive with all the wine you guys plied me with. If I didn't know better, I'd think Dae was trying to get me drunk, so I'd change my mind about bringing in another doctor."

Jase looked pointedly at Dae. "Told you she'd see right through it. And yes, it's always okay for you to stay. Hell, you could move in with us and it'd be okay with me." Jase came over and kissed her cheek.

"Let's not go that far. I've lived with her before, remember? She's way too neat for us," Dae said. While Dae and Jase's house was clean, it was always messy. Brooke thought of it as a loving mess. There were novels piled on tables and the morning's newspaper pulled apart in sections on the floor by the French doors, as if they'd sat in the sunlight to read the paper there together that morning. It could all be tidied within minutes, but that wasn't important to them. Their home was lived in. It reminded her of her grandmother's house in Fergus Bay. The house exuded love. Her house in Cheltenham was more... disciplined.

"Well, I'm heading for bed. Are you off early tomorrow? Sunday surf and all that?" Dae asked her.

"Yep, and if my head isn't too foggy, I'll be gone by five," she said, loading the last plate into the dishwasher.

"Fuck! You can have that," laughed Jase. "I'm sleeping until noon! First weekend off in a month. I'm planning on a lazy day tomorrow." Brooke chuckled, then walked to the couch to grab her handbag. She didn't need to bother with an overnight bag. She kept a spare swimsuit, toiletries, and a change of clothes in the flat, for the nights she stayed.

"Be safe out there," said Dae, kissing her cheek goodnight. Jase reached over and kissed her other cheek. Then, together, Dae and Jase headed to their bedroom. Brooke stared after them, feeling something she couldn't quite put her finger on. Was it jealousy? No. She was happy for Dae and Jase. Happy Dae finally found his person. For a while, she wondered if he'd ever live to see the day to find love.

Stepping out into the backyard, the cool chill swept over her face. She looked up, saw the sliver of a moon, and pined for the cluster of stars which always blanketed Fergus Bay. It would be weeks before she got back down to Tasmania. Sighing, she walked into the granny flat, thankful Jase had put the heat on.

In the small bathroom, Brooke brushed her teeth and considered her life. Sure, she'd married the guy from university, just as her friends had done, but she had no romantic feelings for Dae. Their marriage was a pact between two friends. Besides, she wanted to focus on her career.

She thought about a dinner she'd had with Dae and Jase a few months prior, when Dae and Jase shared their plans to adopt. When Dae looked at her pointedly as he spoke the words, it felt like a punch to the stomach. He knew the decisions she had made long ago. But she was happy for them. They were both great with kids and she'd told herself it was too late for her to have children. It was easier to say that. She had her chance for a family many moons ago. Thinking about the past, and what could have been, was too painful. Much too painful.

Shaking her head, she reminded herself of everything she had in her life. It was a habit she got into when she started down the rabbit hole of self-pity. She had a distinguished career. A successful practice where she loved everyone who worked in it, even Dae on his bad days. She had Jase, whom she loved like a brother. Parents vibrantly living their own lives. A spirited grandmother, who was also her mentor. And two best friends who were there for her through thick and thin. Merritt, a property developer living in Melbourne, who was unfortunately married to a complete git. And Sam, living in Fergus Bay with Brooke's gorgeous goddaughter. Yes, she told herself, she had a good life.

She washed her face, took her hair out of its ponytail, and downed two aspirin with a glass of water. She refilled the glass then carried it to the bedroom. She set her alarm for the morning and crawled into bed, thinking of Dae and Jase again. They had something special. A relationship that only came along once, twice, if you were lucky. She'd missed her chance. She had to be content with her life now. She made her choices. She lived the family life through others. Dae and Jase. Sam and Bee. She had love in her life, unconditional love from her parents and her grandmother Marty, but the feeling she'd felt when she watched Dae and Jase head to their bedroom lingered. Loneliness crept in. Was this all there was to her life?

Turning off the side lamp, she questioned, not for the first time, if she made the right decision seventeen years before.

3

SAM. ISOLATED.

JULY.

Sam stepped into the bitter wind after locking up the last house on the row. The temperature had dropped significantly while she checked for damage. Most of the owners came for just a month or so each year, so they gave Sam the keys to their houses to manage. She wanted to make sure everything was secure. Now, back to Marty's, she felt the cold down to her bones. It had to be hovering around two or three degrees Celsius, and it was forecast to drop even further overnight.

After a quick knock, she opened the front door, hung her jacket on the hook, and found Marty and Bee curled up together under a mock lambswool blanket. They were chatting away like two old hens, while their fingers flew in and around crochet hooks. Sam imagined burrowing her way in between them, hoping to get warm, but she still had things to do. She hovered over the wood stove, her back relishing the heat for a moment. Ned had a prime spot, she mused, curled up at Marty's feet. He was one spoiled dog, that's for sure. Despite being a cattle dog, he'd never rounded up any cattle in his life. Marty stuck one foot out from under the blanket and gave him a rub. Bloody dog.

He knew where his bread was buttered. Turning around to face the heat, Sam rubbed her hands over the woodstove and noticed they would need more wood to get through the night.

"I'm going out to the woodshed. I'll be back in a little while. Keep the fire stoked, will you Bee?" When Bee agreed, Sam headed to the backdoor. She grabbed Bee's black and yellow striped beanie and put on her bright yellow jacket once again. She took a deep breath and braced herself for the elements.

The rain lashed sideways; the wind cutting through her jacket. The storm had intensified again in just a few minutes. It was bound to be another rough night. She could deal if the winds were northerly, but they'd stayed from the southeast. They lived closer to Antarctica than the Great Barrier Reef, and right now, it felt like bloody Antarctica. With the power out, it would not get better until she got more wood.

Thankful that the house blocked the brunt of the wind, she dashed across the courtyard to unlock the woodshed. A sudden gust ripped the door from her hands, smashing it against the wall, the sound ricocheting like a gunshot. She grabbed the door and secured it to the hook with a bungee cord, then stepped into the shed. Should she try the wheelbarrow? Realising it would be another thing the wind would toy with, Sam picked up the metal bucket tucked behind the door. She'd take multiple trips. They'd already gone through a lot of wood with the two stoves burning, and she didn't want to make this trek again in the middle of the night. She filled the bucket with as many logs as she could, then dashed to the woodbin by Marty's back door, thankful it was protected by the wide veranda. She finished the job quickly and relocked the shed. Then she secured the outdoor table and chairs. Looking around, she saw Marty's chickens were smart enough to roost, but Sam did a head count in the hen house just to be sure. All were accounted for and safe, so she headed back inside. Ned greeted her at the door, tail wagging, happy to see she was okay. She leaned down and patted him, then as she hung her jacket once more, he trotted back to the warm lounge room. Bloody dog.

"Dinner will be just a bit longer. Why don't you sit down and get under the blanket, Sam? You look to be freezing," suggested Marty.

Sam stood at the woodstove again, trying to get warm. She turned to heat her backside and shook her head.

"I'm okay here. I'll sit in a little while." Marty reached out and squeezed her arm. The woman was Sam's height, but Sam guessed she'd shrunk a little in her old age. Her hair, a glorious wave of silver, was cut into a chic asymmetrical bob. Her face was clear of makeup, save for the bold pink lipstick she often wore. Her nails, impeccably done, were painted a matching bold pink. Tonight, she wore black slacks, a long sleeve black tunic top, and a soft grey wrap she'd most likely knitted herself, a colour that brought out her sea-green eyes. She also wore the UGG slippers she and Bee had splurged on last Christmas for her.

"You've been moving for hours. Rest up Sweet Pea," Marty chided, settling back down to the couch next to Bee. Bee handed her the other half of her blanket.

"Thank you, Bee," she said, covering her legs. "And thank you for all you did today, Sam." Sam didn't see the need for the gratitude, but she nodded anyway.

"It's a good thing you never had that old cast-iron stove removed from the kitchen when you renovated," Sam said. Between the two stoves, the house was cosy. She was finally defrosting.

"I did that on purpose. I can't tell you how many times the power has gone out. That stove has been used a great deal in the last fifty years," she said, resuming her crocheting.

"You used to hide Christmas presents in there," teased Bee.

"And how do you know about that? That's my favourite hiding place," Marty said, pulling the blanket away from Bee in mock punishment. A brief tug of war ensued.

"Aunty Brooke showed me. She said she discovered it years ago but said nothing."

"Well, I'll have to get on to her about that, won't I?" Marty said.

"I hope you checked it before you put the roast in there," voiced Sam, relieved when Marty nodded. She was teasing, but Sam noticed the older woman was becoming a little forgetful lately. Sam thought that if she ever made it to ninety-eight, she'd most likely be in a nursing home, dribbling into her pudding. The way her stress levels were, Sam had serious doubts she'd even make it past seventy.

A phone buzzed. Bee looked down at her phone beside her, then looked to Sam and shook her head. Wasn't her phone. Sam walked over to the kitchen counter and picked up hers. A message from Georgina. She opened the message.

"Oh shi…. shiz," she'd been reprimanded by Marty enough times to know never to swear in her presence. But this news was worthy.

"What's wrong?" asked Bee, concerned.

"Not good news. The bridge is out. Ah…" she scanned more of the message. "Washed away."

"Oh dear. That's not good at all," said Marty. "Who's the message from? I can call Bill Bishop. He'll know what's what." Bill Bishop was the landowner closest to the bridge and a third generation Tasmanian. His grandfather had built the original bridge that connected Fergus Bay to Orford. It was an old rickety wooden bridge now, barely stable enough to get the traffic across, so it was no surprise it was gone. The council had been sitting on their laurels about the repairs, ignoring inquiries from the Fergus Bay homeowners, along with others who used the road regularly. But now, with the bridge washed away? That would cause some serious issues for anyone living this side of the bridge. They were cut off from Orford. It would take close to an hour, driving via the horrendously corrugated forest road, to get anywhere that resembled civilisation. Sam tried not to panic.

"Don't worry Sweet Pea. There's still a way out," Marty insisted, rising to make her phone call. Yes, but Sam knew her vehicle wasn't up for the road conditions in the best of times, and Marty's truck wasn't either. Crap. What were they going to do?

She heard Marty's voice in the background, but Sam was trying to work out a plan. Suddenly, she felt exhausted and overwhelmed and, looking at Bee, noticed she was back to scratching her arm. Yeah, she felt anxious too. Their house falling apart was one thing. The bridge collapsing was a whole other worry. As if to stress the point, a roar of thunderous wind whipped through the gum trees. Geezus.

"Hello? Hello?" She turned to find Marty staring at her phone. "Lines must be down." Marty was the only shack that still had a landline. Sam looked down at her phone. Two bars but only about 30% power. She looked to Bee, asking the status of her phone telepathically.

"I have two bars and about 60% power. You can use my phone to call him back, Marmy." She unlocked her phone and handed it to Marty.

"Oh, thank you, Bee," Marty said. "He started saying something about the bridge. But that's when we got cut off. While I do this, Sweet Pea, would you check the roast in the oven? Be sure to use the mitts. The handles on that stove get awfully hot."

Sam walked into the vast kitchen and paused while she slowly took it in. She loved this space. Somehow, it calmed her, which was ironic because Sam would never consider herself a cook. Still, it was a dream kitchen. Marty had all the mod cons, but the kitchen retained its cosy feel. The old cast-iron stove, tucked into the original fireplace, contributed to that. On the stove's left side were dual ovens. On the right, the fire pit. There was a special tool that was used to remove the covers over the fire pit, and once removed, you could place a cast-iron skillet or Dutch oven into the openness, and it would cook directly from the flames below. Tonight, though, only the dual ovens were being used.

Sam first checked the fire pit. They'd use this, along with the wood stove in the lounge room, to keep the house warm overnight. Seeing the fire was low, she called to Bee to bring her a smaller piece of wood from the wood stack. She grabbed the oven mitts and opened the first oven. Sam reached in and pulled the pan out, turning to place it on the wooden chopping board. She lifted the foil, releasing the intoxicating aroma of rosemary and garlic. In the centre sat a half a leg of lamb surrounded by root vegetables. Her mouth watered. She tested a potato, gliding the fork through the skin with ease. Perfect. Of course it was. Bee entered the kitchen with two small logs in her hand, while Sam pulled out the baked Yorkshire puddings Marty had also made. They, too, were cooked to perfection.

"Wow, that looks amazing. Why don't you cook like that, Mum?" Bee asked, knowing the answer.

"Because that would mean I'd need time to make a roast from scratch. Not to mention knowing how to make one."

"I love coming to Marmy's house," Bee sighed, leaning over to smell the roast.

"I do too. Just not during a raging storm without power and now, apparently, without a bridge. I'm not sure what that means for us, Baby Bee." She could hear Marty asking the right questions to Bill Bishop and a lot of responses like 'okay' and 'yes, of course'. Sam knew that for her and Bee it would not be good news if the bridge wasn't replaced quickly. But Sam knew the council wouldn't act, since it only affected eight houses and a handful of farms. She'd be surprised if it'd get on the council agenda at all. Their track record with repairing roads in the area was abysmal.

The reality of the last 24 hours hit her. She slowly leaned back against the kitchen island in defeat. The destroyed bridge had her mind running through a series of negatives. It meant no school for Bee since she couldn't get to Orford for the bus. It also meant no work for either of them at Georgina's café, or shifts at the pub for Sam either, since both were in Orford. It all equated to no money coming in. Their lives had just screeched to a halt in one fell swoop.

The forest road was unforgiving, and no match for her ancient Toyota Corolla. The car was barely hanging on as it was. The local mechanic had recently told her she was overdue to replace her fan belt by about six months, and her alternator needed replacing as well. He had mentioned something else, but since it was a couple of thousand dollars to do the work, she'd zoned out on him. She figured she could use Marty's truck if she really needed supplies, but it was just about as old as Sam. She doubted it would make it over the forest road either.

Things were dire. And to make matters even worse, she was out of coffee.

4

BROOKE. UNRAVELLING.

JULY.

The sun was barely up when Brooke arrived at Mona Vale for her Sunday surf. Her head was foggy, more from the lack of sleep than too much wine, but the briskness of the winter morning revived her.

She grabbed her surfboard from the top of her ten-year-old Subaru and hit the sand. The waves were good, robust enough for a decent surf, but not so rough that her body would feel pounded later.

Diving into the icy blue waters, the world gained some clarity. Some mornings, she used her surf time to think through the week. Other days, like this one, she simply sat on her board and meditated. Watching the surfers around her catch wave after wave, there was an order to things. She took her turn, moved when she needed to, but after a few rides, she decided to just sit, and be one with the morning vibe. She moved her fingers back and forth through the water; the motion calming the thoughts that wouldn't disappear.

Her mind drifted back to her thoughts from the night before. Her life wasn't bad. She had everything she planned for. Her medical degree. A medical practice catering to the Korean community. She'd even bought a house on her own in an affluent area, close to her parents, but far enough to give each other some distance. At Sydney's house prices, that was almost unheard of for a single woman, but her grandmother and father had taught her well with their frugal ways.

She'd planned her life out since she was ten. But lately, something kept nagging at her. Was it that stupid biological clock people talked about? No. She'd made peace with that. She wanted children at one point, but nearing forty, she'd ruled that out for herself. She couldn't imagine sharing her life with anyone anymore. That dream had passed.

She shook the thoughts from her head, gazed up, and took stock of everything around her. Be present, she told herself. She felt the salt wrinkling the ends of her fingertips. The seagulls around her either dived into the water, finding their catch, or they followed people on the beach looking for a handout. To her far right, the waves zipped along the shoreline, the sound echoing as the crest-line reached the end of the beach. The sound reminded her of Fergus Bay. She was home-sick, she realised. Homesick for Fergus Bay.

She drove home a little while later, shivering from the cold air, thankful she wore her blue hoodie and an old pair sweatpants, since the heater in her car was acting up. She'd have to get that looked at. Sydney was cold in the winter. It didn't help that her hair was still wet from the cold shower she took to wash the salt off her skin.

After parking her Subaru in her driveway, she unbuckled the surfboard from the roof rack, grabbed her wetsuit, damp towel, phone, and keys, and walked to the backyard. She leaned her board against her blue wooden shed and wrangled her wetsuit over the clothesline, tossing the rest on the grass in the shade. She'd hose the board and wetsuit down, then take them back to Dae's when she went by her parent's house later.

Before she could grab the hose, her phone rang. She wanted to ignore it but saw Sam's name on the caller id. The storm was still on her mind.

"Hey Sam. How are you all doing?" Brooke asked, scanning her board for areas that needed re-waxing. She pulled a strand of stiff hair away from her ear.

"Not good. Worst of the storm is through. But now we're cut off," said Sam. Brooke immediately gave Sam her full attention.

"What do you mean, cut off? Are you okay? How's..."

"Marty's fine," Sam broke in. Brooke released her breath. She didn't know what she'd do if anything happened to Marty. She hated being so far away from them, especially if she needed to be there to help. It was only a two-hour flight from Sydney to Hobart, but it still took half a day to reach them.

"You could even say Marty's over the moon. Seems to be in her element in a crisis," Sam said sarcastically, but then sighed. "We're all okay. Just cut off."

"What does that even mean?" Brooke asked again. She tried to keep the rising impatience from her voice.

"It means that the bridge between us and Orford has been washed away. They're saying the storm is a once in a generation event. Marty had a great laugh about that. I guess they weren't thinking of people her age when they made that statement." Sam was rambling, which meant things were bad. Really bad.

"When will the bridge be rebuilt?" Brooke asked, but she knew the answer. She'd heard enough of Marty's grumblings about the inept local council.

"Probably never. So, unless we go the long way around, we're stuck." Brooke knew Sam's twenty-year-old Corolla wouldn't make it on the 4WD track. Marty's truck might fare better, but it was older than they were. Damn it. Why hadn't they replaced their vehicles? But Brooke knew why. For Marty, she was stubborn and frugal. She claimed the truck ran just fine. For Sam, it was about money.

"How can I help?" Brooke asked.

"Unless you can work on the council and get the bridge fixed tomorrow, not much."

"What if I sent you money to get a new vehicle? Look, you can pay me back later. I know you're strapped, and this is a way I can help. And before you really bitch at me... because I can hear you bucking at my offer, you know your car won't survive the forest track." Brooke's

Subaru was just as old as Sam's Corolla, but Brooke could afford to maintain her car. Sam struggled just to keep petrol in hers.

"Yes. Tell me something I don't know. But even if I took you up on the offer, how am I supposed to get that new car? And how am I supposed to repay you? Because with the bridge being out, I have no income. I can't get to work. Bee can't even get to school…" Sam's voice was tight and high pitched.

"Oh, right. I'm sorry, I didn't even think about that."

"Yeah. Look, I'm sorry too. I didn't mean to snap at you. We're just flailing here. Marty was on with Bill Bishop. You know who he is, right? The farmer closest to the bridge?" Sam continued. "Yes, you know who he is. Anyway, he's trying to arrange a flying fox to get across the river."

"What the hell is a flying fox?" Brooke shrieked, envisioning small fruit bats flying around their head. And how the hell did bats fit into this situation?

"It's like a zip line, but it's a platform that relies on gravity to pulley people across. It's used a lot in flooding situations on the mainland."

"Oh. Well, that's kind of cool, actually. Although I can't imagine Marty zooming across on one, can you?" Brooke asked.

"She was the one who suggested it to Bill Bishop! Anyway, he and some engineers he knows are working it out. Orford is rallying around, organising pickups for us once it's built, offering to take us wherever we need to go. But that won't go on forever."

"That's something at least," Brooke said, her mind whizzing. She was trying to work out what she could do and how fast she could get down there.

"Yeah, it's been a busy morning already. The storm hasn't let up yet. It's downgraded at least, but according to old Mr. Collins, it's not going away for a couple of days. Phone lines are sporadic. It's a good thing, Lach…" Sam hesitated. They had an unwritten rule to never speak Lachlan's name.

"It's okay. What did he do?" Sam sighed on the end of the line. Brooke hated to add to Sam's angst. Lachlan and Brooke had history.

He was a topic they usually avoided, which sometimes got tricky considering how engrained Lachlan was in Sam's life.

"He left a generator for Marty when he did her renovations. He was worried about her if she ever lost power. Marty said she forgot about it until he called to check on us this morning. He'd even checked it last week to make sure it was running okay. Kind of saved the day because our phones were switched to airplane mode to conserve power."

"I'm glad he did that," Brooke said, suddenly desperate to change the subject away from Lachlan. "Do you need me to come down?"

"No. But I have something else I need to talk to you about. Our trip to Sydney." Sam and Bee always planned a trip to visit Brooke during the July school holidays. It was something they all looked forward to and with Bee graduating high school soon, this particular trip was going to be epic.

"I'm not sure we can come. I checked on the house this morning. Part of the roof of the house is gone. So is the fence, which isn't as important, but it keeps Ned contained when we're not around. I have water damage in the sunroom as well, and I think the lightning zapped my fridge. I was hoping it would last another year or two, but that idea is out the window…"

"Oh, shit Sam. But no, I get it. I'm disappointed and I know Bee will be too, but I understand why. Look, let me send you some money to help with the repairs. At least help you with the fridge. The repairs are going to cost enough."

"Lachie said he'd cover the repairs, and you know him, he's always doing the labour for free." Brooke itched to correct Sam that she really didn't know how Lachie was anymore. She hadn't spoken to him in seventeen years, not counting the brief hello at Zed's funeral. She let the comment go.

"Okay, but what about the rest? Please let me help." Whenever they visited her in Sydney, Sam paid only for the airfares, while Brooke covered everything else. Sam fought her on it at first, until Brooke showed Sam her bank account. Brooke laughed when Sam's eyes bulged at the balance. But, as frugal as she was, there were some things she didn't hesitate spending money on, like their trip to Sydney and helping Sam whenever she could.

"If you can help organise a fridge, I'd appreciate that," Sam finally said. "Then I can focus on getting my car fixed."

"What's wrong with your car? Other than it needing a gracious burial," Brooke teased.

"You mean retirement. I only wish it had the running capacity Marty seems to have."

"Sam seriously, if you need money for your car, I can send that to you too. But before you go off on me, I'll at least organise the new fridge. Leave that one problem with me," Brooke said, heading inside to make a note of it, so she wouldn't forget. "I need to wax my board, then I'll get that organised for you." Brooke scribbled the reminder on the whiteboard on her fridge, then went back outside and sat on the back step.

"Now, how's Marty? Is she okay? Or is she in a baking frenzy?"

"Totally. I don't think I've eaten so much cake in my life! Or muffins or bread. She enveloped us like five-star guests," Sam admitted. Brooke could image Sam standing there, skinny as ever, holding her bloated stomach.

"God. Were there chocolates on the pillows too?" Brooke teased, pulling weeds next to the step as they chatted, the sun warming her body.

"No, but I wouldn't be surprised if she thought about it..." said Sam. Brooke laughed at that. She could imagine it clearly. When Marty had guests, she was in her prime. But knowing she was in a baking frenzy, Brooke knew she was extremely stressed, too. Her grandmother loved to bake. But with the amount of baking Sam was talking about, Brooke was abundantly clear on how serious things were in Fergus Bay.

When Brooke finally hung up with Sam, she gathered her thoughts while she waxed her surfboard. After her shower, she'd do some research and organise a new fridge. Then she'd call Pete at the service station and arrange for the bill for Sam's repairs to be sent to her. Sam would have a conniption about it. But it was the least she could do. God, she hated being so far away.

. . .

In the shower, the blow of the rest of the news hit her hard. Cancelling the long weekend was a major disappointment. She needed those weekends with Sam and Bee, just as much as they did. They kept her grounded. Squeezing the shampoo into her palm, she thought of Sam's comments about Lachlan. Just hearing his name, spoken with such fondness, was hard to hear. Sam's struggles with the storm were a good comparison to how it felt when she and Lachlan ended things. Massive destruction and no way to fix it. The feelings she had the night before when she lay staring at the ceiling in Dae's granny flat resurfaced. Loneliness. Wondering if her decisions were the right ones. No. She wouldn't give in to that. She made her choices. By some miracle, she hoped Sam and Bee could still make it to Sydney. She wasn't ready to admit it to Sam, but she felt on shaky ground, too.

Ten minutes later, dressed in yoga pants and a zip up hoodie, Brooke grabbed a quick salad from the fridge. She noticed her mum had been by to restock her fridge with leftovers. Thank God. It meant she didn't have to run to the supermarket on a Sunday afternoon to get groceries. She found a fork in the drawer, then her phone, and headed outside again to her deck to sit in the sunshine once more. She googled some appliance stores in Tasmania, saved some links, and ate her lunch. Satisfied with what to arrange for Sam and Bee, she called Merritt.

"Hi B! I was just thinking about you," Merritt said, picking up after two rings.

"Clearly I was thinking about you too," Brooke responded. "How are things on your end?"

"Damn busy. I feel like I've been running on a treadmill nonstop lately. I've got three deals happening at the same time. Luckily, one will be complete next week, the other closes a week from Friday and the third is about three weeks out. I'll be thankful for a bit of breathing space. How about you? How's the practice?"

"Same as usual. Fighting with Dae over how to run things."

"When is he going to work out that the business is actually yours?" Merritt asked, but she sounded a bit distracted. And a little pissed off.

"Most likely never. But I'm used to it. He's always been a control freak," Brooke said.

"Yeah, I'm not sure what it is about men and feeling like they need to control women," said Merritt in a snarky tone.

"I wouldn't say he's controlling me," contended Brooke, surprised by Merritt's snit. "What's going on? You sound like you're on the attack today."

Merritt knew Dae well, since they had all met at university. She'd even lived with them for a year. So it was weird for Merritt to throw Dae into the misogynist bucket. She knew him better than that.

"Oh, just having some issues with James. He seems, I don't know, wanting more control over some things and letting other details go completely. Something is going on with him, and I'm too busy to stop and think about what it may be." Brooke wasn't a huge fan of James, but when Merritt fell in love, she fell hard. Dae liked to describe James as a schmoozer. He could charm a pensioner out of their retirement with just enough left for them to buy a cup of tea, while making them believe they'd bought the tea farm instead.

"Anyway, enough of my crap. I was going to call Sam later. I read there was a massive storm that hit the east coast, and that Hobart got some snow. Have you talked to them?"

"I have. They're safe. There's some damage to Sam's place. But the worst part is that the bridge between them and Orford has been washed away. So, they're cut off. The only way out is via the forest road. Which is the road we took down to Marion Bay, the last time we were all down there." Brooke watched a kookaburra land on the electrical line, his focus zeroed in on the ground below.

"Oh shit. That road is horrible!" Merritt exclaimed.

"It is! And I doubt Sam's car or Marty's truck can handle it," said Brooke.

"What are they going to do?"

"Seems the town is helping them out. Building some contraption called a flying fox to get them back and forth."

"Oh, that's great. One of my friends growing up had a flying fox on their property. They would use it to get over the creek whenever it flooded," Merritt said. There were some days Brooke forgot Merritt came from anywhere other than the city. She went straight from country girl to city lover as soon as she moved to Sydney. Now she was in Melbourne and Brooke doubted she'd ever leave.

"I hope it works because I doubt the council has plans to fix or rebuild the bridge anytime soon," Brooke said.

"Is there anything I can do to help?" asked Merritt.

"Call Sam. She's pretty stressed, although she won't admit that."

"Yeah. And Zed's birthday is coming up soon too," Merritt said. "I'll call, don't worry."

"Good. I think that'll help," Brooke said, reproaching herself that she'd forgotten about Zed's birthday. It was just around the corner. August second.

"When I heard the news about the storm, I immediately thought about Zed. Sam has got to be freaking out. But then I had a weird thought. I've only known Zed as that. Zed. Never Zayden. How'd he even get that nickname?"

"Always last, always late, just like the last letter in the alphabet. He was always the last one to arrive anywhere and he was notoriously late. It's why no one thought to call for help when he didn't come back on the trawler before dark."

"Ah, okay. He was late for their wedding too, wasn't he?" Merritt asked. Brooke groaned.

"He was. He was out fishing and apparently lost track of time," Brooke said, remembering how she was ready to kill Zed that day. Brooke could hear Merritt shuffling some papers around and knew that Merritt had already checked out of the conversation. She was usually only good for five minutes before she moved on to something else.

"Well, I'd love to chat more, but I have to get this paperwork finished up today," Merritt said, confirming Brooke's prediction. "Call you next week?"

"Sure. Sounds good," Brooke paused, not wanting to hang up just yet, but her friends had lives. "Love you," she added.

"Love you too. Speak soon. Mwah." When Brooke heard the dial tone, she looked up and saw the kookaburra watching her. It looked about as lonely as she felt.

5

SAM. COMMUNITY.

AUGUST.

The week after the bridge collapsed felt like death, as if the world stopped spinning altogether. An icy stillness had taken over. It was just past four in the afternoon and darkness was falling, matching Sam's mood. Twilight came early in the Tasmanian winter.

She had no way of making an income for the foreseeable future, and Zed's insurance money was running out fast. There was no way to get to Orford to work, and Sam knew Georgina had a big event planned at the café. Was it her friend Aubrey's birthday? That sounded right. Sam felt guilty that she couldn't help but she had no choice. With no movement on the bridge repair, she wasn't going anywhere. Even if she could, her car had decided not to start. She was stuck. No, not stuck. She was screwed.

If all that wasn't bad enough, Zed's birthday fell in the mix of it. She and Bee made his favourite chocolate cake, just as they always did, and sat in silence as they ate enormous slices. There were no words. They'd all been said. Except they hadn't.

"Some days I miss Dad..." said Bee. It broke Sam's heart. She didn't know what to say. She was missing Zed too, especially lately. She needed help and hated to ask anyone for it.

"But other days..." Bee continued. "Do you think he regrets it? What I mean is, say he's watching us from wherever he may be now. Do you think he regrets it?"

"Regrets what, babe?" Sam asked, placing her fork down. No amount of sugar was going to help the pit in her stomach.

"Dying on us. Leaving us in the lurch. Fighting with you the night before," Bee said, finishing the last of her cake. Sam gasped. She didn't realise Bee knew about the fight. She'd assumed Bee had been asleep.

"You know about that?"

"Yes Mum. I was fourteen when he died. I wasn't going to my room at eight o'clock every night to go to sleep. And it's hard not to hear everything that happens in this house," she said, then wiped the last of the frosting from her plate with her finger.

"Oh, Bee, I had no idea. I'm so sorry." Sam said, smoothing her daughter's hair away from her eyes. Bee pulled back.

"Why are you sorry?" Bee asked angrily. "You told him something he didn't want to hear. Something he should have listened to. But instead of listening, he got drunk and angry and took the boat out in the storm. He made the mistake, Mum. Not you. You were right. You needed to be more than a fisherman's wife and it's because of his dreams that you've been left to clean up his shit." Bee stood abruptly, scraping her chair back noisily, and took their plates to the kitchen, practically throwing them into the sink.

"Bee," Sam called to her, but her daughter just shook her head.

"Time to take him off the pedestal, Mum. He doesn't deserve the position," she said. Bee stormed back to her room, slamming her door. Sam sat back in her chair, shocked at her daughter's outrage. Where had that come from?

Sam was still reeling from Bee's pronouncement four days later, while she lay in bed for the fourth day running. While Bee acted as if nothing happened the night of Zed's birthday, Sam was flailing. Bee's words haunted her. Clearly her daughter felt like she'd given up. She had though, hadn't she? Bee wasn't wrong. Zed should have listened.

Zed's attitude was probably a result of Jackson's influence. It wasn't the first time Jackson had stepped into the middle of their marriage. Her favourite gem was Jackson's bullshit about letting the little woman stay home while the man went to work. Zed had taken that to heart, insisting she be a stay-at-home mum, even though they couldn't afford it. And look where that got her. Here she was, broke, with no experience, and no way out.

On her dresser, picture frames were lined up, showing the highlight reel of her life. To the left, a photo with her, her mum, dad, and brother Paul. It was taken when she was thirteen, before she lost them all. They stood on the deck of a houseboat her parents had rented, the last summer Paul was alive. It was right before Paul's rugby accident, and three years before her parents died on a foggy highway. Her family was gone, except for her.

To the right of that frame, there was a photo of Zed and Bee, smiling broadly when Zed took Bee fishing on the beach when she was four. Bee had caught her first fish. Their grins were enormous. Now Zed was gone, too.

To the farthest right was a snapshot of she and Brooke, the night they'd gotten their matching Bon Jovi tattoos, when they were thirty. The tattoo replicated the cover of their favourite album: a heart, a sword, and wings. Zed used to joke about it, calling it their tramp stamps. She had no idea then that it would represent her life. She had the sword through her heart at least. But where were the damn wings? She needed those now the most.

She rolled over. Hopelessness overwhelmed her. She hadn't showered in four days. She hadn't walked Ned, even though he came sniffing around at six forty-five every morning for his daily beach walk. When that didn't happen, he decided the pile of dirty clothes in the corner of her room was a good place to sleep, so he spent the day there. The house was freezing cold, despite Bee's effort to keep the wood stove going. Sam suspected they had a hole in the roof somewhere else, but it didn't matter. She didn't have the money to fix it anyway.

She smelled rank. Her hair was matted in a knot of curls. Her face felt greasy from neglect, and her mouth felt furry and probably smelled worse than the overflowing garbage bin in the kitchen. She didn't care and no one else seemed to. Sure, Bee had pleaded for her to get up, but Sam ignored her. At least she brought her food, but Sam suspected it was food delivered straight from Marty's kitchen. Seemed Bee was spending a lot of time over at Marty's these days. Great. She was even losing her own daughter.

Four days. Four days since anyone had called her. Four days since Brooke called and only because it was Zed's birthday. And yet, Brooke called Marty every day to check in on her, according to Bee. Sam was still waiting on the fridge, but assumed Brooke had forgotten, just as she'd forgotten about her. Merritt called for Zed's birthday. Of course she had. She hadn't heard from Merritt for weeks, then the magical call came on her husband's birthday. No one called for any other reason, other than they thought they should. Should. She hated that word even more nowadays.

Even Georgina hadn't called to check in on her. Not about work or how they were doing. The last communication with her was the text about the bridge going out. And Sean, the new owner of the pub, told her to call him when she could manage her way in. Like she had a choice about the damn bridge. He said they'd talk about her job then, but she remembered his nasty, arrogant tone. She couldn't count on her job being there when the bridge was fixed. However long that was going to be.

Lachie called on Zed's birthday. Another obligatory call. But even he'd skipped right past any pleasantries to say he couldn't help them anytime soon. His workload was impossible. Everyone had extensive damage from the storm. Sam's phone sat silent. At one point, she asked Bee to call her phone, just to make sure the service wasn't cut off. She knew it was pathetic.

People probably figured that if Sam had gotten through Zed's death, and yet another birthday, the drama with the bridge would be easy. But it wasn't. It was fucking hard. Her sunroom was destroyed. She had a water leak coming through a light fixture in her laundry, which Lachie promised to fix this week. A fallen branch was pushing her entire fence over. Her fridge sat dead in her kitchen. And with no coffee, everything had gone to shit. She was in a dark, angry place.

Sam couldn't even be bothered to check in on Marty. The woman had been by twice already to take Ned out on walks, making snarky comments about how the dog needs fresh air even if Sam didn't. Nothing like a guilt trip.

In the early afternoon, Sam heard a knock on her back door. Marty's voice rang through the house, asking Bee where Sam was. Shit. The last thing Sam needed was Marty coming by. She'd be appalled at the state of the house. Not to mention the state of her. Ugh. She pulled the heavy covers up around her chin and snuggled down even deeper into her queen-size bed. Her sheets stank.

Before she knew it, the tiny nonagenarian was standing in the middle of her bedroom, hands on her hips. Sam peered out at her through one eye from beneath the covers. Marty looked completely pulled together. Today, she was dressed in dark jeans and an oversized cable knit jumper. And right now, she wore a very determined look on her unadorned face. She moved to the end of Sam's bed, her hands still firmly on her hips, and didn't say a damn thing. Minutes ticked by. What? What did she want? Couldn't she see she was trying to nap? Sam moved the covers back a little to look at Marty, the signal Marty had apparently been waiting for.

"Come on. There's stuff to do. No sense wallowing. The sun is shining. So, get up. When you are done cleaning up yourself, you can help me with my garden. It's a damn mess. Now come on, girly. Get in the damn shower, get dressed, and get outside." Sam looked to the doorway. Her daughter stood there in the door frame with an expression Sam had not seen in four years. Absolute fear.

"Please Mum. Please get up," Bee begged once more. Shit. She could ignore Marty. But she couldn't ignore Bee.

"Come on. We need you," said Marty, her tone now remarkably softer. She wiggled Sam's foot from outside of the covers. "Time to get up, Sweet Pea." Sam looked to her daughter again. The pleading look on Bee's face got her moving.

Fine. At least Marty and Bee needed her.

6

BROOKE. ROUTINE.

AUGUST.

There was nothing more she could do for Marty, Sam, and Bee. It was hard being so far away. She felt frustrated and annoyed. The fridge was one thing, but the bridge still caused a serious issue for all involved. Brooke had even put in a call to the local council, but they'd blown her off because she wasn't a local property owner. Told her that the repair to the bridge was on the list. Seriously? The way they ran the council was like living in the nineteen fifties. It was infuriating.

All she could do was focus on her own life, which was frustrating enough. And right now, Dae was her most immediate problem.

"Either bring on a new doctor or reduce our consultation times to fifteen minutes," he snapped at her. They were in their monthly meeting, discussing practice business. Sue, the practice manager, looked very retro today in her grey trousers and pink jumper, her hair hoisted into a long banana clip. Sitting beside Sue was Brooke's father, Ray, who worked as their accountant. Compared to Dae, her dad looked a mess. His blonde hair stuck out in every direction, and his stark white shirt showed how little sun he'd received lately. Dae's suit matched his attitude. Stiff and unwrinkled. Their third doctor, Dr. Yang, wore his constant serious frown, but Brooke knew, outside of the office, the man was comical. All five of them were tightly seated around the desk in her office. What she wouldn't give for a decent conference room.

"If you want to know if you can add another doctor, from a financial point of view, things are looking great. Expenses are low, thanks to Sue, and revenue is high," her father added. Sue was more of a partner than an employee. She and Brooke had gone into the business with the same mindset: focus on the patient. Sue promised she'd manage the business with an iron fist, and she had. Every expenditure was assessed and accounted for. They didn't pander to the drug reps, who called regularly. They looked to their community for what they needed and delivered exactly that. It's why they were so busy. Word of mouth was a powerful thing, and within the Korean community, it spread like wildfire.

"Dae. We've talked about this." Ad nauseam, she thought. Dae came on a year after they opened, after he'd finished his residency. He wanted part ownership of the practice, but Brooke didn't agree with his business model. His ideas were more mainstream. His focus was on patient turnover. She knew they'd make more money with that setup, but she just wasn't interested in running that kind of practice.

"It's better for the patient," said Dae. "They won't have to wait as long for an appointment." He had a good point, but his pushy attitude was getting too much lately.

"Sure," said Sue, "but you're also talking about reducing consultation times, Dae, and that will cause contention with the patients. They all comment how great it is to have time with each of you. They feel heard." Thank God for Sue. Brooke loved the engagement she had with her patients. She thought Dae did, too.

She'd been considering the new doctor. A reduced workload would be great. They had the space, but there was something holding her back. She just didn't know what. And given how this meeting was going, she wasn't sure if she wanted to take on another opinion. Dae's suggestion of reducing the consultation time was out of the question. Their thirty-minute patient consults allowed them to stick to their schedule. Enough of the appointments fell short of the time allowed, giving them padding for research and to make thorough notes. It also meant they didn't have to take work home, allowing for a better work/life balance, and she knew Dae appreciated that more than ever with Jase in the picture. No, she wouldn't budge on changing the consultation time. They all needed that buffer.

"Let me think about bringing on another doctor. Maybe part time. I'm not sold on the idea yet. But I will not change the consultation times and, to be honest, I'm not sure why you're pushing for less time with patients, Dae?"

"Because we can't get to all the patients now, Brooke. We have a waiting list a mile long. A new full-time doctor will help that and if we reduce the consult time..." she cut him off.

"I'm not reducing the consult time. That's non-negotiable, but I will think about another doctor." Her tone was obvious. Her decision was made.

The meeting was exhausting and ran overtime. Walking out of the office, Sue pointed out the irony that they could absorb the extra meeting time because of the current schedule. Brooke smirked, inwardly delighted.

Four hours later, with the last patient seen, Brooke picked up the phone to call her grandmother. Marty was her grounding force.

"Hello Sunshine. How was your day?" Marty asked.

"Hi Marty. It was great if I ignore the business meeting we had today," she said, picking up a stray pen on her desk and popping it into her top drawer.

"Is Dae still insisting on adding another doctor? Your father told me last week that you don't need it. I'm not sure if he was calling to share the information, looking for my opinion, or just checking up on me to make sure I'm still alive and kicking. I can never tell with him nowadays." Marty had been a force in women's health in Tasmania, one of the few female doctors in the field in the early seventies. Her work on decriminalising abortions in Australia was still discussed in medical circles, not to mention her record of only one maternal death, and a low infant mortality rate during the early part of her career. Her practice had been one of the most successful in Tasmania for women's health. Marty was the reason Brooke pursued medicine. She was and continued to be Brooke's mentor and strongest professional ally.

"The practice is going well. So no, we don't need another doctor. But it would help. I was thinking about this today, after the meeting. Dae is being a pill. In fact, he's being really pushy about it and I'm reacting to that. It's making me want to say no just in defiance. Besides, I don't have time to train a new doctor in how we do things right now."

"How *you* do things, you mean," her grandmother chuckled. "Clearly, it's not how Dae would like to do them."

"Yes. If it were up to Dae, I think he'd be expanding to five more doctors on a rotation. And he'd be reducing the consulting time, even though the extra time benefits him."

"If you'd like my opinion, and if you don't, too bad because I'm going to give it to you anyway." Brooke smiled to herself. This was why she loved her grandmother so much. "You could find balance there. Add another doctor but keep your consultation times the way they are. The time you spend with your patients is valuable. And, let's be honest, patients need a few minutes just to get past the white-coat syndrome. They need the time to relax and open up. If you have the clock going and they feel that pressure, they won't be as open with you as you need them to be. Nor will you have time to read between the lines. A lot of patients aren't that forthcoming. You need to ask the right questions, and sometimes that takes more probing than the five questions we ask, anyway."

"That's exactly how I feel," Brooke said.

"Then stick to your guns, Sunshine," Marty said. "Now, when are you coming down here? We could use a little perking up. Sam is unravelling, and I just know she's going to lose it on me sooner than later. Since we're stuck here together, I think she's getting a little sick of this old woman telling her what to do. But we both know she does not do well when she's idle."

"No, she doesn't. She needs to keep moving, so she doesn't spiral back into that dark hole. I keep asking her if she's seen someone about her grief," Brooke said. Marty snorted.

"She's so busy taking care of everyone else that she doesn't realise that she needs taking care of, too. Zayden's birthday was a rough one. Bee's worried too. She spoke with me the other day. Said her mother had been listening to one song, over and over. What was it? Let me think now…"

"Was it the song 'Chasing Cars' perhaps?" Brooke asked and began humming the tune for Marty. It was Sam and Zed's song.

"Yes, I think that's the one. Over and over. I went over and pulled that stubborn redheaded girl out of her bed. Bee said she'd been there for days. I used my garden as an excuse because I couldn't think of anything else to get her moving. I had to play the guilt card."

"You didn't." Brooke laughed. "Did she come up punching?" Sam hated people telling her what to do. She was independent to the hilt and had been since she met her when they were seven. When Brooke tried to boss her about on the playground, Sam thrust out her chest, flipped her long red curly hair and told Brooke off as no one had before. She'd been the same ever since. Thankfully, they stayed friends since then too.

"No. Of course not. It's me. She's never been that way with me. I told her what she needed to hear. That people need her. I also put a word in with Georgina. Bee said no one has called Sam since the bridge went out. Oh, they did on Zayden's birthday, but otherwise nothing. Out of sight, out of mind, I suppose. I have my age working for me with people checking in. People think I'm going to die at the drop of a hat. But my poor Sweet Pea, it's different for her. Anyway, she's okay. Back in action. I gave her a list of tasks I needed help with. Had to get creative there, but it's worked."

"She is stubborn, and I'm guilty of not checking in. I called the other day and have been meaning to call her again. Getting a fridge to her has been a struggle and I guess I should have let her know what was going on there. Plus, the new tenant just moved into the cottage out the back at home, and that's been a bit of a mess. I have a million reasons for not calling, but they are no excuse. I know how she can get sometimes. I've just been strapped for time this week." But no matter what excuses she had, she needed to call Sam.

"I'll call her tonight. I promise," Brooke said and wondered if

Marty hadn't just played the guilt card with her as well. "How are you doing? Do you need anything?"

"Just a new bridge is all. But no, Sunshine, I have everything I need. News is, they are grading the forest road now. So, it should be a little safer. It was a little slippery through there with all the rain at first. But we're fine. Don't you worry about us."

"I still worry. You know that," she replied. She needed to get down to Fergus Bay and soon. When they hung up, Brooke tidied her desk and shut down her computer. Standing in the doorway, she scanned the office to make sure everything was in place for the next day. Her staff were on top of things, as always. She loved her team. Which reminded her, she needed to watch last week's episodes of New Amsterdam and Grey's Anatomy to keep up with the office chatter. They all loved to nit-pick the unrealistic nuances on the shows. Brooke loved the shows for the characters. She'd marry Max Goodwin or Jackson Avery in a heartbeat. Ah, if only they were real.

Walking out of the building and into the dark just after six, she tightened her scarf to ward off the winter chill. She fell into a rhythm with the other people bundled in their warm coats strolling to the Epping train station. This winter was rough, even in Sydney. When she boarded the city-bound train in Epping, she heard her phone ringing in her handbag. Not wanting to disturb her fellow passengers, she clicked the phone to silent. She noted it was Dae, most likely wanting to do a post-mortem on the earlier meeting. She found a seat on the train and, ignoring Dae and his pushy attitude, tried to enjoy the ride home.

At the end of the carriage, she watched a father with a baby no more than four months old. The baby was strapped to his chest, facing out. The father read to the baby in soft tones, close enough to the baby's ear that only she could hear him. The book was no larger than his hand. But he held it close enough to the baby that it took up most of her vision. She was mesmerised by the images. When he stopped reading to turn the page, she looked back at him with wonder. When his whispers resumed, her focus returned to the page.

She smiled at the simple beauty they shared, but the moment created an incredible sadness in her. Before the melancholy took hold, she reminded herself that she made her choice. It had been a hard choice, and one she thought about too much lately. Dae and Jase's news about adopting rocked her. No. She couldn't think about that. She had chosen her career instead.

When the train reached Cheltenham, she disembarked with only a handful of other passengers. Most would take the line all the way to the city. With only the sound of shoe steps striking pavement, the small cluster made their way out of the station and disappeared into their cars. Brooke weaved her way through the peak hour traffic and away from the station. She turned down her street, dimly illuminated by streetlights.

Opening her front door, everything inside was quiet. There were no sounds of family. No laughter coming from the kitchen. No arguing. No music playing from the stereo. The click of her shoes on the cold tile was the only sound. She removed her grey woollen coat and unwrapped her crimson scarf in the darkness. She left her shoes by her coat for the following morning and padded to the back of the house to the kitchen. She flipped the light switch on, then opened her fridge to stare into the stark cavity. She decided on her mother's chicken satay for dinner and placed it into the microwave to reheat. While she waited, she poured a glass of Shiraz from the open bottle sitting on the quartz counter, then looked out to see the cottage lights were off out the back. Empty there too. When the microwave dinged, she took her dinner to the large, empty dining room table to eat.

The tinging of the fork against the bowl amplified in the quiet. A car honked on the main road a few blocks away, and she heard the low rumble from the rail line.

She looked around her house, thinking of Marty's beach house and how inviting it was. Walls there were filled with cherished paintings. Rugs covered the wood floors, and blankets were flung over chairs to ward off the evening chill. Sam's house, as chaotic as it was, felt cosy too. Photos covered every surface. Paintings from Bee's childhood lined one wall. Even Dae and Jase's house felt the same way. Like a home. Messy, but a messy home. In comparison, Brooke's white walls and simple furnishings appeared stark and empty. She wondered if the plot of her life made sense anymore. What had she been hoping for once she became a doctor? Suddenly, her practice felt like all she had in her life, and what she had of a life, felt like an abandoned warehouse.

As she ate, she looked around her house. Everything she saw felt transient, like a model home waiting for the next owner. Pristine, rarely used furniture, staged with stock photos and immaculate window dressings. There was no impression that a person had actually lived here for ten years. There was no sense of home, like the others. Hers was just a house. Everything in her house was austere. Empty. Including her.

7

SAM. CHANGES.

SEPTEMBER.

Two weeks later, Sam grabbed her bold yellow jacket from the back hook, whistled for Ned, and wandered down the path to the beach. The sun had yet to come up over the horizon. Pink blazed through the sky like wildfire and a mist hugged the hilltops to the north. She loved these mornings. Nothing could be heard but the low chug of fishing trawlers sailing out to sea, the methodical rolling of the waves, and the tweeting of wrens in the ferns. But damn, it was cold. Growing up in Sydney, she was accustomed to chilly mornings, but in Tasmania, it was downright frigid. The winds were calm for now, thankfully. They would come later in the afternoon. You could practically set your watch to it.

Ned played his favourite game running around the beach. He picked up a stick between his teeth, grinning with satisfaction, only to drop it when he found a better one. He could go at it for hours if she let him. She had bought a ball launcher, a few years before, but he'd never been interested. Sticks were his preferred choice.

A movement in the water caught her attention. There it was. She hadn't seen it in a couple of weeks.

"Good morning," she said to the break in the water. She was rewarded by her lone dolphin gliding to the surface, taking a breath of crisp air, before submerging once more. The ritual repeated five times. It was always five times, and always the lone dolphin. As quickly as it appeared, it vanished. Sam was convinced it was Zed. She knew the idea was irrational. She told Bee about the dolphin, right after Zed died, but her daughter rolled her eyes as only a fourteen-year-old could. She told Marty later. Marty smiled knowingly and said Sam was lucky to still have Zed around.

"When I lost my daughter, I saw yellow butterflies," Marty shared a few years before. "The monument out the back of my place, under the cluster of gum trees, is for my daughter." The news shocked Sam. She and Brooke had often wondered whose marker it was. When they asked Marty over the years, she brushed it off, telling them only that it was a family member. Now, Sam knew just how close that family member was to Marty.

"We believe these things because it keeps our loved ones close. Whether it's true, or whether people think we've lost our marbles, it doesn't matter. Whatever we need to believe, to keep that person in our hearts, that's what's important."

Sam missed Zed, especially on these mornings. He was an early riser. He had to be to work on the fishing trawler. He rose early on his days off too, claiming the waves with his surfboard.

They'd met because of these early mornings. Months after her parents died, Sam spent that first summer in Fergus Bay with Brooke and her family. Her nightmares were at their worst back then, and she suffered from acute insomnia. Every morning before the house woke, she walked to the beach. It was better than tossing and turning for a few more hours. The waves weren't huge in Fergus Bay, not like Sydney's beaches, so she was surprised to see the lone surfer riding the small crests. Zed came out of the water a short time later, carrying his surfboard under his arm. He shook the water dripping from his straggly blonde hair and unzipped his wetsuit. The sunrise was gorgeous that morning, but a chill lingered in the air. She was relieved to have worn her puffer jacket and sweatpants. At least until Zed approached her and announced only a tourist would wear so many layers on such a mild morning. His smile enthralled her. After that, they met as often as they could that summer, finding time around his work when he worked as a deckhand on the boats.

The early morning routine continued after Bee came along. They stole precious moments to walk the beach together, leaving Bee sound asleep and cosy under her blankets.

Yes. She missed him terribly. Especially nowadays. Zed was a great distracter when she was having a bad day. But his clichés drove her nuts. 'Everything happens for a reason' was his favourite. Then there was one she was still holding out for, 'Things always work out in the end.' They hadn't worked out great for him, but she still held on to that hope for herself and Bee.

She knew her marriage wasn't great. Sure, it was dreamy in the beginning. Like so many young couples, they were full of fantastic ideas. But once reality came knocking, she realised their dreams lacked in the practical sense. Zed was a dreamer. He insisted on a back-packing trip as soon as she turned eighteen. 'A year or until the money runs out,' he declared, and the money ran out fast. It lasted four months. Two weeks after arriving home, she was surprised to find she was pregnant. But they vowed to travel again together.

"Later, when Bee leaves home, we'll go," he'd promised. He never let go of the dream. Now Sam wondered if they would have lasted that long.

She traced lines in the sand with her foot while Ned happily chased his sticks. Sam thought about their last night. Could she have said something to avoid the fight that made him storm out the door? Maybe. Probably. But the argument replayed so often in her head she felt like there was little room for anything else sometimes. Replaying that conversation, melding into something that should have been, relentlessly spun in her head.

"Do you know what today is, Zed?" she would have asked. Of course, he would shake his head. He never remembered.

"It's the anniversary of my parents' death. Eighteen years. Eighteen years since they were killed in that car accident on the M-1. Yesterday was the anniversary of my brother's death. Twenty-one years since he died in the rugby accident. And you forgot. You forgot both of those things."

"Shit, Sam, I'm sorry," Zed would say in the revised version of the doomed conversation.

"I marked it on the fridge calendar. The same fridge you get your beer from." She would look down at the beer on the table, wonder if she would also tell him how she felt about his drinking too much lately. Alcohol contributed to the accident.

"Do you even notice what matters to me anymore, Zed? We've always structured our life around you. Your wants. Your dreams. You've never considered mine."

"You've never said anything before," he'd say. That would be true, to a point.

"I have told you. Not a lot, no, but when I did, you haven't listened. I wanted to go to university, remember? But back then, it was too complicated because you were working odd hours at the marina. And there were always excuses. We only had one car. There wasn't enough money. Blah Blah Blah." He'd look at her like she was a stranger because it had been too long since she had talked about going to university. But with Bee growing up and not needing her as much, the idea had resurfaced.

"And now? Why don't we move the boat to Hobart?" The conversation would go from there. He'd go kicking and screaming. That's where the actual conversation always resurfaced. The words she'd actually said to him. Those couldn't be changed. How she wanted more in her life than to be a fisherman's wife. With the stack of bills in her hand, she'd try to explain they needed to do better.

Geezus, she'd reworked their conversation so many times. And now she was stuck in that nightmare, with bills she couldn't pay, without his paycheque and now with the dwindling insurance money. She either went to bed worrying about not being able to pay the bills, or she had the reoccurring nightmare of someone's death. It just went around and around, night after sleepless night. And it achieved nothing. He was still gone, and she was still here.

Calling Ned back, she headed home. She'd get Bee up and make eggs for breakfast. Something healthy besides the stale cereal they'd been raiding from the abandoned shacks. The homeowners told them to help themselves to whatever they wanted since the bridge collapsed. But Marty's chickens were a saving grace during their isolation. They were champion layers in normal times. But now it was as if they sensed it was their time to shine. The hens were laying more than the three of them could eat. They were tiring of eating eggs, but there was nothing better to start the day than Marty's homemade sourdough and fried eggs, with the yolk still a little runny. Her tummy rumbled just as she walked through the door.

They were still stuck, but after days lying in bed, Sam needed to take some control. Marty was right to push her. She decided if people weren't calling her, she was going to call them. She'd make damn sure they knew she was still around. She'd called Georgina first, to get an update on the café, and to hear what she'd heard about the bridge repairs, since Georgina always had her ear to the ground. While there was no news on the bridge, Sam was surprised to hear that Georgina had been to Jackson's house every day to check on him. She'd even organised the community to help him with additional meals and cleaning. When she hung up, Sam asked Bee if she knew about Georgina helping Jackson. Bee admitted she did and swore she'd told Sam about it. Maybe she did. The four days in bed were a fog. Maybe they weren't invisible after all.

While she heated the pan on her gas stove, Sam called Jackson. She was most worried about him, especially now he was left to his own devices. He seemed lost ever since the loss of his wife Beverlee.

"Hey Jackson, it's Sam. How's it going?" she asked, as she cracked eggs into the sizzling pan.

"Hi Sam. It's fine. All okay down there at the shack?" she could hear him moving around, then heard the groan of the recliner's springs when he sat down.

"All okay. Saw a dolphin this morning, about fifty metres from the beach," she said. She'd never share with Jackson that she imagined the dolphin as Zed. She'd never live it down.

"You know, I read recently that dolphins are so smart that within a few weeks of captivity, they can train people to stand on the edge of the pool and throw them fish." Sam laughed. Jackson had some terrible lines some days.

"Have you had Meals on Wheels delivered this week?" she asked. Sam made sure he had a delivery a couple of days a week, then supplemented the rest with casseroles, which she separated into individual proportions. It was the supplemental meals Georgina was helping with, but Sam was more worried about the Meals on Wheels piece. They'd had some hiccups during the first few months.

"Yeah. Bah. Those meals are like cardboard some days. Other days? Like mush. And I've had only vegetables and beans for the last couple of deliveries. Where's the damn meat? I didn't fight my way to the top of the food chain to be a bloody vegetarian."

"Are you over-microwaving them again?" she asked, knowing he couldn't work a microwave for the first year that Beverlee was gone. Last year he'd blown up the microwave when he put foil over his plate. It was lucky he didn't burn the house down. The man was hopeless in the kitchen. He even burned his own toast.

"No. I know how to use the blasted thing. I'd starve if I didn't."

"I'll give Meals on Wheels a call and see what's going on. Has Georgina been coming over?" Sam asked, already knowing the answer.

"Yeah, she came yesterday. Brought me some coffee and bread. Even some of those fancy pastries I like to order when I go into the coffee shop."

"That was nice of her," Sam said, and Jackson grunted, but she knew it was for show. She knew he loved those pastries. She made a note to thank Georgina. That really was a kind gesture.

"I'm glad you called Bee yesterday. She seemed happy to talk to you." Sam knew he must be worried for them if he called Bee. He never rang unless it was an emergency.

"She's a good kid, that one. Anyway, I'm fine. You're fine. Now, I'm going to go back to my crossword if it's all the same to you," Jackson said, hanging up abruptly.

"Yeah, okay. Bye Jackson," Sam said to the empty line and called to Bee for breakfast.

Sam cleaned up the breakfast dishes while Bee finished getting ready for school.

Looking out the window, she admired the near-new Toyota Land Cruiser that sat in her driveway. Things changed a lot in two weeks. Once word was out that they were well and truly isolated, the community rallied to help them. A farmer, who lived further up the coast, loaned her the two-year-old 4WD. The sight of it still shocked her sitting behind her car in the driveway. At first, she tried to decline the offer. She couldn't borrow an almost brand-new vehicle! But Mick insisted they use it for as long as they needed. His only request was to return it with a full tank of petrol. As if she'd return it empty. It would be washed, detailed, full of petrol. And even then, she'd find some other way to repay him for his generosity.

"Been stuck myself. Know how it is," said the farmer. His wife, Beth, followed him in their other Land Cruiser. Sam was shocked to find Beth's 4WD was filled with groceries for the three of them, including their mail from Orford. Georgina threw in some other goodies, too. Homemade meat pies from the bakery, Nicole's speciality pastries, and twenty kilos of Georgina's specialty roasted coffee. The coffee finally pushed Sam over the edge as she blubbered into Beth's shoulder. Sam sorely missed her coffee. She was battling a caffeine headache that rivalled the pain of childbirth. She bled the shacks dry of all she could find. She even choked down instant coffee in desperation and had to resort to tea when that ran out. Just that morning, Sam had joked with Bee that she was ready to swim to Orford, as she could not go another day without coffee. Inhaling the intense roast, she had much to thank Georgina for. She suspected it was Georgina who got on the grapevine and made it all happen.

When a beat-up four-wheel drive rumbled down the track three days later, Sam wasn't sure what was going on. When it parked in front of her house, she went out to investigate.

"Have a fridge for you," the guy said, jumping down from the driver's seat. Sam saw a gigantic box sitting upright on the deck. It was strapped more securely than a newborn going home from the hospital. Sam wanted to cry.

"How'd you get it down the forest road in one piece?" she asked as the guy unloaded it from the truck.

"Nice and slow. Plus, I was paid pretty handsomely to do it, so I was getting it to you one way or another. Oh, and I have other stuff for you inside the truck. I'll get that for you after I hook this all up," he said.

She watched as he dollied the old fridge out of the way, then positioned the new fridge in its place. While he took the old fridge back out to his truck, she checked out the shiny silver wonder and realised it was a model she'd never be able to afford herself. It was even better than Marty's! The truck driver yelled out to her from the back door, weighed down by bags of groceries. They still had plenty from the delivery from Mick and Beth. Her eyes teared up, freaking the delivery guy out.

"Some of it is for, um, Marty?" he said, looking down at the bags.

"I'll get it to her. She's just down the track," Sam said, wiping a lone tear from her cheek.

"Is it odd? Delivering a fridge *and* the groceries to go with it?" she asked, as she sifted through the bags to discover what was inside.

"Nah, we get strange requests like this all the time. The fridge is hooked up. Wait a little while until it cools down. Maybe an hour? Then you're good to go. Can you sign here?" Minutes later, the truck was loaded with her old useless fridge and ambling back down the track. She texted Brooke.

Thanks for the fridge! It's gorgeous! And for the groceries. You're an angel!

Brooke's reply came moments later: *Glad it finally arrived! Sorry for the delay. Had some serious challenges.*

I'm sure! The road is still a mess. How'd you manage it?

Meh - called a guy. ;-) Took a while to find him though.

Within the same miraculous week, Bill Bishop finally organised the engineers to build the flying fox Marty suggested. Unfortunately though, they still had to rely on people to get them from the river and into Orford, but Georgina promised she'd organise pickups.

The flying fox was dicey at first. Sam nearly fell out the first time. But once the kinks were ironed out and the flying fox was fully functional, Bee was able to meet her best friend Liv on the other side of the river to meet the school bus. It also meant Sam could get to work.

With Bee dropped at the flying fox for school, Sam drove home. She wasn't due at work until noon, now she was rostered back on, and there were a million things on her list to do before she headed in. She was still trying to get her yard cleaned up. She needed to get the pile of washing under control. And she needed to check her bank account to see which bills she could afford to pay, and which would have to wait. She needed a plan but didn't have a clue what that even looked like. Her mind raced a million miles an hour.

Sam took a huge breath. She needed some perspective. They had all come out of the storm safely. The damage to the house could have been a lot worse. She was grateful to the people that helped them when they desperately needed it. But the reality remained. They were still on the brink of destitution.

She turned up the music, rolled down her window, and inhaled the cold air. It smelled of seaweed and salt, but the scent grounded her. It smelled familiar. Like home. She considered moving after Zed died, away from the sea, but this place was where she was meant to be. Feeling the breeze catch her hair, she felt Mother Nature remind her of where she was. Just be, enjoy the moment, she seemed to say.

Bon Jovi's song, 'Livin' on a Prayer', blasted on the car's stereo. It was one of her favourites. Most days, it felt like the anthem of her life. Singing along, Sam was happy to get some of her life back. Life had been nothing near normal these last couple of weeks. Lachie had arranged for the leak in the light fixture to be repaired, but with the amount of damage to other houses along the coast, she could only hope he would get to her soon for the rest. He'd asked for photos the week before, to see what damage was done. Climbing the rickety old ladder from the shed, she saw the damage was bad, but it wasn't critical. She and Bee patched things as best as they could by stacking bricks on the roof to keep more tin from flying off, but the sunroom was a goner. Lachie would need to rebuild that completely. Driving back down their dirt track, she wondered if her homeowner's insurance would pay for some of the damage? She hoped they would.

Her eyes wandered over to Marty's house as she neared her driveway. The curtains on Marty's bi-fold doors off the kitchen weren't open yet. That was odd. She usually had them open by this time of the morning, to let the heat from the sun warm the room. Especially on such a gorgeous winter day, with the sun shining for the first time in two weeks. Sam looked to the clock on the dash. It was after eight. Maybe Marty was already pottering in her garden?

Sam hopped out of the car and walked to the front fence. Leaning over, she could see clearly down to the front of Marty's house. The curtains were closed there too. Maybe someone picked Marty up for a town run, but she hadn't mentioned it. Maybe she'd just gone for a walk along the beach? Sam looked over to her exposed sunroom and saw Ned curled up, sound asleep in the sunshine. Hmm. He usually went with Marty when she walked the beach as she always enjoyed having Ned's company. Sam felt a prickle on the back of her neck.

She walked back to her porch, grabbing her keys and phone from her handbag. She stepped around Ned, unlocked the door, and tossed her bag on the brown corduroy couch inside. She reached around the door frame and plucked Marty's spare key from the key hook. Ned, still laying in the sunshine, looked to her with his head cocked to the side, as if to ask, 'what's up?' Sam said nothing, but when she patted her leg twice in quick succession, Ned jumped up and sprinted to her side. Together they walked quickly toward Marty's.

Sam looked through the front garden, hoping she'd find the elderly woman, but found it empty. Ned seemed to pick up on the task and began his own search. While he scoured the yard, Sam walked to the door and knocked. No answer. Maybe Marty was out on the beach alone? But no. She always took Ned with her. She had since Ned was a puppy. Sam knocked harder. No answer. She tried the door handle, hoping to find it unlocked. It wasn't. She unlocked the door and poked her head in.

"Marty? Are you here?" The hairs on her neck prickled again. Shit.

"Marty? Are you still asleep? It's a gorgeous day outside. Your garden is calling." Still no answer. She walked to the other side of the house. The master bedroom had a full view of the beach, but Sam saw the door was almost closed, and the room was dark. The prickle was now a full-on panic. Sam pushed the door open, letting the light cast over to the bed.

There lay her friend, curled up as if she were enjoying a delightful dream, a slight smile curling her lips. But Sam knew in an instant Marty wasn't sleeping. She looked around the room. Everything was in its place. Everything but nothing.

8

BROOKE. HOMECOMING.

SEPTEMBER.

The knock at Brooke's office door made her jump.

"Excuse me a minute," she said to Mrs. Park. Sue stood on the other side, looking very apologetic.

"I'm sorry to interrupt, but there's an urgent call for you. It's your friend, Sam." Brooke knew that for Sue to interrupt her, it was an emergency. And Sam never called her on her work number.

"Tell her I'll call her right back. I'm almost done here with Mrs. Park." Closing the door, Brooke switched back into Korean and quickly explained to her patient that she had a family emergency. The woman jumped up, ready to leave, but Brooke wrote a prescription for the woman's reflux, and explained if there was anything else, the front desk would reschedule her for the first available appointment. Brooke apologised for the inconvenience, and gently showed the woman out. As Mrs. Park walked to the reception desk, Brooke motioned to Sue.

"Did Sam say what it was about?"

"No. Only that it was a family emergency." That could be Bee or Marty.

"Okay. Could you please make sure Mrs. Park is taken care of?"

"No worries." Brooke nodded, turned, and closed the door. She dialled Sam's cell number from her office phone.

"Hey Brooke. Sorry to disturb you at work. But..." Sam's tone alerted her that whatever it was, it was serious.

"Who?" It was the only question she needed answered. Sam was silent, and all Brooke could hear was the sound of the surf in the background.

"Marty. I'm so sorry, Brooke. I just found her. I thought she was sleeping. But... I'm at her house now. I've called the Orford police. I'm just waiting for them to come and declare her..." Brooke didn't hear anymore. Sam rambled on, but the words changed to a background hum, like the sound of cicadas in the summer.

Marty. Her grandmother. Dead. She'd only spoken to her late yesterday afternoon. Marty had waffled on about the damage to her beautiful purple bush in her garden. Her Pride of Madeira. Why Brooke remembered the name of the plant, she didn't know. But Brooke had tuned her out since it was the third - or was it the fourth? – time that she had talked about it since the storm.

"Brooke? You still with me?" She heard Sam's voice, but Brooke was speechless. This couldn't be happening. Not yet. She wasn't ready for this. Which was stupid, she realised, given the woman's age. But it was Marty. Her Marty. The woman who guided her through life. The one who inspired her to be a doctor, who pushed her to follow the path Marty had blazed before her. The woman who told her that she needed to go back to Sydney and get her degree, when Brooke begged to stay in Tasmania, so many years ago. No. Marty was still alive. She had to be.

"Brooke. You okay?" Sam's voice was soft, empathetic. Brooke felt the tears on her cheeks before she realised she was crying. The emotion caught in her throat and a sob escaped.

"I'm sorry. I'm so sorry to have to tell you over the phone. Let me call Dae. He can come to you." Dae? Hearing his name brought Brooke back to reality. She looked around her office. She had to go. Dae would look after the practice because she had to go to Fergus Bay. Like, now.

"I'm okay. I'll tell him. I'm going to book a flight. I'll try to be there tonight."

"I'll pick you up from the airport."

"Okay, thanks," she said. Then something clicked. The storm. "Wait. How? Aren't you still cut off?" Brooke vaguely remembered Sam saying something about a flying fox. That was going to be interesting. Getting a dead body... but didn't Sam just say something about a helicopter coming for that? She shouldn't have tuned her out. Brooke shook her head. She had to get there.

"We have a Land Cruiser on loan, remember? We can get to Hobart via the forest road," said Sam. "If I can't be there, I'll send someone to pick you up. Georgina maybe. Or Nicole. Someone will be there."

"Okay. Okay. I'll let you know about my flight as soon as I book it. Are you okay? Did you..."

"Yeah, I'm okay. It wasn't the best way to start a day, I'll give you that. I haven't told Bee yet. She's not home from school. I found Marty after I'd dropped her off..."

"Oh God, she'll be devastated," exclaimed Brooke, and sat back in her chair. Oh, poor Bee.

"Yeah, she will. I just hope I can tell her before someone else does. I think I'll call Liv's mum and see if she can get her from school. The word isn't out yet. But now I've called the police, it will be soon," said Sam. "Just call me when you know your flight details. Look, I've got to go. Keep your cell phone close. Oh, I haven't called your parents yet. Do you want to do that? I can if you'd rather?"

"No, I will. I'll call them now. Dad's away in Brisbane and Mum has a huge catering event tonight."

"Okay. Look, I've got to go. I think the police are here," Sam said, her voice now sounding urgent. "And Brooke? She wasn't in any pain. She died in her sleep. With a smile on her face." Brooke smiled at that. She was glad. That was something at least.

When the call ended, Brooke dove into action. She informed Sue what had happened and added what she would need from her, as she dashed to Dae's office. With Sue on her heels, she was relieved to see Dae was between patients. Brooke was numb, but the logistics kept her focused, allowing her to block out all emotion. The last thing she needed was for reality to come crashing in. She needed to keep it together until she got to Fergus Bay. Although Dae was surprised by the news, he picked up her cue and assured her he had the practice covered, while Sue promised to reschedule her appointments. She asked Sue to book her on a flight to Hobart that afternoon, then turned back to Dae to tell him about some time-sensitive test results she was expecting for a patient. Dae, with tears in his eyes now, told her he had it covered, but added that he would be at the funeral. Sure. That was fine. Yes. Fine.

Not stopping, she turned and headed back to her office, thinking about the call to her dad, realising that of all the days she needed to reach him, this was the day he was presenting at an accounting conference. She called her mum as she packed up her bag with her laptop and notes, but her mother took it in stride.

"It was Marty's time, Danmus," her mother said, using the Korean nickname she'd given her as a child. "We'll be on the first flight tomorrow morning, even if it means flying in separately." Brooke made a note in case she forgot.

"Just remember that the bridge is out between Fergus Bay and Orford," Brooke said, trying to keep the panic from her voice.

"We're well aware. Don't worry, Sweetness," the nickname now translated to English. "We'll work it out. You just get there as quickly as you can. We're right behind you."

Brooke called Merritt when she caught the train to the airport. Her friend tried her best to lighten her heart with a story about Marty from ten years before.

"Remember how I teased Marty about being too old to do tequila shots? I lit a fire with that! She put me in my place quick-smart! Oh, and the look on her face!" Merritt laughed. "She said, hands on hips, that she'd been shooting tequila long before I was a twinkle in my mother's eye! Remember that? She was punchy with those stories of living in Mexico. What was she there for? Relief work? Well, after five shots, I was blasted, and she was still as sober as they came. She earned my undying respect after that, and I had no doubt Marty could hold her own with the best of them!"

Merritt assured her she'd be in Fergus Bay the following day. While the train rumbled toward Central Station, Merritt booked her flight. Brooke was relieved she'd be there. Merritt had spent many of her holidays in Fergus Bay with her and Sam, stopping only when she met James. Merritt's support would help a lot.

Two hours later, Brooke was on a flight from Sydney to Hobart. In her crumpled suit, a coffee stain on her pristine white shirt from earlier turbulence, Brooke sat still for the first time since she heard the news. Reality was sinking in. Sam was amazing for calling the police, then making the arrangements to get the body to Hobart. When she called Sam, right before her flight boarded, Sam told her Marty was taken out in the Westpac helicopter. The funeral home couldn't get to her house with their hearse. Marty would have loved that, she mused. But it was Sam who was on her mind. Telling Bee would be the hardest part. Bee was as close to Marty as Brooke was. She would be a mess by the time she got there.

Freycinet appeared in the distance from her window. She was almost to Hobart. She knew this area like the back of her hand. She scanned the coastline. It weaved in and out with thin lines of white sand and inlets, its border dotted with native gum trees. The water colour changed from turquoise, close to the shore, to a dark navy further out. She narrowed in on Maria Island, which meant Fergus Bay was nearby. Brooke looked down, hoping to catch a glimpse of Marty and Sam's houses, but a cloud blocked her view. Disappointed, she looked back, catching a last glimpse of Freycinet before it too disappeared behind a cloud. She sighed.

Turbulence bumped the plane, and someone swore behind her. The flight attendant hung on while clearing the last of the rubbish. Brooke sat back, knowing that in less than fifteen minutes, she'd be landing at Hobart airport.

Then what? Sam's last comment was she didn't know who'd be at the airport to pick her up. Sam would be tied up with Bee. Georgina was down south, visiting friends. With Bee and Sam out, Nicole was short staffed, so she was out as well. Sam's last comment rang through her head: *someone will be there*. She had to trust her. Sam had done a lot already. Wait. Didn't Merritt say something about hiring a car when she flew down? Why hadn't she thought of that? It would have been a lot easier on Sam. She'd look into that. She felt bad for whomever had come all the way to get her.

Coming to Hobart was like flying into a big country town. It was hard to think of it as Tasmania's state capital. Following the line of passengers, Brooke took the stairs to the tarmac. There was no jet bridge here. Once inside the terminal, she turned right and continued to the far end of the building where the one baggage carousel serviced the entire airport. As it spat out suitcases from her flight, the biosecurity beagle weaved its way through, sniffing luggage for banned substances.

"Brooke." She heard the voice but refused to connect it with the person saying her name. No. It couldn't be. Would Sam really send ... no. She wouldn't. She turned. But there, standing only four metres from her, was the man who had left her and taken her heart with him.

"Lachlan."

"Hi. Look, Sam sent me. She said you needed a ride. Since I was heading that way..."

The last time she had seen Lachlan was at Zed's funeral, four years before. Now he was sporting a full beard and his hair was long. No, not all of it. The sides and back were shaved, but it was long on top and pulled into... was that a man bun? He definitely had a hippie tradie vibe going, especially with his blue dockers, work boots, and the grey hoodie emblazoned with his company logo, Jones Custom Constructions. Brooke never imagined this look for him, but somehow it worked. But right now, with his hands in the pockets of his hoodie, he looked nervous. Good.

"And she couldn't send anyone else?" She knew her tone was tight. Of all people Sam could have sent...

"No one else was available, I guess. I'm not that thrilled either, but since it's about Marty..." She'd kill Sam. Lachlan stood in front of her, his blue eyes piercing into hers. Those eyes. She hadn't remembered the gold flecks around his pupils. How could she forget that? She looked away, down to the baggage claim area.

"Do you have a bag?" he asked, bringing her focus back to look into those damn eyes.

"Yes," she said, and turned back to the baggage carousel, overflowing with suitcases. She needed to focus. She didn't need this distraction. She needed to get to Fergus Bay and Lachlan was merely a way to get there. That's all. She didn't have to speak to him.

She reached down for her hot pink wheelie bag. She had been embarrassed to buy it, but turned out, it was easy to spot when she travelled. Lachlan reached the handle at the same time she did.

"I've got it," she spat at him, a little too harshly.

"I'll lift it down and you can take it from there," he said. Oh yeah, she'd forgotten how chivalrous he was, and how much they'd bashed heads over it when they were together. She could handle this, and he knew it. Still, it wasn't worth the fight. Not today.

"Fine," she said and left him to it. She noticed the flex of his muscles, even through the thick hoodie. He was more fit than she remembered. Just pure muscle. Ugh. She felt the emotions rise. No. No. No.

"There you go," he said, extending the handle for her and backing away, hands raised in surrender.

"Thanks," she mumbled, then took the handle and strode toward the exit. The cold air blasted her when she left the terminal. Realising her winter coat was packed inside her suitcase, she kicked herself but refused to stop. She'd deal. She shook her hair from the ponytail, and pulled her suit jacket up around her neck a little tighter. Lachlan sighed behind her. She turned and scowled. What was that?

"Welcome back to Tasmania. Had quite the weather lately," he said. Great. He wanted to talk about the weather. Just great. She pulled her jacket closer around her chin and kept walking. She sped ahead, trying to gain some distance between them, but her bag caught the lip of the footpath, twisting it in her hand. The suitcase lurched sideways.

"Shit," she exclaimed, mortified. Lachlan reached forward to help her.

"I've got it," she snapped. She had to have her shit together. To prove to him she was capable. That she was okay. That she had survived without him.

9

SAM. NAVIGATING.

SEPTEMBER.

She hated to do it. Hated it just as much as she hated calling Brooke to tell her that Marty was gone. Brooke was going to be furious with her. She could almost feel the seething animosity emanating from the airport, and it was over an hour's drive away. She imagined the look on Brooke's face when she found Lachie waiting for her. But Sam had no choice. But Sam had no choice. She was tied up with the police, the coroner, and the homeowners offering their shacks to be used as needed. When Sam called Nicole, to let her know she wouldn't be coming in, Georgina arrived less than two hours later to help prepare for Brooke's family. Sam appreciated Georgina's help, but had she known Georgina was coming to Fergus Bay, she would have asked her to stop at the airport instead of Lachie.

It was while Georgina was there that Sam finally lost it. When she walked back into Marty's house, her eyes zeroed in on the half-finished shawl Marty had been working on, the knitting sitting beside her chair. Georgina held her for a long time when her sorrow took over. Sam grieved, just as she had when she lost her own mother when she was sixteen. The maternal figure in her life was gone. But Marty was more than that to her. Marty was her friend. She was wholly engrained in their lives. How were they going to cope?

It was an insufferably long day. The police arrived to conduct their inquiries, then took over two hours to work out how to get the body to Hobart. They'd finally sent the Westpac helicopter. She'd answered what questions they had, knowing Brooke and her parents would answer the rest. But it was a day she hoped never to repeat. Zed's death was terrible, but she couldn't remember dealing with this part. The police. The declaration. Maybe she had? Her memory was blank to most of that first week after his death.

Telling Brooke this news was difficult. But now she'd have to deal with Brooke's wrath over sending Lachie to pick her up. Oh boy. This was going to be fun.

She fished her phone from her back pocket when it buzzed. A text from Brooke. Oh shit. Here we go.

On my way. My ride was a surprise.

Well, okay. That was a veiled swipe. The rest would come.

Can't wait to see you. And sorry. Will explain when you get here.

This should be good, Brooke immediately responded.

Sam knew the connection would be sporadic once they drove out of Sorell and into the forest. Maybe there was a silver lining. She called Merritt. She needed to share the news and maybe Merritt would have some advice for dealing with Brooke's ire.

"Hey, it's Sam," she said when Merritt picked up.

"Hi. How are you doing? Brooke called me earlier and told me about Marty. I'm so sorry." Sam wasn't sure if Brooke would think to call Merritt. She wasn't surprised she had. Brooke was closer to Merritt, mostly because they'd known each other longer. Now though, Sam needed to skip over all that and get Merritt's advice on how to handle the situation with Brooke.

"Yeah. Look, I think I fucked up. I need to know what to do," she said and explained about Lachlan.

"Oh shit. She's going to blow her stack! Was there no one else?" Merritt asked. It sounded like she was typing. Sam needed her full attention.

"Nope. No one. What do you suggest? They have to go the long way around, so it's going to be a while before she gets here. But that means longer in the truck with Lachie."

"Is she speaking his name yet?" Merritt asked. More typing.

"Nope. What are you doing? Are you typing?" It irritated Sam that Merritt's attention span was forever fleeting.

"I'm looking for a rental car for tomorrow. Dae and I are both going to rent one, so I'm checking availability on 4WDs while he deals with the practice stuff."

"Oh. Right. That's a good idea," said Sam. She hadn't thought about people getting to Fergus Bay. She'd thought about cleaning the houses, but her mind blanked on the rest of the details.

"Okay, found a couple. Let me book them. I would hate to miss out. You know how it is with rentals at Hobart Airport," Merritt said. Sam waited impatiently while Merritt's mouse clicked.

"Okay, back to Brooke. Just give her space. Don't press her on it. She'll be pissed, but she'll mostly be thinking about Marty. Just apologise and let her vent if she needs to. I mean, if you sent James to pick me up, I'd be pissed too, but that's a whole other story. Brooke isn't likely to hold this over on you forever."

"Okay. I figured that's what I needed to do. But just warning you as well. Lachie will be hanging around while we work all this stuff out. He and Marty were close."

""That part won't make her happy, but we'll buffer. What else can I do? I'll be there tomorrow. My flight from Melbourne comes in around the same time that Dae, Jase, and Mi-Young arrive from Sydney. Ray will be on a flight from Brisbane, but he'll be getting in a little before our flights arrive. So, we're all coordinating."

"Can you stop in Hobart and get some booze? Stocks are low here and I figured everyone will need it to get through this. The bridge debacle has put a spanner in the works in getting supplies. I think we have enough food. Georgina said she was going to help with that. I'm sorry to ask since it means an extra trip for you. I'd normally manage that, but I've had to stay here..."

"I'll talk to Dae about it. Might be an idea for Dae to drive Brooke's parents straight to Fergus Bay, and Jase and I will deal with the rest."

"Yeah. Yeah, that's a great idea. Thanks Merritt. That will help a lot," Sam said.

"Okay, let me get back with Dae, and I'll text you later with the plan. Let me know how it goes between Brooke and Lachie. Brooke won't be happy, but you had no choice. She'll understand that... eventually. Maybe have a shot of whisky before they arrive?" Merritt chuckled. Sam didn't want to admit she'd already had one after they'd loaded Marty's body on to the helicopter.

Just over two hours later, Lachie's truck came down the road. They were later than she expected. Visions of an all-out fight on the side of the road and a potential murder kept her worried.

"Is that Uncle Lachie and Aunty Brooke?" asked Bee, standing at her bedroom doorway. A long line of red flamed while she scratched her arm. Her voice was hoarse, and her eyes were bloodshot. The news of Marty's death upset her as badly as Sam expected. It took Sam an hour just to calm her. Now, she still looked a mess, barefoot and dressed in her school uniform, her ponytail skewed. Sam's heart broke just looking at her. She'd lost another person she'd grown close to. Another piece of her own life puzzle lost forever. Sam knew Bee would break down again with Brooke's arrival.

Had Brooke broken down after she heard the news? Sam pondered that as she walked to the back door. Probably not. Brooke faced tragedy with clinical detachment. She was a rock when Zed died. Besides, Lachie was here. Brooke hardened to stone around Lachie. No emotions. Ever. But she couldn't second guess her decision to call him. He'd been her absolute last resort.

A car door forcibly slammed shut outside. That would be Brooke. Sam opened the back door and walked into the sunshine. Lachie waved to her, his face sporting a grimace. He walked around to the back to help Brooke, but she already hefted her suitcase halfway out of his truck.

"Hi guys. How bad was the road?" Sam asked, trying to sound light and failing miserably.

"Hey Ginger," Lachie said, using the nickname he'd called her since the day they met. He was the only one allowed to call her that. "It was better than it has been. They've finally graded it. That helped. We, um, stopped on the way." So, they had a roadside fight after all, just as Sam feared.

"We stopped at the funeral home in Sorell," said Brooke, coming to her for a hug. Sam saw how wrecked Brooke looked. Her whisky brown eyes were tinged with red. Her hair was uncombed, sporting a kink from a long-worn ponytail. Sam was surprised to see the stained shirt under her rumpled grey suit. It was unlike Brooke to look so dishevelled. It felt a lifetime ago that Sam called her with the news, but now, Sam felt the ferocity of the hug. Was it out of relief or grief? Whichever it was, a healthy amount of rage was mixed in.

"Brooke, I'm so..." Sam began, as Lachie walked past them to her back door.

"Don't say it. It's not like we weren't expecting it at some point. She was ninety-eight, after all. No spring chicken." Ah, okay. The doctor was in. That would explain the invisible mask, the 'I'm fine! Every-thing is fine!' mask she wore with Lachie here.

"Do you want to stay here, or over at...?" Sam began, but she couldn't bring herself to finish the question. If Brooke said she wanted to stay at Marty's, she'd ask Lachie to take the suitcase over for them. She'd had enough of being in Marty's house today.

"Here for now. I don't want to go over there yet," Brooke replied. Sam nodded.

"Hey kiddo," Lachie said to Bee, behind her. "You doin' okay?" Sam didn't hear what Bee said, but she was glad Lachie was here. Bee needed him now more than ever. Whatever she had said to her daughter hadn't worked so far to ease her hurt, but at least she'd stopped crying. Bee was close to Brooke, but not nearly as close as she was to Lachie.

"You'll be okay. Promise. And look, I want to stay, but I've an emer-gency up in Triabunna. But text me later, okay?" Sam highly doubted there was an emergency. Not today. It was more likely Lachie was escaping Brooke's wrath. He looked as sad as Bee did when she turned to look at them. When Bee nodded, he hugged her, then pinched her chin as he always did when he bid his goodbye, then turned and walked back toward his truck, ignoring Brooke on the way past.

"Bee baby," Brooke said, and moved in to hug Bee. Sam knew Bee would be a blubbering mess in Brooke's arms within minutes. She didn't want to leave Brooke to deal with that for too long, but she needed to talk to Lachie first.

"Lachie, wait up," she said, and walked over to Lachie's truck. He was already reaching for his door.

"So, how'd it go with Brooke? I'm really sorry to have asked you," Sam whispered.

"It's alright. Someone had to pick her up, but we barely said two words to each other. Other than her asking to stop at the funeral home on the way. That's why we were delayed. She wanted to view the body. But it wasn't there."

"No. It's still at the morgue. They have to issue the cause of death certificate before they can release the body to the funeral home."

"Ah, okay. Brooke seemed to know more about it. Like, she wasn't surprised it wasn't there, but she wanted to check anyway. So, I waited in the truck. Her instructions." He looked pained. He was just as stubborn as Brooke, but Sam knew he still loved her.

"Look, don't worry about Brooke. She's got a lot on her mind. I'm sorry to have asked for your help. I know you were busy. I just ran out of options."

"Yeah, it's no problem," he said. "No word on the bridge yet?" Sam shook her head.

"Shame. Well, I'm off to meet my crew at the flying fox, so if you need anything from Orford, let me know. I'll be back later on this side to pick up my truck."

"Thanks. Georgina was over today. She's been great. Not only with this, but with the bridge bullshit, too. And Merritt is organising an alcohol run from town when she gets in tomorrow."

"Okay. I'll be back out tomorrow, so if you need anything else, just text me. I'm here for whatever you need. You know how I felt about Marty." Sam noticed he said nothing about Brooke. "Oh, and I wanted to talk to Brooke about, you know, making the casket. But I didn't get there."

"I'll broach it with her. I'll let her know what you and Marty agreed to."

"Thanks. I believe Ray knows. Just not sure about Brooke. When I spoke to Marty about it last year and showed her the plans, she said she was humbled, which..." Lachie said, his eyes tearing up. He cleared his throat.

"It's kind of my way of saying goodbye, you know? She was the closest I ever came to having a grandmother." Lachie said, forcing a smile. Then he waved, got into the driver's seat, and reached for his seatbelt. Sam nodded, closed his door, and stepped back, then waved when he put the truck in gear.

The unspoken words lingered: even if he hadn't married the woman's granddaughter all those years ago.

10

BROOKE. REALITY.

SEPTEMBER.

Brooke sat on Sam's brown corduroy couch with Bee's head in her lap. She gently ran her hand across Bee's head, smoothing her hair away from her face. She'd only said two words to Bee before the girl collapsed into her arms, sobbing. Brooke felt every ounce of the girl's pain. So much had happened since that morning. When she was stuck in the truck with Lachlan, she realised it was Sam who was left to deal with the body. She hated to think of the trauma that raised for her. No one had thought about that piece when the time came for Marty... Oh shit. She hadn't even asked Sam if she was okay. She'd been too pissed about her ride.

The back door slammed. Sam walked over and gestured she would take over consoling Bee, but Brooke shook her head. She was fine with Bee. She could take Bee's emotions and heartache. She was a doctor. She was trained for this. Besides, she needed the reassuring touch herself.

"Is he gone?" Brooke asked Sam. Sam nodded with such a guilty look that Brooke nearly laughed out loud. God. That was a royal blindside!

"Why the..." Brooke began, then looked down at Bee. The girl was seventeen. Surely, she'd heard the word fuck before.

Brooke felt sorry for Sam, but the moment of sympathy vanished. With Sam conveniently standing in front of her, Brooke's anger resurfaced. She knew it was wrong. Sam was hurting too. But sending Lachlan? That was too much.

"Why the fuck did you send Lachlan?" Brooke spat, and Sam's jaw dropped; her eyes grew wide. Brooke rarely swore, and never in front of Bee.

"Sorry Bee Baby. I'm just..." but Bee wasn't listening. She was in her own world of hurt.

"I'm so sorry, Brooke," Sam said, tears forming. "I tried everyone. Jackson even offered to come in and get you, but..."

"He can't drive anymore. But it may have been preferable to bloody Lachlan!"

"I know, I know. I'm truly sorry. I called everyone I could think of. But then Lachie said he was coming out here anyway, so he agreed to get you on the way through. I knew you'd hate it, but I really had no choice. I wanted to pick you up myself, but there was no one else to deal with... the rest."

Sam's revelation doused her anger.

"It's fine. I was just surprised." Brooke said, finally realising that Sam wouldn't have sent Lachlan unless she really had to. Not today of all days. The reality hit her hard.

"And I know, I should have warned you. But you were already in the air by the time he responded."

"I won't have to deal with him anymore, so we can just let it go." Sam slumped heavily in the seat across from her. The wood stove crackled, making her jump.

"Here's the thing. Lachie..."

"Let's just agree not to speak his name," said Brooke, stopping Sam in her tracks. Brooke ran her hand across Bee's hair once again, stroking it softly. It used to calm her when she had tantrums and, gauging by the reduced tears and the deeper breathing, it was doing the trick. Brooke needed something to calm her own anxiety. Maybe she'd take a run on the beach later. She could hear the waves crashing on the shore and, if she just closed her eyes, she could imagine herself riding the waves.

"Why don't you want to speak his name, Aunty Brooke?" Bee asked in a voice that reminded Brooke of when Bee was five. Bee sat up when Brooke didn't respond right away. Her face was mottled, and snot ran beneath her nose. "What's up between you and Uncle Lachie?"

"Go blow your nose, Bee. I'm sure Brooke doesn't need that on her suit. Besides, she doesn't want to talk about him right now." Bee slowly got up from the couch. Lines from the corduroy creased her arms.

"Or ever," Brooke grumbled as Bee walked back to the bathroom.

"I'm truly, truly sorry, Brooke, but I have to say this. Lachie... well, you know he and Marty were close."

Brooke sighed. Fuck. She hated the closeness of this community sometimes.

"What does he want?" she asked. She needed wine. Or whisky. Anything. "Wait. Don't tell me yet. Do you have anything to drink? I think I need alcohol to deal with anymore of today. And I'm sure there's a lot you need to fill me in on."

"I have red wine, whisky, Baileys, and I may even have some left-over gin from summer," said Sam, crawling from the depths of her chair to go to the kitchen.

"A shot of whisky, then wine," Brooke said and followed Sam. She picked up her handbag near the front door and grabbed her Chapstick and her phone. She needed to let her parents know she'd arrived, and that Marty's body was still with the coroner. She didn't want them to waste a trip to the funeral home, either.

"Do you want me to just spill today's events or...?"

"Let's have a drink first. Is Bee okay?" she asked, looking back toward the bathroom.

"She'll be okay. It may be hard for her to hear the details, so I'll suggest she go in for a bubble bath."

"Are you talking about me?" asked Bee, coming back out of the bathroom.

"Yes, actually. I was just saying to Brooke you might like a bubble bath. What do you think? Light some candles, put on some music?"

"Are you trying to get rid of me?" Bee asked.

"Well, do you want to hear all the gory details of today?" Sam asked. Brooke really admired the honesty and openness of their relationship. It reminded her of the mother-daughter duo in Gilmore Girls. These two were a united front, especially since Zed's death. She was just glad to be a part of their circle.

"Ah, no thanks. I'll go have a bath. But I have one question for you, Aunty Brooke. It's kind of morbid."

"What's up, Bee?" Brooke asked.

"When they prepare Marty for, you know... the funeral, can you make sure her nails are painted? I know they do makeup and all that, but can you also make sure her nails are painted too?"

"That's an odd thing, Bee," Brooke said.

"I know, but Marty always had her nails painted. Always. Her nails were never chipped. You never noticed that?" Bee asked. Brooke looked at Sam with a puzzled expression.

"She's not wrong. Now I think of it, Marty never went without nail polish. They were always immaculately done," Sam said.

"Don't worry Bee," Brooke said. "I'll make sure they're painted. Can you help me with the colour?" Bee nodded.

"Thank you," Bee said. It seemed as if the weight of the world was lifted from her shoulders for such a small thing. "I just kept thinking about that. Ever since..." Brooke stepped over and hugged her goddaughter.

"I've got you covered, Bee. Leave it with me," she said.

"Are you two having wine? Can I have some?" Bee said, now being a little cheeky. She knew the answer was no. She still had four months before reaching the legal drinking age. Still, it helped lighten the mood.

"Nice try," Sam laughed. Bee shrugged, kissed her mother's cheek, hugged her quickly, then left them to it. Brooke opened the bottle of wine while Sam went to the cabinet and grabbed glasses for the drinks.

"I would have given her wine. It may help calm her down a bit," said Brooke.

"From the doctor's lips? Oh my!" Sam said, smiling. She poured a healthy dose of whisky into the tumblers.

"Sometimes a little helps. Besides, she's almost of age. She's probably sneaking whisky behind your back." They heard Bee pottering around before finally closing the bathroom door.

"She's not like we were," Sam said, picking up the wine bottle and pouring the deep red liquid into the wine glasses.

"Doubt that. Bee is a replica of you, only taller," Brooke said. "You should have started marking the bottles years ago." Sam rolled her eyes.

"Okay, spill it," Brooke said, then turned her head toward the bathroom. "God, what is she listening to?"

"Funk Rap. Don't ask," said Sam, and handed Brooke the whisky glass. They both downed their shot, then carried their glass of wine to the lounge room.

"Let me just stoke the fire. It's going to be cold tonight," Sam said, opening the wood stove and adding another log.

"I know I should go to Marty's tonight. But I just... can't." Brooke felt hollow. Like a piece of herself was missing. They always congregated at Marty's house, but it would be all too real if she went there. She wasn't ready for that. Not yet.

"It's fine. I get it. Just means you have a choice of sharing a bed with me, or with Bee. Or you can snuggle with Ned on the couch," Sam said, securing the latch to the stove. Ned perked up at the mention of his name.

"Sorry Ned," Sam said, curling up in the deep lounge chair again. The dog put his head back down.

"Do you remember when your mum and dad died and how you slept in my bed for two weeks? You said you didn't want to be alone," Brooke said, taking a sip of her wine. "I get that now."

"My bed it is then," Sam said, giving her the look she needed. It wasn't sympathy. Brooke had enough of that today. It was a look of understanding. And God knew, of all people, Sam would know what this emptiness felt like.

Sam recounted every single detail about the day's events. Everything from the questions the police asked to how they'd got Marty's body into the helicopter. She left nothing out. Brooke thought it bizarre to think about getting Marty into the helicopter, but it was fitting. Her grandmother would have loved it. Her last grand adventure.

"I need to talk to you about one last thing, and sorry, but I have to say his name. Lachie has built Marty's casket. He and Marty talked about it before, and she was okay with it. He said he'd spoken to the funeral home to make sure it's legal. And it is. He's been working on it for a while, knowing this day would eventually come. I think your dad is aware, but Lachie didn't think you were."

"Her casket?"

"He is a master carpenter, remember? And Lachie's work is amazing. Whatever he has made for her, it's bound to be beautiful. Worthy." At this, Brooke crumpled. The weight of the emotion finally caught up with her. Lachlan's kind gesture was the last thing she expected.

11

SAM. REMINDERS.

SEPTEMBER.

Sitting behind Brooke and her parents for Marty's funeral, Ave Maria played overhead. She dug her fingernails into her palm, fighting the urge to flee, praying to any God that listened, to end the fucking awful music. It was too much. Bee sat next to her, straight as a board, her cheeks tear stained. And right now, she was back to scratching her arm and looked to be damn close to drawing blood. She reached for Bee's hand. Bee turned, attempted a smile, but the smile didn't reach her red-rimmed eyes.

Sam desperately wanted off this depressing roller coaster. First her brother's funeral, then her parents', Zed's funeral four years ago, and Beverlee's a year later. It was the ride that never ended. This music played at every damn one of those funerals. She tried to skip it for Zed's funeral, but Beverlee insisted. Why was this music a requirement of every damn service? A large, callused hand took hers, startling her out of her turmoil. Lachie looked over to her and knowingly gave her hand a squeeze.

She'd been running for days. Ever since she found Marty. But now she'd stopped. She'd been forced to, for yet another funeral. When the minister spoke, the horrible music finally ended. Thank God for small favours. Sam inhaled deeply, catching her breath once again. She listened to the minister without hearing the words. Gathered today. Loving memories. Cherished life. Much loved. Blah blah. Same shit, different funeral.

A memory flashed to a scene with her mother when she was about seven or eight. She stood on an old wooden stool next to her mum in the kitchen. Flour dusted the floor and covered every counter. Music was playing in the background. The record player was always on in their house. What music played that day? Was it Billy Joel? Probably. Her mother loved him. His records were well played. Her mum was telling her a story, but what were they making? Was it bread? A pie? No, it was a cake. A carrot cake. Her dad's favourite, Sam remembered. Her mum was saying something about the mess they always made but she was laughing as she said it. She was always smiling or laughing. Until she wasn't.

All that changed when her brother Paul died. There was no more baking. No more music playing in the house. Sounds of laughter and joy were replaced with silence. Sam felt as if she lived in a library. She always had to be quiet. When her dad begged her mum to try counselling, she went screaming. Literally. She didn't want to talk about how she was feeling.

"No one understood this kind of pain," her mother screamed. Sam remembered the words vividly. The therapy hadn't helped either. It only sent her into a deeper depression. It was a surprise to all when her mum agreed to attend her Dad's cousin's wedding on the Central Coast. It was the trip that had cost them both their lives. Sam didn't want to think about what life would have been like, had they not gone.

She remembered little of Zed's funeral. She sat completely still during that service, so much so that she remembered her back aching later. She didn't shed a tear the entire day. People said to her later how much it surprised them. Why would it? She was used to death by now. Her people died, as simple as that. She remembered Beverlee blubbering into her hanky. Meanwhile, Jackson looked like he'd been hit by a truck, sitting still in silent agony. His famous one-liners buried for the moment with the tragic loss of his grandson. She was comforted by those one-liners. But where was Bee that day? She didn't remember Bee being at Zed's funeral. But she must have been.

Sam looked over to her daughter again and saw tears creep down her cheeks. She hated for Bee to bear this pain again. She squeezed her hand. Bee lay her head on her shoulder, snuggled in a little.

To someone on the outside, she, Lachie, and Bee might appear as a family huddled together. And they were, of a sort, but not in the traditional sense. That type of family stopped existing for Sam. She had lost so much. She glanced at Lachie. His eyes were fixed on the back of Brooke's head. Sam knew he'd rather be sitting next to her, holding her hand instead, comforting her. That's the family that should have been.

Marty's casket rested majestically at the front of the room. The smell of Huon Pine filled the air. Lachie built the coffin completely by hand. He painstakingly etched flowers into the longer sides of the casket. It must have taken him weeks, months. With his hand holding hers, she felt the dryness of his skin. It felt contradictory that a hand so rough would make something so delicate and beautiful. She knew Marty would have loved this casket. Would have been touched by the work and the love Lachie had put into it.

"It's beautiful Lachie. She would have been honoured," Sam whispered to him. He turned to her, surprised she was speaking while Brooke's father delivered the eulogy. But he smiled warmly, nodded, and returned his gaze back to the podium. Sam turned when a rumbling began from the back of the room. The Premier of the state, a tall, bald man with a well-seasoned face, moved to the podium and spoke of Marty's service to the Australian medical community.

"Did you know about all that?" Bee whispered to her when the politician finished his speech. Sam whispered that she knew of some of it. Marty was a different woman to the outside world. To them, she was simply Marty. Her adopted grandmother. Bee's great-grandmother, by love rather than blood. Avid gardener. Crafter. Baker. Mentor. Friend. She was so much more, but the feelings were trapped in her chest.

Bee released her hand and walked toward the front podium. It was that time already? She knew Bee was scheduled to speak. She asked

Brooke's parents if it would be okay if she said something at the funeral. Of course, they said. Sam watched her daughter smooth the folded piece of paper she pulled from her dress pocket. She looked out and found Lachie. She scratched her arm. Lachie held her gaze, and dipped his head slightly, as if to say, 'you got this.' Bee cleared her throat.

"When Mum told me Marty passed away, I was shocked. I mean, we all knew it would happen. She was old after all," there was chuckling in the aisles. Bee settled a bit. Her eyes locked on Lachie's again.

"But then it hit me... Marty was my grandmother. Well, great-grandmother really. She patiently endured tea parties with me when I was little. She built sandcastles down at the beach with me while Mum and Dad worked on the house. She taught me how to bake, because, well, she was better at it than Mum." More chuckling. "She taught me how to sew, knit and crochet, skills I treasure more than I can ever say." Her voice cracked. Sam smiled proudly at her girl as she looked down at her notes, then back at Lachie.

"But the biggest thing she gave me was my name. I was named after my dad's grandmother, Beverlee, but it was Marty who gave me the name Bee. She told me time and time again that I was a little bumble bee that spread love wherever I went. But it was Marty who did that. She spread the love. Thank you."

Bee raced back to her seat. Sam held her arms out and enveloped her in a hug when the tears came.

"That was beautiful, babe. You were brave to get up there and say all of that. Marty would have loved it," she whispered. When mother and daughter separated, Lachie, with tears in his eyes, reached over to Bee and squeezed her hand.

"On point," he said simply.

When the service was over, Sam sped back into go mode. She followed the mourners into the reception area. Dignitaries said a few words to Brooke's parents and left. Dae and Jase stood beside Brooke, speaking softly, rubbing her back. Sam mouthed to her, 'You okay?' Brooke offered a discreet nod.

"Hey Ginge. Georgina wanted you to know that there are hot hors d'oeuvres under the cloches, and sandwiches and cakes on the opposite tables. Everything is ready," Lachie said quietly beside her. "And I hope you know what cloches are, because I have no damn clue." Sam smiled.

She could not have gotten through this week without Georgina's help. She and Nicole rallied the troops to get food to Fergus Bay for the family, then organised the catering for the funeral, based on Marty's wishes. No one needed to ask for help, they simply got to work.

Lachie too, although how he had time to work and finish the casket, she had no idea. He must have been burning both ends of the candle. The dark circles under his eyes confirmed it. She knew her eyes matched his. Even with help, the preparations took their toll. Sam walked over to Brooke's parents, Ray and Mi-Young, to let them know everything was ready. Georgina opened the doors to the reception area.

"Hey," Merritt said, surprising her. "Are you okay?"

"Hi," Sam asked, ignoring the question. If she didn't stop and think, she was fine. Just fine. Looking at Merritt, Sam smoothed her hands over her shirt, trying to get out the wrinkles bound to be there. In three-inch heels, Merritt made it to Sam's eye level. The woman was dressed impeccably in a black suit that hugged her curves beautifully. Her blunt-cut blonde hair was glossy and smooth. Even her makeup looked professionally applied. Sam always felt like a scrappy home-body next to Merritt, although today she managed to wear makeup and wrangle her red curls. She doubted her efforts came close to matching Merritt, but it was the best she could do. Her black pants and kimono-style blouse, what she referred to as her funeral clothes, had been ironed at one point, thanks to Bee. The only place she ever wore them was to funerals. Zed's. Beverlee's. Now Marty's.

"What do you need help with?" asked Merritt.

"Just make sure Brooke keeps standing," Sam said.

"You and Bee too. This is hard for you guys as well. How can I help *you*?" Merritt asked. Sam looked over at Brooke. Dae was beside her, directing her where she needed to go. Between the four of them, she, Dae, Jase, and Merritt, no one had left Brooke's side since she arrived. It was like they were all waiting for her to crack open.

"You're already helping. I'm glad you and Dae thought to rent the

4WDs. That's helped immensely in navigating the forest road back and forth. And getting the alcohol. That's helped a hell of a lot, too." Merritt smiled.

"Just keep an eye on Brooke. She seems to have finally gone from doctor to grieving granddaughter," Sam said, locking eyes with Brooke and watching the tears form.

BROOKE. CARVINGS.

SEPTEMBER.

The music calmed her. She just wished everyone would leave her alone for five damn minutes. She felt suffocated from all the hovering. Sitting in the front pew beside her parents, the smell of pine and flowers filled her nostrils. Marty had been very specific about the flowers she wanted. Stocks in vases, and an arrangement of native wildflowers to cover the casket.

The casket. It sat only a few metres from her. Closed, thankfully. Lachlan had called her father, once he'd arrived in Fergus Bay. It was another thing Marty had noted in her wishes: she requested the casket made by Lachlan. It was a beautiful gesture. Brooke expected a simple pine box with some fancy joinery. Certainly not the exquisite carving depicting Marty's love for her garden. Sam was right. It was an extraordinary work of art. It broke her heart to know it would burn later, with Marty's body inside.

She stared at the wooden roses climbing the sides of the casket as the minister prattled on. They were fully bloomed and intertwined with other cottage-type flowers, flowers that were always present in

Marty's garden. Next to the roses were the sunflowers she grew, representing summer. And at the very end, a gorgeous eucalyptus tree, paying tribute to the tree in Marty's backyard. The one with the gravestone at the base of it. Whose gravestone was that again? She had no idea. Some long-lost relative.

A dignitary from the city got up and talked about Marty's service to Tasmania. More prattle.

Zinnias were etched into the lower left, with jasmine winding around in delicate spirals, almost identical to the jasmine that smelled so intoxicating along Marty's veranda. Lachlan clearly studied the garden closely. He included everything Marty loved most about her garden.

Brooke startled to see Bee standing at the podium. She looked older than her seventeen years today. Her hair was down, the loose curls framing her lost face. Tears left streaks in her makeup, but she must have worn waterproof mascara since her lashes were wet, but there were no black trailing lines. Bee cleared her throat, told the stories of Marty as a grandmother, bringing back similar memories of her own. But when Bee told the story of how her name came to be, Brooke could no longer contain her tears. Her mother handed her a tissue that she refused earlier. She hated to make a scene. This wasn't like her.

When one of Marty's gardening friends stood at the podium and spoke of the beautiful casket, Brooke's attention returned to her surroundings. Her eyes zeroed in on the detailed woodwork in front to her.

"It'll be okay, Sunshine." Brooke heard Marty speak as if she was sitting right next to her. "Look around. There's love in the room. You're going to be okay." Brooke turned in her pew between speakers and looked around. Dae and Jase sat on the other side of the room, two rows back from the front, Merritt sitting next to them. Dae stared worriedly at her. Her lips curled into a gentle smile, trying to convey she was okay. And she was, wasn't she? She continued looking around. She turned and gasped when she locked eyes with Lachlan right behind her, sitting beside Sam and Bee. She hadn't seen him come in. He looked handsome in his dark suit. The colour enhanced his cornflower blue eyes. He tried to smile, but this wasn't the place for smiles. Only sadness. She struggled to hold on.

After hours of shaking hands with people she didn't know, thanking countless people for coming, she needed air. People still hovered around her after returning to Marty's, asking her if she was okay. She was a doctor, for God's sake. Yes, she was okay. She dealt with death all the time. She knew how it worked. But now she craved space.

She stood alone in the spare room at Marty's house, hearing voices from the other side of the door. How could she get outside with no one noticing?

"Brooke?" Sam called from the other side of the door. Another hovering body, but at least she could tell Sam what she needed. She'd get it. She cracked the door and pulled her friend in. Sam started to ask her if she was okay, but Brooke held her hand up.

"What's the matter?" Sam asked.

"Don't ask me if I'm okay. I am so sick of that question," Brooke said. Sam nodded instantly. Good, she got it. "I need fresh air. I need to go for a run. Can you cover for me?"

"Yes. Go," Sam said.

"Thank you. Where's Bee?" Brooke asked, stripping out of her suit, pulling her running clothes on.

"Home. Liv is over for a bit. They're hanging out in her room. I think Bee's had enough of the adults for a while."

"Haven't we all," said Brooke, lacing her sneakers. "Sure you're okay for me to do this?"

"Yep. I've plied your great aunt with whisky. Your mum and dad have opened another bottle of wine. Merritt is entertaining everyone with another Marty story. And Dae and Jase are in the kitchen organising dinner. All good."

"Thanks," Brooke said, and opened the door a little. Seeing everyone distracted, she dashed to the back door, snatching one of the two yellow jackets that hung on the nearby peg.

Brooke walked down the sandy path to the beach while gathering her hair into a ponytail, securing it with a band from her wrist. Brooke relished the icy breeze on her skin. Air. It felt good to inhale it, to carry it with her. She stretched out her arms as she passed the sea daisies and coastal spinifex, bowing greedily towards the late-afternoon sun. Life slowly flowed into her. Running was how she dealt with death at work. It reminded her that life went on. Today was no different.

At the shoreline, she stretched, warming up her muscles. But she was impatient now. She reminded herself to start slow.

She headed south, feeling the southerly wind bite at her face in the coldness of the afternoon. But it felt good. Exhilarating even. She picked up her pace and headed closer to the waterline. Her feet pounded over the pipi holes that pocketed the wet sand. Oyster-catchers watched her carefully as they bobbed in the shallow water for their evening meals. Terns flittered back and forth between the waves, their legs speeding ten times faster than Brooke's fastest pace. She smelled the seaweed where the tide always left it piled along the shore. To her right, the resident sea eagle rested on his favourite spot. He watched her run by from the dead branch on the huge gum, not bothered at all.

Brooke flittered through her memories, but she let them go. Thoughts of Marty could wait for a while. Instead, she would stay in the moment. She needed this time alone to just be. A heaviness threatened to overwhelm her otherwise, like a dark cloud ready to burst and soak her to the skin.

She continued her pace for a kilometre down the beach. The oyster-catchers yipped at her when she got too close. The seagulls darted and swooped as she passed, never quite gauging the proper distance of safety. Not the brightest of birds, she thought. Salt formed on her lips although she didn't dare lick them, knowing that would dry her mouth out and she still had to return. She'd forgotten to bring water.

Ahead of her, she saw a figure sitting on the beach. Odd. She expected to have the place to herself. Maybe it was someone free camping, further down the forest road? It wasn't unheard of. Lots of people did that all over Tasmania. Her safety didn't even cross her mind, not here, but she didn't want to turn around. She certainly didn't want to talk to anyone, either.

The figure stood, brushed sand from their pants, then turned toward her. Lachlan. She slowed her pace.

"Sorry. Didn't think anyone would be down this far," he said when she finally reached him. He was still wearing his suit, the pant legs rolled up a little, exposing his bare feet. They had to be freezing. He wore a black woollen skull cap fitted down over his ears.

"No, I'm sorry. I didn't mean to disturb you," she said. "I didn't think anyone would be out."

"Needing fresh air, huh?" he asked, putting his hands into his pockets.

"Yeah. Was getting a little too..." This was more conversation than they'd managed in fifteen years. It felt weird.

"Stifling? Lots of people were hovering around you today. You used to hate that," he said, bringing back their past.

"Still do," she admitted.

"Hard day," he said, and it was then she noticed the dampness on his cheeks. He'd come down here to cry.

"Yeah. The casket was beautiful, Lachlan. Shame it was... you know," she said, regretting the words immediately. "It must have taken you ages. Did you sleep at all?"

"I had most of it done. Figured that even if she lived another ten years, I'd have ten years to keep working on it." That made sense. "I'm sure you weren't happy to have it in your face during the entire service. Didn't think through that part."

"It was actually a good distraction. I tuned out all the sad stories. It was, is, hard enough. Bee did well, though. So proud of our girl."

"She's a good kid. Ginger has done well with her," he said. Brooke laughed at the nickname.

"You're the only one that has ever gotten away with calling her that, you know. Dae..." she said.

"Let's not talk about Dae," Lachlan said, cutting her off. She nodded, saw pain in his eyes.

"Sorry."

"I know you will hate me asking this, but are you okay? I mean, really? I'm not asking as a courtesy. I'm asking you because I know how much Marty meant to you. And I watched you today, trying to keep it together. But this is me, Brooke."

She felt the lump rise in her throat but couldn't push it down. She stared at Lachlan and ever so slowly shook her head, but she couldn't stop the tears from falling. He stepped forward and took her into his arms. His arms were familiar and foreign at the same time. He smelled the same. Sobs broke free into his shoulder. Her knees buckled, and he caught her, cradled her, rocked her back and forth while she let the pain release. Lachlan rubbed her back, soothing her. His comfort was the last thing she expected, but somehow it was the comfort she needed. He said nothing. He simply held her as the tears flowed. Eventually, she pulled back and noticed the trail of snot on his jacket. It smeared when she tried to wipe it off.

"Don't worry about it," he said, handing her a cotton handkerchief from his jacket pocket. "It's unused. I have two."

"Thank you. Sorry," she said, wiping her nose.

"Why are you sorry? It'll come out when I get it dry cleaned."

"Sorry about that, too. I meant, sorry about losing it on you," she said.

"No need to apologise. You needed to let it out. You can't be the doctor all the time," he said and smiled gently. "I'm going to head home. That forest road is a bitch in the dark. You okay from here?"

"Yes. I'm going to walk a little further, then head back. Thank you, Lachlan," she said. He stepped forward, hugged her quickly, then turned and walked down the beach, his head down, lost in his own thoughts.

13

SAM. CHALLENGES.

SEPTEMBER.

Now the funeral was over, and everyone was settled in for the night, all Sam wanted was a four-finger tumbler of whisky and to take her damn shoes off. Merritt and Brooke sat in her living room, an open bottle of red wine between them. Nostalgic tunes from their teen years played quietly in the background. Bee had gone to bed after Liv went home, wanting some peace of her own. Sam wouldn't mind that herself, but that would come later. For now, she wanted out of the funeral clothes.

"Be right back," she said to her two friends.

Within two minutes, she'd thrown the funeral clothes on to the chair in her bedroom and tugged on her grey sweatpants, her favourite Bon Jovi hoodie, and her UGG boots. In the kitchen, Sam picked up the bottle of whisky from the kitchen counter, took a sturdy whisky glass from the cabinet, and joined her friends in the lounge room. She wrapped the soft yellow blanket Bee knitted around her and plopped into her favourite chair.

"What are you guys talking about? I hope it's something normal. I can't deal with any more death or crying today," Sam said. She winced when she saw pain shoot across Brooke's face. "Sorry."

Brooke shook her head.

"It's okay. We were just talking about how brave Bee was today," Brooke said, then took a sip of her wine. "I should have said more about what Marty meant to me, but I could only focus on the facts. If I opened the emotion can, it would have been the end of me. Besides, there were so many people." Sam nodded. She'd never been to a more packed funeral.

"I forgot it was Marty who gave Bee her nickname," Brooke continued.

"I remember Marty telling me the story of how Bee's nickname came to be," said Merritt. "But didn't Marty give you all a nickname?"

"Yes. I was Sweet Pea, named after her favourite cottage flower. Maybe it was her way of telling me I was her favourite?" Sam teased Brooke.

"Or because sweet peas are a climbing flower, and you drove her up the wall?" Brooke countered.

"Well, I guess it could go both ways," Sam said and raised her glass to Brooke.

"You had one too, didn't you Brooke?" Merritt asked, kicking her insanely high heels off and curling her feet under her on the couch. How Merritt was still comfortable wearing her suit, Sam had no clue.

"I was always Sunshine. Because I spread sunshine wherever I went. So, I was like Bee that way, I suppose," said Brooke. "Let's talk about something else. I need a distraction." Sam agreed. Emotions had run high all day.

"I heard Georgina talking about her photography with someone today. She's planning a exhibit?" Merritt asked.

"Yeah, she's in the middle of all the planning. She's handing the café over to Nicole," said Sam. "I'm just glad she's finally doing it. Her work is amazing, and it took a trip to Spain for her to decide to do something with it."

"Is that the Camino thing she kept talking about?" asked Merritt.

"Yeah," Sam said.

"But what is the Camino?" Merritt asked, drinking some of her wine.

"It's a long distance walk across Northern Spain. She did it earlier this year. I think it's like eight hundred kilometres. It took her just over a month to walk it," said Sam. "She absolutely loved it."

"Bloody hell. That sounds like a nightmare!" said Merritt. Working out was never Merritt's favourite thing, Sam knew. She tried to get her up to walk the beach in the mornings when she came down, but Merritt preferred her bed.

"I don't know," said Sam. "She came back a different person. It really did her a lot of good."

"Would you do it Brooke?" Merritt asked, drawing a zoned-out Brooke back into the conversation. "Walk this trail across Spain, like Georgina?"

"Maybe," Brooke said, snapping back to them. "We talked about it when I was here a few months ago. She said she loved it. That it changed her life. Georgina said it gave her a lot of clarity."

"God knows I could use that!" said Merritt. "I feel like my life is completely off track lately."

"Tell us about this eco-lodge you're wanting to build," said Brooke, sitting up a little straighter. Changing the subject meant she was re-engaging. That was good.

"An eco-lodge?" Sam asked. She knew Merritt was a developer, but she thought it involved corporate buildings, mostly. An eco-lodge was a vast pivot.

"Yeah. I've been wanting to build one for ages. James doesn't agree," said Merritt. She sighed deeply before taking a long drink of her wine. "To be honest, he's being a downright dickhead about it."

"You mentioned something going on with him. Did you figure it out?" asked Brooke. Sam remembered Merritt saying something to her about troubles with James, but with all the funeral arrangements, she forgot to follow up. She was surprised, though, that they were having issues. They ran a successful property development firm together for years before marrying eighteen months ago.

"To start, we have different visions. I think the eco-lodge, or even a fuller eco-resort, is essential to our portfolio. He wants to focus on the corporate side. But more pressing," she began, taking a deep breath, "he's been cheating on me for the last year with some woman he met at the gym. So now, I'm torn. I don't know if I want to continue working with him. I'm wondering if I should just kick him to the curb completely. Obviously, our marriage is over. Professionally, I don't have the money to go it alone. James secured the investors, and it's the part of the business I know little about. It's a mess. Everything is up in the air right now."

"I say kick him to the curb," said Brooke. "He cheated on you for most of your marriage! I'd kick him out professionally, too. You'll work out a plan and you'll be successful at it. You've got more business sense than most people I know."

"Thanks. Guess I'm just reeling with the personal stuff. It wasn't like our marriage was really solid. I mean, after the honeymoon was over, it hasn't been great," said Merritt, picking some of Ned's dog hair from her pants.

"You were rebounding," Brooke said. Sam looked confused.

"Yeah. I'm realising now that I shouldn't have gotten involved with James in the first place. I think I was lured by his charm and intelligence. But turns out, he just thinks with his dick. Men are not for me. Should have stuck with women."

Sam was confused. Women? What did she miss?

"What do you mean, should have stuck with women?" asked Sam.

"You remember Kendall, Sam," Brooke said. "Merritt's great love before James."

"She was in a fog back then," said Merritt. She turned from Brooke to Sam and said, "I've always been with women before James. Kendall and I were together for fifteen years." Sam thought Kendall was just Merritt's best friend from Melbourne, but Merritt hadn't mentioned her since... wow, a while. Sam figured their friendship had simply run its course.

"I had no clue. I thought you were just friends," she admitted. "Goes to show how much of a bubble I live in." Too much of one, clearly.

"Dad asked me today what I wanted to do about Marty's house," said Brooke, changing the subject, her voice trailing off.

"What do you mean? Like, sell it?" said Sam, feeling even more blindsided by this news than Merritt liking women.

"Yeah. But I don't know. It's hard, you know, especially since..." Brooke was hesitant to walk into Marty's house, let alone admit Marty died there.

"Brooke. You love it here. You love the house as much as she did. She wouldn't want for you to sell it."

"Then you have it," snapped Brooke. "I can't face it."

"You can't give it to me! Look, I know how hard this is. Trust me, I know." She hated to pull the Zed death card but selling Marty's house was insane!

"Shit. Yes, I'm sorry. I know you do. I just.." Brooke took a large gulp of wine. Sam had watched the doctor unravel, re-twine, and unravel again over the last few days. She thought she was on the re-twine stage again, but apparently not.

"I get it. But you also need to give yourself some time. But you know as well as I do, you cannot sell that house," Sam went on.

"I know," Brooke said, the weight of the words blanketing them all.

Sam couldn't believe they were even considering selling Marty's house. If only she had the money, she would buy it. Sam knew the place would sell quickly, and to someone who would probably let it sit vacant, eleven months of the year. What a shame. Of course, that meant she and Bee would be alone for most of the year in Fergus Bay. Wait. No. It would only be her. She'd be alone. Bee would be leaving soon too, to start her own life at university. The thought of being so alone crushed Sam.

"We'll deal with it tomorrow," Brooke sighed.

"I wish I could stick around," Merritt chimed in, "but I have a shit show to work out. I need to go back to Melbourne tomorrow." They were quiet for a few minutes. The fire crackled in the background, and Ned's snoring, low and deep, filled the silence.

"What's happening with the bridge, Sam? Any word?" Sam was grateful Merritt was changing the subject. She sipped her whisky.

"Nothing. It's been out for almost four weeks now. The council hasn't lifted a finger. They don't care. We're just eight houses in the bay with a handful of farms around us. There's no money here, so they ignore it. Lach…" She didn't see Brooke flinch for once. Maybe the ban on his name was lifted.

"The Man Whose Name Shall Not Be Spoken offered to get his crew out to make repairs. He wouldn't be paid, but he knows the burden it places on us. The council said he's not qualified for bridge building, so they wouldn't approve it."

"Are you still not talking to him, Brooke?" Merritt asked. Oh shit. Didn't Merritt realise she was jumping into the shark cage with that question? "I saw him today. He was watching you, making sure you were okay. He still cares about you. Isn't it time you just let it go?" Brooke sat next to Merritt and said nothing, staring into her wine glass instead.

"That would mean they would need to have a serious conversation about what happened. And it's been years. I'm not holding my breath," said Sam, daring to weigh in. If Merritt went there, so would she. Fuck it. She was done with their drama.

"Why are you so angry at him?" Merritt asked. "I'm sincerely asking. I don't get it."

"Because he left me at the airport," Brooke mumbled sadly.

"Years ago! When you told him you were married to someone else!" Sam said. "He had to find out from Zed that it was a marriage of convenience. Because you somehow left that part out. That's why he's been angry at you all this time." Brooke shot daggers in Sam's direction.

"There's more to it than that," Brooke whispered.

"Well, it sounds like something you need to work out with him. It's time, because it's obvious to everyone who knows you that neither of you have moved past it," said Merritt. "Anyway, I'm heading back to Melbourne tomorrow to face my own challenges. I will let you both know what happens with James. And Sam, I know you have challenges too. You're cut off without a way to support yourself and that's rough. But I think you have a bigger issue than that." Sam raised her eyebrow. Oh she'd love to hear this.

"You going to need to keep the guys at bay with Bee. If you're not already. She's growing up way too fast. I can't believe she's almost finished with high school!" Merritt added.

"Geezus, I know," Sam said, draining her whisky. Brooke continued to stare absently at her lap.

"Maybe a walk across Spain would do us all some good!" Merritt laughed, raising her glass in a toast. "Shit. I must be drunk to suggest that!"

14

BROOKE. LETTERS.

SEPTEMBER.

The sun coming in through the windows blinded Brooke as she sat on Marty's bedroom floor. Everyone had returned to their lives, but Brooke remained in Fergus Bay. She wasn't ready to leave yet. It took her nearly a week, but she finally worked up enough courage to walk through Marty's front door alone. It had been one thing while everyone was there. It was noisy. Busy. But alone? That brought forward the reality, and it was too hard to think about.

She'd been sorting through Marty's things since before five. She couldn't sleep. She'd had a dream about Marty, Lachlan, and Dae, all trying to talk to her at once. But she couldn't understand a word they were saying. Even now, hours later, the dream spun in her head as she tried to analyse it.

Shaking it off, Brooke crawled back into Marty's large walk-in closet and pushed aside a box marked 'Winter'. Her father asked her to look for a letter for Sam and another one containing Marty's bank password or a PIN number. Marty had compiled the important paperwork into a tidy bundle before her death, leaving it with a note for her father, so it wasn't like Marty to overlook such an important detail. And she had no idea what the letter to Sam was about. Since her parents needed to get back to Sydney for work, it was up to Brooke to find the information.

In the far corner, she found a small wooden chest with beautiful carvings. It resembled a hope chest, but it was smaller and more compact. A gift from Lachlan? Possibly. It looked handmade, but it seemed old. Brooke had never seen it before, even though she'd spent many of her young days in Marty's closet, tucked away from the adults, reading books. She would have remembered this chest. Maybe Marty had stored it elsewhere and moved it later? But where else would it have been? It's not like she could get into the attic. Maybe Lachlan...

Lachlan. Why did his name keep popping into her head? First her dreams, now with this chest. It was bloody annoying. Still, it made sense to think Lachlan was involved.

She lifted the lid and found bundles of letters. One stack was tied with blue ribbon, several stacks tied with red, and a couple of other random envelopes tossed in. She shuffled through the random pieces of mail, until she came upon one with Westpac Banking printed on the top left corner. This had to be what her father was looking for! After a quick scan, she recognised the PIN number. Of all the places. She'd call her father later with the details. She was curious about the other contents in the box.

She picked up the blue bundle and saw they were letters she'd written to Marty over the years. Every single one of them. She was touched that Marty kept them. Setting that bundle aside to look through later, she picked up one of the four stacks of letters tied with red ribbon. Odd. The envelopes, old and faded, were addressed to a Gilly Scott, but at the Fergus Bay address. The postmark showed the early nineteen sixties.

Who the hell was Gilly Scott? A relative, clearly, given she had the same last name as she and Marty.

Brooke took a letter out and flipped it over. All that was written on the back of the envelope was a name. Henry Finlayson. Finlayson. Why did that ring a bell? Did she dare find out who these people were? Moreover, did she dare read the letters? It seemed like an invasion of privacy. But whose privacy? Not Marty's, since they weren't addressed to her. So, who were these people? Her grandfather's sister? But wasn't her name something like Helen?

"Knock knock." Sam walked into the bedroom. "Geezus, what's going on in here?" Brooke looked up. Stacks of jewellery, letters, and an assortment of bits and bobs she'd found, were scattered all around her. Some items were set aside for her mother. Things she knew her mother would want. Brooke made a pile for herself as well. Her father had given instructions for her to go through everything. She looked at her phone. It was already half-past nine. How had she lost track of so much time so quickly?

"I was looking for some info my dad needed and clearly got distracted. But I have something for you. Dad said to make sure you got it. It's a letter from Marty."

Brooke handed the letter addressed to Sam. Sam took it hesitantly and looked at the crisp white envelope with profound sadness. "I'll read it later. I can't deal with it today."

"What else have you found?" Sam asked, folding the envelope, and sliding it into her back pocket. She settled onto the floor next to Brooke.

"I found these old letters in the back corner of Marty's closet. Do you know who Gilly Scott might be?"

"No idea. Sounds like a relative?" Sam suggested, taking a bundle from Brooke.

"Yes... probably. But why would Marty have these letters?"

"No clue. What do they say?" Sam asked, turning the bundle over in her hands.

"I don't know, I just found them. I'm scared to read them. Especially if they're not Marty's. Seems like an invasion of privacy, doesn't it?" Brooke asked.

"Yeah, kind of. Except..." Sam picked up another bundle, turned it over. "Do you know who they're from?"

"Someone called Henry Finlayson. I might ask Dad before I open them," she said. Sam nodded and peeked into the box, digging her hand in to the bottom. Brooke didn't mind in the least. Sam was as much a part of her family as anyone.

"Geezus, there's all kinds of stuff in this box. Look... photos. Holy... look at this one of your parents. They looked so young and fresh!" Sam declared and handed Brooke the photo. "It looks like it was taken in Korea."

"Likely. They met there. Mum was a tour guide in Seoul. She'd just finished culinary school and dad was backpacking after finishing uni. He said he was taking a gap year before starting work. Dad didn't speak Korean, so Mum, who spoke English, helped him out. It was love at first sight. Her parents weren't too pleased apparently, but he somehow convinced mum to join him on the rest of his travels. Later on, they moved to Australia. Her parents were certainly not pleased about that."

"I've never heard that story. I only knew they met in Korea. They told me that when I first started living with you guys." Sam looked down at another photo. "Wow, they were before their time, weren't they? I mean, backpacking around the world in the late seventies. They would have been considered hippies back then, wouldn't they?"

"Yes. They have some amazing tales from their travels. They're talking about reliving them next year when dad finally retires."

"If they ever retire," Sam said, shaking her head. "You're dad, maybe. But not your Mum."

"Would they move here?" Sam asked, picking up another photo. Brooke shook her head.

"Doubt it," said Brooke. "Dad's been on the mainland since he was eighteen. Says it's too cold down here for him now. It's why they bought the place in Queensland, I think."

"Have you thought more about selling?" Sam asked. Brooke shrugged. "Marty knew how you felt about this place. This has only ever been a holiday house to your parents. But for you? This has always been home to you."

Brooke considered that. It was true. She felt grounded here. At peace. It's where she did her best thinking. Even her creative side came out. And she felt less competitive being here. In Sydney, it was all about the business. She was always running from one place to another.

Yes, her practice was successful, but what about the rest? The highlight of her week was her Sunday surf. Here, she could surf every day. Here, she could relax and be the person she truly was, not just Doctor Choi-Scott. She was missing so much from her life being in Sydney, even though she had every opportunity there. She didn't fit there like she did here. Maybe she never did? She'd been running so long that she never stopped long enough to notice. Not until the last year or so.

"I know selling is on the table. But you should consider what this place is to you before you decide. Is it just a house? Or does the house have greater meaning for you?"

Brooke stayed silent, weighing her words.

"Anyway, I'm heading to work. Have an afternoon shift at the café," Sam rose, pulled her shirt over her black pants. "Jackson had his car delivered to the other side of the flying fox, so now we don't have to rely on anyone to pick us up from the other side. Do you need anything before I go? Anything from the market?" Brooke shook her head.

"No, between Mum and Jase, I think we have enough food to last a month. Oh, I may need milk. I found an espresso maker buried in Marty's pantry, so I've been using that."

"She had an espresso-maker? How did I not know that? No. Don't answer that. The woman was an obsessive tea drinker. She believed coffee was for sailors and wharfies," Sam joked, wrangling her unruly curls back up into a ponytail.

"The woman was wicked smart, but she had her quirks," Brooke said, then stood and stretched her arms over her head.

"You know, I think I could use a change of scenery," she added. She stood and stretched her arms over her head. "Mind if I hang out at the café for a while?"

"You can hang out all afternoon if you want," Sam said, looking down at her phone. "But I've got to go in the next five minutes, or I'll be late."

"Give me three. I may take a long walk around town. I need to move." Her legs were stiff from sitting too long. She bundled up the letters, grabbed her computer, and ran a brush through her hair. At the back door, she put old tennis shoes on. Orford was not Sydney. She didn't need to dress up. She was comfortable hanging out in old jeans and cardigans here.

"Grab a coat and a beanie. Wind's up and it's cold outside."

Brooke spent the first few hours in the café catching up on work. She chose a quiet spot in the corner, far enough away from the roaring fire not to overheat, but also not in the way of the tourist crowd. The wooden tables were large enough for her to spread out and, if she guessed, were the work of their resident carpenter, Lachlan. Nope, she wasn't going there again. The letters remained bundled before her. She was still unsure about breaching someone's confidence. Brooke did a Google search for Gilly Scott and Henry Finlayson. With little else to go on, all she could find was a nurse in Scotland who looked younger than Brooke, and a mathematics nerd from the last century. Neither fit.

By three, Brooke needed a break, so she headed off for a walk. Orford was a laid-back village. It had a small supermarket, a post office called the Orford Hub, and a satellite library, along with the three cafés, including the one Sam worked in. Surprisingly, it also had a golf club, a bowling club, and a pub to support the vast number of holiday homes and Airbnb's. Last time Brooke investigated, there were about seventy AirBnbs in the immediate area, which sadly sat empty for most of the year. Tourists kept the cafés going, but Orford wasn't a bustling tourist destination, which probably explained why the Airbnbs sat empty. For Brooke, Orford, and Fergus Bay by extension, were as close to heaven as she'd ever found.

Passing those empty houses sitting along the Prosser River, Brooke walked east, toward the elephant sized, geo-textile sandbags. Marty explained they were placed there to prevent erosion. Brooke remembered Bee jumping on them, like they were a trampoline, when she was little. She loved the days when Bee was small. Sam probably did too, knowing she'd be leaving for uni next year.

Brooke turned from the sandbags onto Millingtons Beach. The Antarctic winds howled on this side of town. The waves were nearly big enough to surf. Tempting, but even a full winter wetsuit wouldn't protect her enough from the erratic winds. Normally people were running their dogs off-leash here, but today, the weather deterred even the most die-hard Tasmanians.

She really liked the vibe around Orford. The locals were mostly retirees, content to live and let live. It was the type of place where you stopped to chat with a neighbour outside the Orford Hub for twenty minutes before you continued with your day, all without missing a beat. She missed that connection in Sydney. But right now, she appreciated the quiet. It gave her time to think about the last week. She felt Marty's absence in the mornings especially. Surfing most mornings, Marty always had a full breakfast ready for Brooke when she returned. Now, she returned to an empty house, the same as in Sydney. Brooke wondered if she'd ever have the feeling of home again with Marty gone.

Zipping her jacket up to her chin, Brooke continued along the beach as far as the creek inlet. She cut back along the trail through Our Park, but she wasn't ready to go back to the café yet. Knowing Sam wasn't done until after five, Brooke followed the bridge over the Prosser River, then followed the path toward Raspins Beach. Some locals were out gathering firewood for their woodstoves, or walking their dogs, before twilight came. At the bird sanctuary, the pelicans slept on their nests while the nearby oystercatchers wiggled their bottoms, digging for their evening meal in the soft sand.

The school bus approached just as Brooke reached Raspins Beach. She expected to see Bee in the window, chatting with her friends, since her stop was in front of the café. She was such a good kid, Brooke thought. Since she wasn't working today, Brooke expected to find Bee deep in her schoolbooks by the time she returned.

To her dismay, when the bus pulled away, Brooke watched Bee walk toward a young guy leaning against a work truck. When she saw Bee's smile, Brooke was suddenly grateful to be hidden by the trees along the path. She watched Bee kiss the guy, and not a simple peck on the cheek either. Bee hadn't mentioned anything to her about a romance, and they had a pact. She could talk to her about anything, especially things she didn't want her mother to know about, so Brooke wondered if Sam knew. But Sam hadn't said anything to her either. And something like this, Sam would have definitely said something.

At least teased Bee about it. No, this was something Bee would tell Brooke, the older, wiser aunt. The trust between them was strong, and this kind of stuff fell right into that category. And the little vixen hadn't said a word about a guy. She'd ask tonight.

When Bee got into the passenger's side of the guy's truck, Brooke gasped.

Jones Custom Constructions.

Whoever this guy was, he worked for Lachlan. She'd definitely be asking Bee questions now.

After dinner, Brooke washed up with Bee, while Sam went to deal with the laundry.

"Hey. I was out walking today, down at Raspins." Brooke hesitated a beat. "Who's the guy?"

Bee spun wildly, splashing water everywhere, to see if Sam was around.

"She's in the laundry, don't worry. I take it you haven't told her about him yet?" Brooke asked, picking up a plate to dry. Bee shook her head.

"Any reason? It's not like you to hide stuff from your mum, is it?"

"He's older," whispered Bee, as if that explained everything.

"Um, hello? Your dad was older than your mum when they started dating. Like nearly five years older. Do you not think she'd understand?"

"I don't want her to think I'll end up like her," Bee said, placing a well-washed glass in the draining rack. "She's always going on about how worried she is that I'll end up like her."

"Pregnant, you mean?" Bee nodded. "Are you that serious with this guy? Are you having unprotected sex?" God, Brooke hoped not. Seeing Bee's instant blush, she worried they were. Maybe she just wasn't saying so. They talked about birth control only six months before, and Bee told her she wasn't ready and was still a virgin. With what she saw today, she was ready to write Bee a prescription right now.

"No. We haven't... done it yet. But we're close," Bee said. "I was going to ask you..."

"We'll make an appointment for you tomorrow. I can write you a prescription, but I think you're better off seeing a local GP. And you need to talk to your mum about this, Bee. She's going to find out. Orford is not that big of a place and if he works for Lachlan..." Just saying his name felt weird. But after the funeral, she'd put aside some of the anger.

"I will. I'll talk to mum."

"Have you talked to your Uncle Lachlan about it? He's got to know by now," said Brooke.

"He knows. Or he suspects anyway. We haven't been seeing each other for very long. Mostly we meet in the city," she said, pulling the plug on the water. Oh goodie, Brooke thought, secret rendezvous. They always worked out so well. She would know.

"What's his name?" Brooke asked.

"Declan. He's Irish," Bee said, and her voice softened. So did her face. She looked... swoony. Oh shit.

15

SAM. RUMOURS.

SEPTEMBER.

Sam stopped at Jackson's on her way to work. Her father-in-law was still active, but he was a cranky old goat without wheels. She couldn't fault that. She'd become a cranky old goat herself, since she'd been stuck for the last few weeks without a way to get around.

She liked Jackson. He was one of the wittiest people she knew, always delivering one-liners with the timing of a professional stand-up. She heard Bee repeat a few, which she needed to remember to talk to her about. It was one thing for Jackson to do, since he had the personality to match, but coming from Bee? She just came across as a smart ass. Sam needed to nip that.

She pulled up to Jackson's house. She swore the gardener was scheduled to come by this week, but the weeds were sprouting through the unruly lawn with a vengeance. She needed to call and find out what was going on. Reaching the back door, she knocked, then let herself in.

"Jackson? It's Sam."

"Geezus. You scared the shit out of me. Are you planning to kill me

for my money because I'll warn you now: You'll be sorely disappointed," Jackson said from his worn brown leather recliner. The chair was
older than Sam. Beverlee fought to get rid of it for years, but now she
was gone, the chair would be rolled out with Jackson's dead body.
Beside him was a side table, piled high with books, crosswords, a
coffee mug, and three different remotes. She guessed the mug was half
filled with his morning coffee. He often forgot to finish it.

"Sorry. I knocked. How are you doing?" She noticed the house was
reasonably tidy. There were some dishes beside the sink, which was
fine. Zed had installed a dishwasher for his grandparents not long
before he died, but Jackson never used it. Ironically, he thought it
wasted water.

"Fine, fine. I have people coming and going all the time. It's a pain
in my bum. Let's just say some people, like Bee, bring happiness. But
others? Happiness occurs with their departure." She laughed, understanding very few of his quips were actually directed at her.

"Do you need anything? I've got a freezer full of food from
Brooke's mum when she was here. I'll drop some off tomorrow. I'm
back at work so I can swing by every day again. No more strangers."

"Thank God for that. I can't even say they are strangers. They're
people I've known most of my damn life. Oh, Georgina is fine. She's
in and out. I can handle her. But the rest? They're just widows
looking for someone to coddle. They can stick to their damn knitting
circles. Don't need 'em." The chair squeaked angrily, as if in agree-
ment when he reached for the remote to mute the television. His
flannel shirt looked clean, but it had clearly seen better days. She
bought him new clothes for Christmas, but he told her to return
them and not waste her money. His were just fine, thank you very
much.

"I know it was a pain, but I needed their help when I couldn't get
here," she said, "so I'm grateful they stepped in to help. Speaking of
which, thank you for the use of your car. It's been a life saver. We're
glad to be back to normal."

"What's normal?" Jackson grumbled. "Nothing's been normal in
four damn years."

"Yeah, I know. I'm feeling that a lot myself lately."

"You and Bee okay out there otherwise? Any damage to the house with that storm?" he asked.

"Nothing we can't handle. Lachie is on to it." Jackson was the last person she'd talk to about her money woes.

"Sorry to hear about Marty, too. She was a good egg," he offered. Sam nodded. It was too hard to talk about the loss with Jackson. He'd lost almost as much as she had. First his daughter when she ran off. Then Zed. Then his wife Beverlee, who died of breast cancer a year after Zed's death. Although Sam still believed she'd died from heartbreak. Zed had been everything to Beverlee.

Sam checked Jackson's fridge and pantry, then walked back into the lounge room.

"Looks like you need milk and more bread, so I'll drop them by later. Oh, and I'm going to call the gardener. Your yard is getting out of control."

"Oh, he was here yesterday. Told me he was going to trim the hedge and weed the garden. Told him to get lost," Jackson said, picking up his glasses and crossword.

"What? Why?" she asked.

"Because I reckon God must love stupid people because He sure made a lot of them! The gardener included!" She smiled at his wisecrack, but she'd call the gardener to find out what really happened. It was likely Jackson was just in a foul mood and didn't want to spend money on something he couldn't do himself anymore. But he seriously needed his garden worked over, and Sam didn't have the time, or the tools, to do it.

"Okay. I'm off. I'll see you later. I'll be by tomorrow to do your washing and I'll drop off those leftovers. Alright?"

"Yep. Now off you go. I have words to play with," he said, and was focused again on his crossword before she was even out the door.

As she drove to the café, she called the gardener, and it was as she expected, Jackson ran him off before he could even unload his mower. Thankfully, he could complete the work while Jackson attended his weekly lawn bowl game tomorrow. One thing down.

She called Merritt to see how she was. A week passed since she'd received a text. Merritt's last message read, *'can't talk now. Volcano erupting'*, whatever that meant. Now the phone rang out and went to voice mail. Damn it.

"Hey, it's Sam. Haven't heard from you for a while. I'm now officially worried about you. Call me when you have a chance. Okay? Love you." She hoped she'd hear back from Merritt soon.

Georgina was neck-deep in conversation with Nicole when Sam entered the café five minutes later. Georgina was still transitioning the business over. Nothing was actually changing but ownership. But now she was back, Sam had been asked to manage the café, while Nicole learned the business side of things. That was fine with Sam. It gave her purpose. And it gave her a steady income again.

It still wasn't enough to dig her out of the financial hole she was in. The last month was rough. The pub had a new owner and had placed her on standby, rather than her regular roster of four shifts a week. She had a good relationship with the previous owners and couldn't afford to lose that additional income, but all she could do was wait and see. Bloody story of her life.

"Good morning!" a voice rang out on the other side at the counter. Sam concentrated on the coffee machine and couldn't see who was there.

"Morning. Hang on, I won't be a moment," she answered.

"No worries," Sam finished the order and turned to the voice, happy to see Georgina's friends, Pam and Jack. They had bought a piece of property on the other side of the river from Fergus Bay. It had originally belonged to Georgina's husband's family. Georgina mentioned they were coming in today to meet with Lachie. She looked to the clock and saw it was ten minutes to twelve. Bloody hell. Where had the time gone?

"I'm sorry. I'm terrible with faces," said Pam. "Wait. You're the one having a hell of a run lately." Sam flagged Kyra over to deliver the coffee to table eight.

"Georgina told us it's been a crazy time for you, with the bridge and the news of your neighbour," Pam said.

"Yeah, it's been pretty chaotic, but we're managing," Sam responded.

"Is there anything we can do?" asked Jack. The question threw Sam. She met these people only a few times before, yet here they were, offering help. "I don't cook, but I can cut firewood." The smile on his face was genuine. She remembered them more clearly now. Jack was lovely. He was witty, and so in love with Pam. She remembered Pam now, too. She looked like a sweet grandmother, but the woman swore like a sailor. In fact, she would have given Zed a run for his money. But these two were like a pair of giggling teenagers. If Georgina hadn't clued her in, she'd think they were having an affair! They were masters at public displays of affection!

"Oh, thanks. But we're okay. Lachie restocked all the shacks on our row with wood and kindling. With the bridge out, no one is coming out to their shacks, so we'll be okay for quite a while."

"If you run low, just call. We're around for another week, but we'll be back. We're about to meet with Lachlan to finalise the details on the house."

"So he told me. That's great. He's got an amazing reputation for quality builds for a reason. Anyway, he's not here yet, so grab a table. I'll be over shortly to take your order."

"Hopefully, you've got some of those amazing fish burgers," said Jack. With a chuckle, Sam assured him they did. It was a staple on their menu.

"Just ring if you need anything. We mean that," said Pam, before steering Jack to a nearby table.

Sam finished up the coffee orders and, after placing a lunch order with the kitchen, went over to serve Pam and Jack just as Lachie walked in.

"Hey Ginger," he said, placing his satchel and jacket on the spare chair.

"Hey Lachie. Coffee?" she asked. He nodded. She didn't have to ask what kind. It was always a triple shot espresso. She then took Pam and Jack's drink order, then waited as Pam stared at the menu. Jack had made his choice for lunch abundantly clear.

"I have a question for you after your meeting," Sam said to Lachie. "It's kind of important."

"You two go ahead and talk," said Pam. "I'm still trying to decide on what to eat."

"Are you sure?" Sam asked. "I don't want to interrupt." Pam nodded and waved them away. Sam walked back to the counter, handed their drink orders to Kyra, now manning the coffee machine, and directed Lachie out of earshot.

"What's going on? Everything okay?" he asked, looking concerned. She ploughed in.

"Do you have someone new working for you?"

"Yeah. A young bricklayer named Declan. Been working for me for about six months now. Why?"

"Because I heard a rumour about Bee from Geraldine Bishop, Bill's wife. You know how she loves to talk. Bee has said nothing to me, but I wondered if you knew of anything going on between them?"

"What's the rumour?" he asked, thrusting his hands in his pockets. Crap. She knew when he was skirting a subject.

"That's the fun part. Her granddaughter told her that Bee and this new guy are sleeping together. Geraldine asked me if Bee was using protection because, and I quote, 'we don't want her ending up like her mother, now do we?'" Lachie's expression morphed from concerned godfather to pissed off friend in about zero point two seconds. "Yeah. Geraldine didn't hold back. Like I said, Bee hasn't mentioned it, and I would think she would. I don't know if she's said anything to Brooke, but they have a pact. Brooke only shares confidences with me if Bee is in danger. But I don't want Bee's reputation ruined if this guy is sprouting rumours about her. What do you know of him?"

"He's a good guy. But he's older than she is. Twenty-one, which is why, if they *are* sleeping together, I'm now the concerned godfather. But I also know that he's hardworking, honest, and I don't see him taking advantage of her. Or spreading rumours."

"Okay. So, if there is something going on..." she began but didn't quite know how to continue. She needed to confront Bee, and she hated to do that. She would rather her daughter confide in her, but the rumours worried her.

"Let's be real. Neither one of us can judge the age difference between them, if there is something going on," he said. Lachie was right. She'd been sixteen when nineteen-year-old Zed had asked her out that morning on the beach. Brooke and Lachie had an even larger age difference, since he was a year older than Zed.

"I don't know if there is, but I think it might be the start of something," Lachie continued, rocking back on his boots. "I'm kind of pissed that he's not said anything. He knows I'm close to her. But I've seen them together and I suspect there may be something going on. Do you want me to say something to him?"

"I don't know. You think he's a good guy? Would you pick him for her?" She nervously twisted a rogue curl that sprang from her ponytail.

"Well, he's a young Irishman and in love with Tasmania, so I think he's solid enough," he said with a smirk. "Actually, his dad is friends with Pam and Georgina. Tom's his name, I think?"

"Hmm, I'll ask Georgina about him. And I'll talk to Bee tonight. But if you can try and scope it out with Declan then let me know, I'd appreciate it."

"Yeah, course. I'll try not to kick him all the way back to town, but I'll do what I can." Sam gasped. Lachie smiled. "I'm kidding. I'll be gentle."

"Heard another rumour about the new owner at the pub. Sounds like he's rubbing everyone the wrong way. You doing okay over there?" Lachie asked.

"Oh yeah. Sean's a git," said Sam. "I've only been back a week. I worked Saturday night and last Thursday afternoon. He put me on standby, which irks me. What really pisses me off though, is he's told me I need to 'polish it up'," she said, using hand quotes. Lachie shook his head.

"I heard he told Jane she needed to do a double shift at the last minute," he said. "When she told him she needed to find a babysitter, he told her she should consider whether she wanted the job at all if she couldn't be flexible."

"Yeah, Jane told me about it," Sam said, shaking her head. "It's going to be interesting."

They headed back to the table, and Sam took their lunch orders.

"I meant to tell you this earlier," Jack said. "We were in at the council chambers this morning to submit the permits and such. We overheard someone, who looked official, talking about rebuilding the bridge. That's great news, right?" asked Jack. Sam lit up.

"Unfortunately, I wouldn't count on it," said Lachie, pulling the laptop out of his satchel. "Sorry Ginger. I heard the same thing. They are merely rumblings right now." Sam's shoulders dropped. Of course. What did she expect?

Sam rehashed her conversation with Lachie in her mind as she worked through the lunch crowd at the café. The stuff going on at the pub really bugged her. She took jobs where she could find them, especially in the last four years. There was something about Sean that she couldn't quite put her finger on. He wanted to bring in big city ways to a seaside village, and the community was bucking. But the rumours didn't stop there either. The guy's ethics were questionable.

When Bee came in for her shift at four, Sam was finishing up a phone call with the new waitress.

"Looks like you're on your own. Just got a call from Tracy. She's not coming back. Got a job at the pub, apparently." The news made Sam nervous, considering her 'on call' status. Tracy was new to the area, moving recently from Melbourne. Since Sam hired her to work for the café, she also knew she had experience with some high-class pubs there, exactly what Sean was looking for with his upscale plans. She already had the 'polish' thing down.

"At least she called," Bee said. "But I doubt she'll last over there. She's too much of a flake." Sam had to agree. She hadn't been the most reliable waitress.

"What's the deal with the new owner, anyway? The rumours are flying," asked Bee, grabbing a rag to clean a table.

"Same stuff I've been experiencing lately," Sam said, passing a tray to Bee for the dirty dishes. "Seems all kinds of rumours are flying around today. Some a little closer to home."

"Will you be able to keep your job there?" Bee asked, giving her a strange look. Sam shrugged, disappointed that Bee skated around her subtle hint. Sam was far more worried about the situation Bee was in. Bee had blown her off and Sam was curious why.

Twilight settled in outside. At closing time, Bee stacked chairs on the tables and swept the floors while Sam closed out the till.

"Why don't you go and buy fish and chips for dinner while I finish here?" Sam suggested.

"Really?" Bee asked, but the tone was laced with suspicion. Usually, they only ate out on special occasions. Well, tonight she needed to talk about Declan, so she'd made the exception.

"Grab my wallet. Crap, wait. No cash," Sam said, remembering they were a cash only takeaway.

"I'll pay for it," Bee offered reluctantly in a bitchy tone. The girl hoarded money like she owned a bank.

"Thanks. Here are Jackson's car keys," she said and watched her daughter amble outside. Glad for the space, Sam still had to work out what the hell she was going to say.

While she waited for Bee to return, Sam called Merritt and was disappointed to get voice mail again. What was going on with her? She quickly texted Brooke and asked if she'd heard from Merritt lately. Brooke's response was instant.

Nope, and I've called her a bunch of times. Am getting worried.

Sam responded: *Me too.*

When Bee returned, Sam placed clean plates on the counter in the café's kitchen.

"I got two pieces of fish, chips, and potato cakes. Hope that's okay?" Bee said, placing the bag on the counter. Sam noticed the overly helpful daughter had returned. Sam couldn't keep up with the dizzying pace of her mood swings.

"Yep, works for me," said Sam, and unwrapped the paper. Once they settled on to the bar stools, Sam took a deep breath and ploughed right in.

"I wanted to ask you something," she began and started cutting her fish into bite-size pieces. "I was wondering when you were going to tell me you were dating Declan?" She asked and looked straight into her daughter's eyes. Shock, guilt, then relief passed through them in a split second.

"I was going to…" Bee began. She pushed the fish around her plate, stalling.

"What were you waiting for…?" Sam asked. This was the one piece she couldn't figure out. Why hadn't she said something?

"I was trying to work out how to tell you. I figured you'd be mad. But I thought it through a million times. Not only was there more of an age difference between you and dad, than there is with Declan and me, but you were also sixteen when you guys started dating. So it shouldn't be a big deal. Plus, I'm almost done with high school."

"All true. So why the secrecy?" Sam asked. Bee looked at her plate again. Sam hadn't eaten a bite.

"I don't know," Bee responded.

"I'm not mad, Bee. Not that you're dating him, anyway. But are you dating him, or just hooking up?" The shocked look on Bee's face almost made her laugh out loud. Okay, they weren't just hooking up. But somehow, that made Sam even more nervous. "The rumours are flying, Bee. That concerns me."

Bee kept her head down, looking defeated as she mashed her fish with her fork.

"What I'm mad about is you didn't tell me. I had to hear it from Mrs. Bishop and when I asked Lachie…"

"Uncle Lachie knows?" Bee shrieked, horrified.

"I'm sorry. You're more upset that Lachie knows your secret than me knowing about it? What the hell Bee?"

"It's not that Mum. It's just I didn't think you'd talk behind my back?"

"Oh, that's one for the books. Look in the mirror, Bee. You're seeing Declan behind mine!" That stopped her daughter short. "That hurts, Bee. After everything, knowing you couldn't tell me this?"

"I was going to. Really. I just didn't know if it was… I don't know, real or not."

"And is it?" Sam asked, scared but curious of the answer. She didn't want her daughter to end up in the same situation as her.

"I think so, but I've already told him I have plans after school," she said. "I'm not staying in Fergus Bay. Maybe not even Tasmania." There it was. The thing that Sam was happiest to hear, but also the thing she feared the most. Her daughter was leaving. She was getting out. But it also meant she was leaving her. Leaving her alone in her miserable life. There was silence for a while.

"Okay," said Sam.

"But I do like him, Mum. Like a lot. Declan is a lot like Uncle Lachie," said Bee. "He has ambition and drive and ideas." Not like her. The unspoken words sat like a volcano about to crack.

"Okay. Well, now I know," she said. Her food was cold, mostly untouched.

Bee stared at her, expecting her to say more, but Sam felt like her legs had been kicked out from under her. She rose from the chair wordlessly and wrapped up the rest of their food. Maybe she'd be hungry later, but she doubted it. Bee's words swirled in her head. She liked him. Leaving Tasmania. Ideas. Ambition. What Bee felt for Declan was real. So, her daughter would leave, and given Declan was Irish and still finding his way, she'd follow him. She'd lose her daughter completely.

"Let's go home," she said.

Sam tried to say something more, anything, while they cleaned up. She knew silence was the worse type of punishment. Her mother used to do the same thing to her when she'd been a rebellious teenager. That ate at her every single day. But now she understood why her mother stayed silent. She simply didn't know what to say or how to react. There were too many emotions, too many feelings, too many words. It was hard to sort through the noise. So, you said nothing.

They made their way home. Silently.

Sam replayed their conversation as she lay in bed. Bee's plans were news to her, too. When the hell had they become so disconnected? They'd been close until... when? Time had flown by lately. Bee was almost eighteen. Almost done with school. Then she'd be gone.

16

BROOKE. DISTRACTIONS.

SEPTEMBER.

Brooke leaned back against the bed's footboard in Marty's bedroom. The house was too warm since she'd mismanaged the wood fire earlier. Now, with the bedroom windows open, she could hear the seagulls outside the window and the rush of the waves crashing on the shoreline. Brooke looked down at the bundle in her hands. For a minute, she doubted herself. Should she? Did it matter anymore? She pulled the red ribbon and unwrapped the bundle with a shaking hand, considering the weight of it all. No. It wasn't right. She carefully placed the stack of letters down on the rug and reached for her latte instead. She stared at the envelopes. No, she couldn't. It was like reading someone's inner thoughts.

She picked up her phone and checked her emails. Dae had everything under control from what she could see. Sue updated her daily and reported things were running smoothly with the practice. That was good, she supposed. No emergency meltdowns to attend to. She felt drawn back to the letters.

She picked up the top letter. It was addressed to a stranger named

Gilly, someone she didn't know. If the letter was to Marty, or from Marty, she didn't know how she would deal with that. But she didn't know these people. Resolute, she pulled out the handwritten pages. The paper was yellow, delicate; the creases showing it had been read many times over. The handwriting was beautiful, full of swirls and the words slanted uniformly. Every word was written out in full, like Tasmania, rather than its abbreviated initials.

Taking a deep breath, ignoring the feeling that she was invading someone's privacy, she began reading.

January 16th, 1961

My Darling Gilly,

Oh God. It was a love letter? Who was this woman? And why did Marty have these stacks? Brooke kept reading.

It has been three weeks since I have seen your smile. The days stretch before me interminably. I am counting the days until I see you again. I feel like I am a man crawling through a desert in search of water. But it is you, my love, who is my only water source, my lifeline. You've asked me to give you time and I assure you; I am trying.

So, with that in mind, I will fill the pages with what I do have, so as not to dwell on what I don't. (Although I wish you were here on this adventure with me). I'm having such a marvellous time, seeing old friends, experiencing unknown places. It's only that I feel something is missing, like a constant absence of something important.

But that is not as I promised. I am sorry. Let me continue to regale you with my adventures. As you can see, this letter is sent to you from San Francisco, so you know I made it to the conference.

It has been quite the adventure to get here. I began the journey flying back to Sydney, as you know, to celebrate the Christmas season. Oh, what a joyous occasion it was. From there, I flew on to Fiji. What a terrific way to enjoy a layover for three days. Nothing but cocktails by the pool and a marvellous party atmosphere! After spending spring in Hobart, the humidity was brutal. How do people live in this kind of climate all the time?

From Fiji, it was on to Honolulu for the New Year, which was truly a tropical paradise. But I admit, I could not get you out of my mind. I imagined you in your blue bathing suit, splashing in the ocean in the morning, then returning to our hotel suite for an afternoon rest. Oh how I would love to share Hawaii with you some day, my love. The dinners were an amazing experience, and the Hawaiian delicacies were heavenly.

But the conference beckoned in San Francisco, my last leg. We had some unexpected turbulence. One gent ended up with the air hostess in his lap and red wine everywhere. It was unintentional, of course. And thankfully everyone took it in great stride. Otherwise, it would have made for a very uncomfortable journey indeed. Still, the smoke from pipes and cigarettes is something I am still washing from my clothes. It hadn't been so bad on the previous flights. Ah, but that's air travel for you.

The letter continued with details about the conference. Brooke determined he was a doctor, but she couldn't figure out what speciality. He must have been a sought-after specialist, to be flying to the U.S. for a conference, especially in those days. The letter skimmed much of the details, focusing on his feelings for Gilly and how much he missed her.

But who was she? And why did she need time? Time for what? And who was Henry? Was he a friend of Marty's? He had to be if he was a doctor from Hobart. It baffled Brooke. She read to the end.

I am awaiting the day I return to you, my darling. I count the days. Heck, I have even worked out how many hours. It's fair to say you are constantly on my mind.

Until March, I will remember your smile until I can see it again for myself.

You have my heart. Always.

Henry

Brooke read through another ten letters. They were all from Henry. They told of his adventures in the United States until late February. Each letter was written two days from the last. Every letter spoke from the heart and of how much he missed her.

So, whomever these people were, they were clearly in love. Or at least he was with her. Brooke didn't know the other side of the relationship, since all the letters were addressed to Gilly. That frustrated her. She shuffled through the envelopes. There had to be over a hundred letters and, looking at the date stamps, they covered eighteen months in total. A brief love affair, then? Or something else. She looked for anything from Gilly. She found one letter, only one, addressed to Henry. It was the last letter in the stack. It was addressed, sealed, but clearly still unsent. Brooke left that one for now. She wanted to read the rest first. She was eager to find out what their story was. Maybe it would shed some light on who they were. She looked to the box again. If the box was in the attic, or even buried in the shed, they had to belong to another relative. Maybe her father would know who they were?

She looked down at her phone and saw it was just after five o'clock. The house was bitterly cold. She closed all the windows, berating herself for not doing it earlier, stoked the fire, then grabbed her yellow jacket from the back rack. She popped her phone into her pocket and walked to the back door. Ned was stretched out comfortably, meaning Sam and Bee weren't home yet. She'd take care of Ned, so they had one less thing to worry about. At her approach, Ned jumped up, tail wagging. She bent down to pat him, then turned to lock the door, laughing at herself for doing so. It wasn't like anyone was coming out this way. Habit, she realised, from living in Sydney.

"Come on Ned. Time to stretch the legs and think about these damn letters. Other than chasing warm spots in the sun, I bet you've hardly moved today." Ned dashed to the gate, ready for his freedom. She crossed the dirt track and made her way to the narrow path leading to the beach. The sides of the walkway were covered in daisy bush and coastal wattle, both now in full bloom.

Brooke tossed her shoes aside and felt the cold sand bite at her feet. It was probably too cold, but she'd always taken her shoes off in the sand, unless she was running. Shoes didn't belong on the beach, Marty always said. No shoes on the beach and no shoes in the house. Well, except slippers.

God, she missed her grandmother. Sorting through her house was heart wrenching. Her clothes still smelled of her and she had half-read books all over the house. Some had bookmarks. Others had receipts rammed in between pages. And her knitting! Brooke found a pair of knitting needles in the laundry only yesterday. She'd found half written letters to old friends stacked on her ancient roll-top desk. When she was looking for some work gloves in the mudroom, she'd found seed packets in an enormous box, along with a journal of what she'd planted and where. Stacked in the pantry were boxes and boxes of tea. Ginger and Lemon, Earl Grey, even Peppermint. She was as much a tea snob as Sam was a coffee one. These were the little things that made Marty who she was. Brooke couldn't face moving any of it or taking anything to the thrift shop. She had made a pile the knitting stuff to give to Bee. She knew she'd love that. And the seeds would go to Sam since she had been Marty's apprentice gardener. Well, more like her free manual labour, but Brooke knew Sam was keen about her garden. Oh, how she missed her grandmother. More than she could face.

Wiggling her toes in the sand, she yelled over the wind for Ned to fetch a stick. He dashed down the beach like a dog on a mission, returning before she reached the waterline with a stick in his mouth. His wagging tail shook his entire body. She threw the stick and imagined her grandmother doing this very thing every single day.

Ned zipped back and forth as they walked the long stretch of empty beach, and her thoughts returned to the letters. Gilly. She'd never heard her father mention anyone named Gilly before, not that he mentioned his family all that much. Since he was an only child, and Marty only had one sister, a spinster ten years younger than herself, that made sense. Maybe Gilly was a nickname for her sister? But no. The last name on the envelope was Scott. So, it had to be someone on her grandfather's side, but she was sure they all lived in England.

Maybe it was a visiting family member? But since the letters were written over a long period, had Gilly moved to Australia at some stage? To Hobart?

She thought of the words Henry wrote. They were so hopelessly romantic, filled with love and admiration. There were none of the emotional barriers people put up nowadays. No baggage, just raw emotion. At least from Henry's side of things. She wished she knew how Gilly felt.

Oh, to feel that kind of affection. Was it the romanticised notion of that period? Did that kind of love even exist anymore? She considered her parents and knew the answer. It existed. Her parents were still in love, even after all these years. And Brooke had experienced that deep connection once, a long time ago. But she didn't want to go there today. She'd had enough of her own past lately. The moment on the beach with Lachlan confused her. Had they simply called a truce for that one day? Why hadn't the anger and hurt tainted it? It would make things easier for her heart. But they were long over. He was just being kind.

She thought about her call with Merritt earlier that morning. She was alive. That was something, at least. She said that the marriage was well and truly over, not that there was much of one to begin with. Merritt had the connection Brooke dreamed about with Kendall. Brooke thought that was the relationship that would outlast them all. She was still amazed that Sam didn't know how deep their relationship was, but then Sam had lived in the Zed and Bee bubble for years. Maybe that was changing?

Brooke gazed in awe as the sun set. The sky was bathed in a diffuse orange glow, as if a soft-focus filter had been applied. The bay mirrored the silky orange, the water as smooth as a warn stone in the still air. But the temperature was dropping, and it would drop further quickly. She should have started Sam's fire for her, so they had a warm house to come home to. But given Brooke's penchant for creating more smoke than fire, it was probably good she didn't.

She turned to make her way home when her thoughts returned to Sam and Zed. They, too, had the connection that Henry wrote of, in the beginning of their relationship. But there had been tiny ripples, ones that were hard to see at first. But like a flat stone that skipped across the still water, the ripples spread and grew. Sam gave up so much for Zed. University. A career. Zed either failed to see it or ignored it. Their life revolved around his dreams and his focus of owning his own fishing trawler. Brooke watched Sam's resentment build over the years. Her friend had struggled with it but rarely said anything. Brooke tried to say something when she first noticed it, but Sam refused to hear the words, especially once they'd bought the house in Fergus Bay. It was so hard to watch. It was *still* hard to watch. Where had her friend disappeared to? That red headed spitfire she'd met when she was seven. Where was she? Now, even though Zed was gone, Sam had gone from living for Zed to simply existing.

But was she any different? Wasn't she merely existing too? Maybe it was time to find her way back.

17

SAM. EXHIBIT.

OCTOBER.

The café was buzzing for Georgina's inaugural photography exhibit and, judging by the number of attendees, the night was an enormous success. But by nine o'clock, Sam's feet were killing her.

"Come on, girls. Time to get some bubbly and celebrate Mum's success!" said Nicole. "We'll leave the rest until later. There's not a lot more to do, so we'll get it done quickly." Sam was happy for the break and eager to check out the exhibit.

When she left the kitchen, Sam smiled at Georgina's shell-shocked face. It didn't quite express the celebration that tonight should bring, but Georgina had been nervous about the exhibit. Sam strolled along the displayed photographs and saw every frame sporting a red dot, indicating what had sold. She looked around for Georgina to offer her congratulations but found her talking to people she didn't recognise. She continued surveying the room. Brooke chatted with Jackson over in the corner and, looking to her left, watched Merritt saunter toward her. Brooke and Merritt had surprised her when they arrived an hour earlier. She wasn't expecting either of them to accept their invitations.

"Hey," said Merritt.

"How do you dress so fabulously all the damn time?" Sam asked. Even if Sam wore her best dress, the one she kept aside for special occasions, she'd still look like a frump next to her curvaceous friend. When she wasn't dressed in her work uniform, Sam lived in yoga pants and hoodies. It worked just fine for her, but it showed the contrast between her life and that of her friend.

"My feet hurt just looking at those shoes." Merritt stood eye level to Sam, thanks to her three-inch heels.

"The secret is not to be standing too long," said Merritt.

"I'm surprised you're here," Sam said, then looked a little closer. "Are you okay? You look more tired than I feel. Underneath the polish, you look like shit." While Merritt looked fabulous in her bold maroon dress, she looked pale and the dark circles under her eyes told the actual story. Her eyes were dull and there was exhaustion behind them. She hadn't heard from Merritt since the funeral, and when Brooke called to say she'd finally heard from her, Sam stopped worrying. Maybe she shouldn't have. It was clear the drama with James had taken a toll on her. It was why she was surprised to see Merritt at Georgina's exhibit, in particular.

"Can't say you're looking much better Sam," commented Merritt.

"Just wiped. Been a long day. And things with Bee are awfully strained right now. She's dating someone who works for Lachlan." She shook her head, trying to get the conversation back on track.

"Seriously though, what's going on Mer? Are you okay?" she asked. Merritt studied a black-and-white photograph of an abandoned wharf encased in fog. Sam turned to the photo. It was one she'd seen many times before and found it to be both breathtaking and haunting.

"Other than my life falling apart?" said Merritt, her voice cracking a little. Merritt picked up another glass of champagne when a server walked past with a tray. Georgina had gone fancy for this exhibit.

"This week has just been fucking insane, but it's not the time or place to talk about it," Merritt said, shutting the conversation down when Brooke walked up behind them.

"Hmm. Okay. Later, then?" Merritt nodded.

"How's it for you, Brooke?" Sam asked, turning to her, but Brooke seemed distracted. Ah, yes. Lachie was here. "How are you doing now that you're back in Sydney?"

The question snapped Brooke back.

"Confused. Tired. Sad. Running on fumes," she said.

"Confused? Why?" asked Merritt.

"Because of the letters I found at Marty's house. I took them back to Sydney with me. I just don't get it. I still don't know who the letters are between."

"Still?" Sam asked.

"Yeah, I need to put them away, but reading them is like eating chocolate. You can't just have one small square and be done with it. You have to keep going," Brooke said, then shook her head. "I'll work it out, eventually. How are you Merritt?"

Sam tried to read Brooke, too. But Brooke was a master at deflecting.

"I'm okay," but Brooke stared at Merritt, like she was waiting for the actual answer. Sam wanted to ward Brooke off, but it seemed like Brooke was looking for a distraction from Lachie's presence in the room. Maybe the letters were regurgitating some feelings?

"Bullshit. You said nothing on the drive here. What's happening with James?" pushed Brooke.

"Ugh. Fine. I'll give you the short version for now. It's been a roller-coaster. I've filed for a divorce, and he's agreed to end the business partnership. But he's the one who manages the finances and manages our investors, so that was the point of contention. He was getting nasty about it for a while, but then I found out he's moving on with his... whatever, and he's moving to America. That means he has a deadline to wrap things up, which works in my favour. So, now he knows I'm aware of his plans, James has agreed to a smaller settlement. I give him the larger property we own together in Melbourne, and he'll give me the business. Apparently, she's a real estate mogul in New York. In a nutshell, he will be out of my life in all aspects and now I'm looking at how I want to run our business moving forward." Merritt shook her head and smiled for the first time since she'd arrived. "*My* business. But one thing is for sure, the idea of the eco-lodge is out. At least for now."

"Holy shit," exclaimed Brooke. "That's why you went silent." Sam was reeling with the information herself. It was no wonder Merritt looked exhausted. Sam only wished she could have helped her through the maze.

"Yeah. Sorry I didn't tell you all what was going on. It's been crazy. I don't think I've slept more than a few hours each night since I got back to Melbourne."

"Can we help at all?" asked Brooke.

"Not at this stage, but thanks. I just need to figure out what's next," said Merritt, downing her champagne.

"Well Georgina looks to have done well," Brooke said, bringing attention back to the exhibit, but a trailing scent of Chanel No.5 wafted behind Sam, transporting her back twenty-five years. She turned quickly and watched Georgina's friend Aubrey walk away. Tonight, she looked exactly like Sam's mother from the back, especially with her auburn hair down. Sam shook her head, ridding herself of the ghosts.

"She sold everything," whispered Brooke. "Her work is incredible. How did I not know how talented Georgina was? I bought two pieces. One for the practice in Sydney and one for Marty's house. And yes, before you ask, I am keeping the house. How could I sell it? It's part of me." Sam was relieved at the news and hugged Brooke, being careful not to spill any of the expensive champagne down her friend's back. Sam turned back to the artwork, then almost spat her champagne out when she noticed the prices. Brooke laughed at her shocked reaction. One framed photo was like three mortgage payments for her.

"I know, it's not cheap, but it's amazing work," said Brooke to Sam's response.

They heard a cheer behind them and turned to find flutes filled with champagne lifted in Georgina's direction. Georgina smiled hesitantly. It was great to see she was moving forward with her talent. Who knew that it would take two perfect strangers on a walk across a country, halfway across the world, for her to take the leap?

"I like Georgina's friends from her Camino. Especially Pam. When Georgina is with them, she lights up. Except tonight. Looks like she's back to her insecure self," Sam said, finishing the last of her champagne.

"I noticed that she's been a lot more confident this year. I vaguely remember us talking about the Camino after Marty's funeral, but did the experience really have that much of an impact on her?" Brooke asked.

"Yep. She said it helped her see things with more clarity," Sam said, and noticed Nicole walking back to the kitchen. "Anyway, looks like the exhibit is over, so we need to finish cleaning up."

"Can I help?" asked Brooke.

"If you can collect whatever needs washing up, that'll be great. I think we'll be another twenty minutes?"

"I'm on it," Brooke said, and set to the task.

Sam headed back into the kitchen. Tom, Aubrey's partner, stood at the sink with his hands buried in dishwater. Kyra and Bee laughed at something he said.

"Poor Aubrey. Stinging nettle hurts! Good thing you were around! So, how did you two meet?" Bee asked. Sam listened as she packaged up some leftover cheese.

"In Spain, earlier this year," Tom said, his Irish accent dancing in the air. "Walkin' the Camino de Santiago. I saw Aubrey for the first time hikin' up a mountain with Pam and Georgina. She took my breath away. But I was starvin', you see, and determined to get to O Cebreiro, so I hurried on. I thank my lucky stars that I caught them later in the pub." He rinsed the pot and placed it on the draining mat.

"I thought you'd been together for years," said Bee. Sam thought this line of questioning was odd, coming from her daughter. Her questions suggested she was familiar with Tom. As far as she knew, Bee had only met him and Aubrey in the café. But since Declan was Tom's son, maybe they'd met elsewhere?

"Feels that way," Tom said. "Now tell me, Bee, that's an unusual name for a lass. How did ya come about it?"

"I'm named after my great-grandmother Beverlee. She and my great-grandfather, Jackson, raised my dad. Jackson was the old man nursing his whisky in the corner. Probably making inappropriate comments to people who stopped by to say hello."

"Ah, aye. I chatted with him. I asked what he did before he retired. He mentioned an old sawmill. Said he always thought he wanted a career, but it turned out he just wanted the pay cheques. Said it was fishin' that was his grand passion, and that he misses it more than his wife." Tom chuckled.

"That doesn't surprise me. My dad was a commercial fisherman, but he died four years ago during a bad storm," Bee shared.

"Aye, I heard that. I'm sorry for ya loss. That's hard for anyone." Sam coughed behind them as she loaded plates into the industrial washer.

"You shouldn't be in here helping us, Tom. You should be out with the guests," Sam said.

"Maybe so, but if it's all the same to you, I'd rather be here helpin'," he said.

"Well, thanks. We appreciate the extra hands," she said. "Georgina mentioned you and Aubrey were looking for property around here. Seems we've become a hot spot with... what does Georgina call Aubrey and Pam? The..." Sam asked, handing him another saucepan.

"The Lovelies. It's a term they started on the Camino. The three of them. And, aye. We are looking for a place to call home. We searched around Victoria, around Bright and Myrtleford way, but found nothing to our likin'. And so we came down to see my boy, Declan. Now we're here, we're lookin'. Aubrey, you see, has a vision of what she wants. I'm just happy to be wherever she is, but I need quiet to write. We like Tasmania for that. Just haven't found the right place. We'll keep searchin'."

"Have you looked over in the Huon Valley?"

"No. I don't believe so. Where is that?" As they washed dishes, Sam filled him in on the various areas around the state that may interest them. If they stayed, Sam reasoned, then maybe Declan would too. And if Declan stayed, then maybe Bee wouldn't fly away too far.

18

BROOKE. KEEPSAKES.

OCTOBER.

The letters were really getting under her skin. She'd read every one of them at least three times. She couldn't get the unsent letter out of her head. The one from Gilly to Henry. Her morning run shook off some of it, but now she was back in Marty's house, she felt Henry and Gilly's presence. But that was stupid. She still had no idea who they even were. She sat on the rug in Marty's bedroom. It had become her favourite spot to read. She reread the last letter, trying to gain a sense of who Gilly was.

April 24th, 1962

Henry,

Writing these words makes our reality even more difficult. The past year and a half have meant more to me than I can ever express. But you know that. It's the last two months which have been so unbearable. Decisions need to be made, and this one is the hardest.

Henry, my love, I must end our relationship. I know this is a shock for you. My last letters were filled with joy and excitement, knowing that I was with child. Our child. It is with great sadness that I tell you our baby was not to be. I lost her two months ago. She came early. Too early to survive.

I know that there was an absence in my letters, and I apologise for that. The grief has been unlike anything I have ever known.

I am heartbroken. I never imagined having more children. It was not part of my plan. I chose my career. Something my husband did not agree with, as you know.

Brooke suspected Henry and Gilly were having an affair. When Henry moved back to Sydney, outlined in one of his letters, it seemed to strain the relationship. *'I chose my career.'* This line unnerved Brooke. The parallels she shared with Gilly did not go unnoticed. But more so, it was the grief that pained Brooke the most.

But Henry, the pain goes deeper than simply losing the baby. Yes, the loss is all-consuming, and I must give myself time to grieve. Not only for the baby, but also as your partner and for our plans. I'm struggling with this, but every time I think of you, all I think about is our baby, and it's too much.

I am sorry, Henry.

I will love you 'til the end.

Gilly.

Brooke placed the letter on the table and sadness overwhelmed her once more. She looked down into the handmade box again. Maybe there was a photo of Gilly and Henry that she hadn't found yet.

Brooke's past slammed into her when she found a photo at the bottom of the box. There she sat in Lachlan's lap, his hand on her knee, and their heads pressed together. The love between them was obvious. As she stared at her long ago past, a song came on the kitchen radio that reminded her of the night they first came together, and again when they parted. "She Will Be Loved" by Maroon 5. The song had haunted her ever since. The memories shoved their way into her heart.

Brooke knew exactly where this photo was taken. Marty, already a legend in the medical community by then, and her grandfather, Bert, a prominent fixture in the political world, always threw a New Year's Eve party in Hobart. Billed as the event of the season, Hobart's high society never missed it. The yachtsmen who stayed after racing from Sydney to Hobart were usually the life of the party.

Sam was at the party, but she was already off somewhere with Zed. They'd been together for a while now. Brooke had invited Lachlan and, knowing he'd be arriving late, wandered the party. Sam invited her to join them in the pool, but she wanted to wait. She looked to the gate again, hoping to see Lachlan. It was funny that it took a year to meet him, after Sam and Zed had gotten together, but Lachlan was always working when she visited. They finally met six months before and hit it off immediately.

Brooke anxiously hovered near the patio when she saw him. He looked lost, not quite knowing what to do with the bottle of wine in his hands. He wore cream linen shorts and a black button-down shirt. She smiled. She'd told him not to bother bringing anything. Her grandmother always hired professional caterers and offered an open bar. But it was sweet for him to think of it. His thick, dark brown hair was cut very short back then. The style enhanced his bold blue eyes that scanned the crowd. Looking for Zed. Looking for her. She waved as she approached and finally caught his eye.

"There you are," she said, nervous at seeing him standing there. Tonight, he was going to meet her parents.

"Oh, Brooke. Thank God. I thought I was at the wrong party for a minute." He looked around. His anxiety was palpable.

"Come on, I'll get you something to drink. Thanks for bringing this. We can drink it later," she said. She took the bottle of wine from him and gave it to a server, asking them to put it in the kitchen.

"Sorry, I didn't realise it was such a fancy event," he said, clearly embarrassed. They got drinks from the bar, and she introduced him to her parents. But since they were so involved in helping Marty and Bert play host, they barely had time to chat. Lachlan looked quite relieved. Hand in hand, they strolled back to the pool where they found Sam and Zed playing water polo with another couple.

"Let's find somewhere quieter. It's so noisy. I hate these parties," Brooke said. She took his hand and led him deeper into the garden, to what she considered Marty's secret oasis. A wooden bench was nestled beneath a canopy of jasmine. It offered the perfect place to read a book, and to escape from this annual party. Lachlan beamed when they took a seat, his eyes taking in clusters of summer roses and the vast delphinium garden surrounding them. Like her, this was more his style. His shoulders relaxed in the quiet.

They talked about surfing and music, but eventually the conversation turned to their plans. Brooke was always surprised by his ambition. He was working part time at the Triabunna sawmill five days a week, and now, with his recent 'service of alcohol' certification, he picked up shifts at the local pub. His goal was to earn as much as he could before starting his building and accounting courses in February. He already had a carpentry qualification under his belt, which allowed him to help a local carpenter as needed. He may have looked like a lazy surfer from the outside, but he had as much ambition as she did.

She told him when they first met that she wanted to follow in Marty's footsteps and become a doctor.

"That's a huge goal. Good for you. I guess that makes you the brainy one of us then?" he teased. She didn't know about that. He was no slouch. He wanted his own construction business someday. That took serious acumen too.

"It's what I've always wanted to do," she admitted. But on this night, as music from the party floated on the summer breeze, she told him about the course load for the upcoming year. University was challenging, but she enjoyed it. She told him she found it interesting that he never mentioned university. He was smart enough to give her engineering friends a run for their money, but he was happy with his plan.

After a while, the conversation turned to Sam and Zed. They were heading off to go backpacking the following month. Brooke was worried Sam was in too deep with Zed. He seemed a dreamer, and Brooke worried that Sam was too quick to give up her plans for Zed.

"What happened to his parents?" Brooke asked. Sam said Zed lived with his grandparents, but never mentioned his parents.

"His mum was a drifter. No one has heard from her since Zed was born. Just took off one day. And his dad, well, who knows. I'm not even sure his mum knew who his dad was. She was, ah, what they used to call a girl about town. At least that's what Beverlee calls her." It painted a clear enough picture. "He's a bit of a dreamer, too. It wouldn't surprise me if he just takes off one day. This dream of his, about backpacking around Europe, has been in the cards for ages. But he's got a steady job at the marina, so I think the money will bring him back."

Brooke had already picked up on the dreamer characteristic with Zed. Sam mentioned the backpacking adventure to her months ago. With everything Sam had dealt with in the last few years, she knew Sam was fragile under all the bluster. But the last thing she needed was for Zed to leave her high and dry in pursuit of a nomadic life. Brooke just had to trust Sam knew what she was doing and be there for her if everything fell apart.

Lachlan, on the other hand, was practical. And smart. She'd already met his parents. They were a lot like hers. Hard-working, running their own business. His Dad ran a plumbing business in Hobart, while his mother was a part-time primary school teacher, when she wasn't helping with the plumbing business. Having a shack in Orford allowed them to get away on the weekends and the holidays.

Brooke and Lachlan spent the summer together before embarking on a long-distance relationship. She spent her uni breaks at Fergus Bay. She balanced textbooks in her lap, sitting in his truck while he worked. They alternated cities over long weekends. Eventually, Brooke got frustrated with the toll it took on them. She asked Lachlan to pursue something worthwhile, like studying engineering with her at uni. But he remained adamant. Carpentry was the life for him. Back then, she wondered if he was a dreamer, like Zed.

Looking down at the photo, she realised how wrong she was. Now, Lachlan owned a very successful custom home business. He created bespoke pieces, like the tables in the café and Marty's gorgeous coffin.

He even had time to manage custom renovations, like he had with Marty's beach house. He made his dream a reality.

Hunger pains rumbled, so she shook off the memories and headed to the kitchen. She was amazed to see the microwave clock showing it was almost ten. She had one day left in Fergus Bay before she returned to Sydney. She wouldn't be back until Christmas and for Bee's birthday. Opening the fridge, a strange noise outside caught her attention. Was that a lawnmower?

She peered out the window and noticed someone mowing the back section of Marty's yard, up by the cluster of gum trees. Strange, she hadn't arranged that. She pulled her cardigan tighter around her and stepped out on to the back deck. Further down the track, she heard someone trimming the shack next to Sam's house. Maybe Sam arranged for all the shacks to be mown? She took the steps down to the lawn and walked toward the back gate. She was surprised to see Lachlan coming from behind the trees.

After the night of the funeral, she'd seen him a few times in Orford. Brooke tried to avoid him, but that was nearly impossible in such a small town. She couldn't decide if she was still angry at him for leaving her at the airport, or if they were now friends. Should she say something or just go back inside? The confusion held her hostage.

Lachlan looked up and, seeing her, released the handle to kill the mower. Brooke took it as a sign and walked through the gate toward him. Seeing the grave marker right behind him stopped Brooke in her tracks. She'd seen the headstone a million times over the years, but the name etched into the granite made her gasp. Mae Finlayson.

"Everything okay?" Lachlan asked, noticing her distress. She slowly peeled her eyes from the stone and nodded.

"It's been there for years," he said. "I remember the stories you and Sam used to spin about it when we were younger."

"I think it was the daughter of a woman named Gilly Scott and Henry Finlayson," Brooke said.

"Who are they?" Lachlan asked.

"I don't know exactly. I found some letters tucked in a box at the back of Marty's closet. They're all addressed to Gilly Scott. I've been trying to work out what they mean and who they belong to."

131

"And they were in Marty's closet?" he asked.

"Yes. All the way in the back corner. Did you make her the box? It looks old, so maybe not. Can I show you?" she asked, although it felt strange asking for his help.

"I can tell you straight up it wasn't me that made it for her. But I can probably tell you when it was made." She turned back toward the door expecting him to follow.

When they were in Marty's bedroom, Brooke handed him the box.

"It's really beautiful. The work you did on the house I mean. I know Marty loved it," she said as he looked over the box. Did she dare tell him? "She left the house to me."

"Rightly so. You loved this house back when…" he began but didn't finish the sentence. He traced his fingers along the edges of the box. "The box was made at least fifty years ago, looking at the workmanship." He flipped it over and saw a marking on the bottom. He rubbed his finger over it, scrutinised it.

"Looks like… 1961," he said.

"Where? I didn't see that?" he pointed out the markings, her eyes zeroing in on it. In their closeness, she caught the faint scent of saltwater underneath the smell of fresh grass on his body. Like he'd been for a surf that morning and hadn't showered afterwards. She pulled back quickly. Her eyes caught his. He looked away first, then he inhaled sharply. The photo of them together at the party lay on the floor. The one where she was on his lap, their heads together.

Then he asked her the one question she thought he knew the answer to.

"Why didn't you tell me Dae was gay? Why didn't you tell me it was a marriage of convenience?" His voice was barely audible.

"I did tell you," she said. He slowly shook his head.

"No, Brooke, you didn't. I found out from Zed."

They both jumped at her phone ringing on the bedside table. Dae's face appeared on the screen.

"Speak of the devil," Lachlan said. "I'll leave you to it. I've got work to do," and before she could say anything, she heard the back door slam.

19

SAM. EMPTY.

OCTOBER.

Sam found herself with a rare day off and was glad to have it to herself. Brooke was back in Sydney, Merritt was in Melbourne, and Bee was spending the afternoon in Hobart with Declan, once she finished her morning shift at the café. Sam had officially met him the weekend before, when they invited him for dinner. At least she wasn't being kept in the dark anymore.

Despite her list of things to do, curling up on the couch and binge watching something stupid on television held more appeal. Maybe she'd do that. Anything to shut out the pain and memories swirling in her head.

"Geezus Ned. Where the hell is your damn lead?" Sam asked, while looking under the cushions on the couch. Ned thumped his tail at the mention of his name, watching her from the back door. The lead had been lost for weeks now, but Sam could hear Marty's voice in her head: *It's nesting season.*

"It's not like I even have to worry about you with the birds," she continued, dumping the 'catch-all basket' on the floor and sorting through it for the umpteenth time.

"Right? You hate the birds. Ha. More like you're terrified of them. All you care about is your damn stick and the freezing cold water." At the word stick, Ned shot up, circled, then sat eagerly, his tail hitting the floor like a methodical countdown.

"Fuck it. Let's go," she said and dumped all the contents back into the basket. The lead wasn't there, and she was done looking for it. She'd ask Bee to pick up one while she was in town today. With Declan. The omission of the romance news still stung, and Bee wasn't sharing any details about the romance either.

She snatched her jacket from the hook, unlocked the back door and almost tripped over a very excited Ned going out. On the way down to the beach, she found two sticks, which were guaranteed to keep Ned out of the nesting area altogether. There, that settled it.

The water was calm this morning, with each wave racing itself down the beach before flattening out. The sun glowed eerily on the horizon behind dark grey clouds blanketing the sky. Sam felt the weight of them.

She let her eyes roam the flat water, hoping, needing, to see her dolphin. She needed to talk to Zed. He was a great distracter when she felt disjointed. And boy, did she feel disjointed.

Nothing but smooth water to the horizon. Crap.

Sam tossed the stick as she strolled the beach. Ned jumped in, ignoring the frigid temperature, and when he returned the stick to her, she swore he was smiling. He would play this game for hours if she let him. As a five-year-old cattle dog, he had energy to burn. Unfortunately for him, her arm gave out after a while, so she found a place to sit on the beach. Ned came and lay on the sand beside her, his tongue out, panting, looking up to her happily. She stroked his head and looked to the water again.

The beach was empty all around her, at least of the human variety. It was just her, Ned, and the birds that scared him. The oystercatchers and terns were at one end of the beach, picking their way along the wet sand, while the seagulls soared just above the water. Even the waves were low key, making a soft splash when they fell over themselves. There were no boats on the water. It was even too early for the Maria Island ferry.

With the quiet morning, the memories invaded. She'd been trying to avoid them by staying busy. She wanted to remember Marty's smile, the way she was before she found her, but the memory loading her on to the helicopter soon replaced it. Marty's body. Lifeless. Just like when they'd taken her brother off the rugby field when she was thirteen. His body then had been lifeless, too.

Sam shivered. She hated thinking of that time. She tried not to think of it, because what she remembered most about that day was her mother screaming. A guttural, soul-bending scream. A scream Sam had replicated the day they'd found Zed's body. Nope, didn't want to think about that day either. The only saving grace in her life was she wasn't there when they'd pulled her parents from their car wreckage. When the semi-trailer hit them head on, while they were driving to Newcastle for a wedding. The truckie had fallen asleep at the wheel and, since it was foggy that morning, they hadn't seen it until it was too late.

She'd been so lost after her parents died. First her brother, then her parents three years later. If Brooke's parents hadn't taken her in, she didn't know what would have happened to her. Technically she was fine to live on her own at sixteen, but since her parents rented their house, there was no house for her to stay in.

With all she had lost, despair knocked, but she pushed it down. She didn't want to think about what she'd now lost with Marty. It was too real. Marty was her adopted grandmother, her friend, her mentor. She was the one who had taught Bee all the things Sam could not. She was the one who had taken Bee into her arms and let her cry when they'd lost Zed, when Sam was in her own world of hurt. What would they do without her?

Sam never realised just how much of their lives involved Marty. Since her death, the wind had been taken out of their sails. Bee had stopped knitting, which threw Sam off. Bee had been knitting since she was six. She'd lost the joy, she said, when Sam asked her about it the week before. Spring meant veggie gardens were prepared and planted, but Sam hadn't even done that. They'd be screwed over summer without their summer garden, but she couldn't bring herself to bother. It was a task she'd always done side by side with Marty. She'd be shocked to remember anything the woman had told her over the years about gardening anyway.

Stroking Ned's head, she knew he was feeling the loss too. She'd found him three days ago sitting on Marty's front porch, like he was waiting for his friend to take him to the beach. When Sam called, he wandered to her like he was carrying the weight of the world on his shoulders. It was enough to push Sam over. She sat on the back porch with Ned's head nestled on her lap and cried for over an hour.

Life felt vacant, like it had when her parents died. Even after Zed died, she'd not felt as alone. She had Bee to look after. Now she wouldn't have Bee for much longer, no matter how much she wanted her to stay. It was a big, wide world out there. Fergus Bay was just a blip, a sheltered blip, from the rest of the world. Right now, it felt like everyone was leaving her. She couldn't even count on Jackson to be around for much longer. Then what?

"Yeah Ned, then what?" she asked, her voice heavy, weighed down with melancholy. But Ned had been lulled to sleep by her stroking hand.

She stood and slowly dusted the sand off her bottom to head home. The beach remained empty, the water still, and the thought lingered. What *was* next for her? She had to do something different. But reality hit her over the head like a two by four. She was nearly forty. She had no skills other than working in pubs and cafes, and did she really want to do that for the rest of her life? She was stuck. But somehow she felt Marty poking her, saying once again, "Come on Sweet Pea, time to get up". She just didn't know if she could this time.

20

BROOKE. DREAMS

OCTOBER.

Brooke opened her eyes slowly, feeling like she emerged from another world. Her dream was... weird. She reached over and checked her phone on the nightstand. Eight? Already? Great. That ruled out a morning surf, but she always had tomorrow. Right now, the dream rattled her. Maybe she could talk about it to someone. Make sense of it. But who would be available? Sam? No, she'd probably be at work by now.

She edged out of bed and walked to her bathroom. She thought about Merritt. Maybe she could ease into the conversation and get an update on what was going on with her plans? Wait. No. Merritt was in Brisbane for the weekend, hooking up with someone she'd just met online. Nothing like rebounding quickly, she thought enviously. Brooke couldn't even remember the last time she'd had sex.

She turned on the cold water tap and looked at her reflection in the mirror. She looked as worn out as she felt. Dark circles lingered under her eyes. God, the dream seemed so real.

What about Dae? No, he would laugh her off, even though he was in the dream. Besides, he was with Jase and her mother in the Hunter Valley this weekend at some food festival. Crap. Jase would be great at making sense of the mind-boggling scene running through her head. Could she tell her mum? Yeah, no. They were close, but not that close.

Fuck it. She'd try Sam. If she was off, she'd be back from the walk and hopefully not sleeping in, although it was Labour Day weekend, so who knew? Or was the public holiday just for New South Wales? She could never keep track. God, she was all over the place. She needed to talk to someone and now. Taking the risk, she dialled Sam's number and walked to the kitchen. She was shocked when Sam picked up.

"Hey, it's me. Where are you? Do you have time to talk?" Brooke grabbed a fire engine red coffee cup from the cupboard and started her kettle.

"Hi. I'm sitting at my kitchen table, drinking coffee, and staring at my planner."

"You have a planner? Why? You never plan anything," said Brooke. She regretted the comment immediately, knowing it would set Sam off.

"I do, and that's because I have a complicated work schedule," Sam said defensively. "More so lately, it seems. I was just trying to work out when my next day off is."

"Sorry. I didn't mean it the way it sounded. I had a weird dream that's spinning me out," she said. Brooke paced while waiting for the water to boil.

"It's okay. Didn't mean to be bitchy either. I can't complain. I'm happy to be working again," Sam said.

"Are you going in to work later today?" Brooke asked.

"No, I have the day off. And by the looks of it, it's the last one for at least…. a month," Sam said. Brooke heard her take a huge gulp of coffee, then push her chair back. Most likely to make another cup. The woman was a caffeine addict.

Brooke's kettle screamed. She took the ground coffee from the pantry and loaded her French press. She needed a shot of caffeine herself.

"I won't keep you long. Just wanted your take on the dream I had. You're always good with that stuff," Brooke said, pouring water into the glass beaker. Sam whispered her name away from the phone. Bee was up.

"Hey Aunty Brooke," she heard Bee call from the other end of the phone before asking her mother, "What time is it?"

"Um, just past eight. I thought you were working this morning before heading to town with Declan?" Sam asked.

"Yes, at nine. Just need coffee and to get dressed," Bee responded. Brooke waited patiently for their conversation to finish. Meanwhile, she made her coffee and popped a slice of bread in the toaster.

"Sorry," said Sam, "just needing to coordinate."

"It's okay. How's work going anyway?" Brooke asked.

"Café is good. Pub, not so much. Sean is a complete dickhead. I'm not looking forward to my shift at the pub tomorrow night. Thursday night, he dressed me down because I gave Bill Bishop the best table we had. Bill, I might add, is a regular and had reserved the table, but Sean decided he wanted that table for some VIP he had in."

"What did you do?" Brooke asked, expecting her fire-eating friend to have read him the riot act. Brooke smeared butter and vegemite on her toast, picked up her coffee and walked to her dining room table.

"Bill and his wife were already eating by then, so there wasn't anything I could do. And I couldn't argue about it. He's the owner now. I can't afford to lose the job," Brooke was shocked. The Sam she knew would have stood up to Sean.

"Anyway, can't let it get to me. I need the work." Brooke worried that if Sam kept going at this manic pace, pushing everything down, she was eventually going to explode. She didn't envy whoever was on the other end of the collapsing super nova. She'd experienced the impact twice, so she changed the subject to safer territory.

"How's Bee? She told me she's stressed about her exams," Brooke said.

"Yeah," said Sam. "She's a delight to be around at the moment."

"Did you talk to her about Declan?" Brooke asked. She knew Sam was perplexed why Bee hadn't shared anything with her. But so was

Brooke, especially after the conversation she'd had with Bee in their kitchen.

"Yeah. They're out in the open now, but she's still not talking about it. Between exams and Declan, her mood swings are killing me."

"Oh?" asked Brooke.

"She is either moping, being incredibly bitchy, or she's Doris Day. I was working the other afternoon while Bee studied in the café, waiting for me to finish my shift. At one point, she got really huffy with me. I don't know what it was about, but she said she wanted to go over to Jackson's. When I told her she couldn't, that he'd taken the shuttle into Hobart for his doctor appointments, Bee swore at me. Told me I was doing a lousy job looking after him. I mean, I was already feeling guilty not taking him in for the appointment myself, but what she said? I was speechless."

"That's not like Bee," Brooke said before taking a bite of her toast. She heard the faint hum of Bee's hair dryer in the background.

"It gets better. When I called her on her attitude, she said she wanted some space because I was in hers. So, I walked away and left her to her studying. Then, just as I was sweeping up, her phone rang. I have never seen her pounce on the thing so fast. It was then that I figured out what was going on. Declan hadn't texted her all day. Because after that, Doris Day emerged all perky and happy. Total one-eighty. Even offered to wash the floors for me."

"Damn."

"Yeah. You know how it is with young love. We've both been there. I guess there are certain things you don't share with 'the olds'," Sam said. Brooke laughed.

"God, I haven't heard that term in such a long time! Zed loved that phrase when referring to parents."

"I don't know what the kids call parents now. Parental Units? Who knows?"

"Don't ask me," Brooke said, continuing to eat her toast.

"I just don't know how to handle this version of Bee. I don't understand why she's not talking about Declan. I mean, I'm not upset about her dating him. But not telling me what's going on is killing me."

Brooke couldn't decide if it was anger or hurt that was causing the quivering in Sam's voice, but the ravaged emotions coming from Sam pained her. She knew Sam's relationship with Bee was the most important thing to her. She also knew how fragile Sam was at the prospect of Bee heading to university.

"Just remember, the Bee you know, she's still in there. Her exams will be over soon, and you'll get time with her afterwards. As for the Declan thing, maybe she's trying to work it out for herself before she can express what she's feeling to you?" Brooke hoped she sounded more like a friend than a doctor with her advice. Sometimes it was hard to know which tightrope to walk with Sam. Brooke heard Sam inhale, take another gulp of coffee, then slap her planner shut.

"Tell me about this dream," Sam said. Brooke exhaled. At least Sam wasn't slapping at her.

"You sure?" asked Brooke, but she was dying to spill it. Sam knew her better than anyone, and it was really weighing on her.

"Yes, it's an excellent distraction from my circus," answered Sam.

"Okay," Brooke puffed up her cheeks, blew out a deep breath, and sat back in her chair. "The dream was weird. I am walking down a cobblestone street with Dae through an old city, like Pamplona or Rome. I have a leather hold-all in my hand, and I'm heading to the airport to meet someone. Someone I've been wanting to be with all my life. He's told me he's free and he asks if I am too. But this man is faceless. I can't see him. I just know he's there. Until now, he's been with another woman. But this is the weird part. The woman he's been involved with is standing in the entrance of a restaurant near me, in this old city. She looks a bit like a young Nicole Kidman. She's talking to Dae at the top of the stairs. Dae knows the woman, but I don't. She's explaining to Dae how the faceless man broke it off with her, telling him she'd be better off. I can hear them talking, but I'm not actually part of the conversation. I'm on the footpath at the bottom of the stairs. The woman tells Dae she's okay with it all. She's with a musician now, who wears crusty boots and smokes like a chimney... and she's never been happier. As soon as she says this, my phone rings. It's the faceless guy. He's asking where I am. He's waiting. Then, the dream ends."

Sam was silent.

"What do you think? What the hell does the dream mean?! It's driving me nuts. I think it's the letters. They're screwing with my head."

"Yeah. It's got to be the letters," Sam said, but something in her voice made Brooke wonder if there was something she wasn't saying. She wasn't sure she liked this version of Sam. The one who held stuff back.

SAM. SECRETS.

OCTOBER.

For a smart woman, Brooke sure was dense sometimes. Her dream was obviously about Lachie. The fact Brooke didn't see that completely baffled her. Those two were meant for each other, but somehow, they couldn't find past their anger and hurt. Sam tried to intervene early on, but Zed insisted it was up to them to figure it out. If they really wanted to be together, they'd work it out. Except it was now fifteen years later, and they were still circling each other.

Had she told Brooke about Lachie and Morgan? She didn't think so. She thought she'd kept that to herself, but hearing Brooke's dream, maybe she had told her. The dream was spot on. Morgan did look like a young Nicole Kidman, so Sam must have said something. It didn't matter. The dream wasn't about Morgan. It was about Brooke and Lachie.

What frustrated her, more than anything, was Brooke and Lachie didn't appreciate what was right in front of them.

Her lingering doubts about moving on without Zed quickly turned to anger. She was a widow in her late thirties, hanging on by a thread, while Brooke and Lachlan had a whole life to live for, together. They were just too damn stubborn to fix it. She'd give anything to have Zed back.

"Knock knock," the booming voice from the back door made her jump.

"What the fuck?" She stood quickly. Lachie came in through the back door.

"Sorry, thought you would have heard the truck drive up. Must have been deep in thought." Ned wagged his tail as Lachie scratched his ears. Great guard dog he was.

"Yeah, sorry. Coffee?" Sam asked.

"Please." Ned sank to the floor and rolled over, looking for a belly rub. Lachie chuckled, shook his head, then kneeled to oblige.

"Was I expecting you today?" she asked, heading to the kitchen. There was nothing in her planner, then realised she had written very little down since before the storm. Other than bills tucked in the back, and a letter Brooke had given her from Marty, which she couldn't bring herself to read just yet, the pages were blank.

"Yeah. Starting on the sunroom. That okay?" She nodded and poured him a cup of coffee. But that killed her plans for the day.

"Declan's with me. Told him to get going on the demo," he said, leaving Ned for the coffee.

"I didn't realise what time it was. Feels like I just got back from dropping Bee off, but crap, it's nearly ten." She needed to get a load of laundry started. Maybe she'd head into town. The noise from the demo would do her head in if she stayed.

"Thanks," he said, taking the coffee.

"I'm off today, but I need to run into Hobart for some shopping," she said, tidying up the table from the pile of bills she'd been juggling.

"We'll be here all day, so I'll pick Bee up this afternoon. Don't worry Sam. Declan's a good kid. I trust him, even around Bee, and you know that's saying something. I've talked around the subject of dating and while he hasn't outwardly said anything, I think there's serious interest. Not just…" He began to say more but stopped there. Probably best.

"Thanks. She needs to study this afternoon. Exams start in two weeks," she said.

"Got it covered. Okay, then I'll get started. Can I show you what we're going to do today, so you don't freak out later?" Lachie asked. She nodded and headed outside with him. Lachie looked toward Marty's house with his brow furrowed for a moment. He returned his gaze to Sam.

"It's quiet out here in the bay. I mean, without Marty. Not that she was a hellraiser, but..." he said. "You okay?"

"Yeah," she said, kicking a rogue weed poking out of her scrappy lawn.

"Your head still spinning with Marty's death?" Lachie asked.

"That and a million other things." She hesitated to share what she was really thinking.

"Things will work out, you know. Speaking of, there's news on the bridge. The council have approved a footbridge. So, I've pulled together a work crew. We'll get started on that in a few days. Just waiting on supplies."

"Well, a footbridge is certainly an improvement. Brooke and Merritt hit the champagne harder than I realised at Georgina's exhibit, so it was interesting getting two drunk women across the river. Merritt almost fell off the flying fox, she was giggling so much." Lachie laughed softly. "Although I guess that would probably be just as likely with a footbridge."

"I wish I'd been there to see that," he said. "Look, I know the footbridge is not the best solution, but it's something. And we'll build it high enough that it won't wash out in the first big rain. You'll still need to use Jackson's car, but the footbridge is at least more solid than the flying fox. If all goes according to plan, I'll have it built in a couple of weeks."

"Thanks, Lachie. That's great news. Really." She hated to think about what she would do without his help.

"You need to worry less, Ginger," said Lachie, picking up the stick Ned laid at his feet, his tail whipping left and right. Lachie threw it for the stout dog long down the track. "Things suck right now, but you have people on your side. You've got a big heart and a sharp mind. Isn't that what Marty used to tell you?" He looked at her pointedly.

"Yeah, she did," she said, smiling. Marty always told her that when she doubted herself. "But God. How do I even get to that better place? I work part time in a café. Even the pub job looks ambiguous right now. Sean is a fucking nightmare to work for."

"Yeah, I've heard that. Bill Bishop told me about his reservation mix-up when I ran into him at the Orford Hub yesterday." He continued to throw the stick for Ned down the track. A waft of sand exploded into the air when Ned screeched to a halt to pick it up.

"There was no mix-up. Sean just had a conniption because Bill reserved the table. He wanted it for someone else. Anyway, it's not good. Things are grim on the money front too, especially with Zed's insurance money running out. I just keep thinking I'm screwed. I just..." God, she hated the high-pitched whine in her voice. She shook her head. "Sorry."

"What can I do to help? Do you need money?" She always needed money, but she wouldn't be taking any from Lachie or from Brooke. It was hard enough accepting their help in other ways.

"No, and you know I'd never take it from you. As I said last week, I can't even pay you for the repairs right now."

"We talked about that, Sam. This is my way of helping. But if you're stretched elsewhere..."

"That's the thing though, Lach. I'm always stretched. I don't know how to get out of the mess I'm in. I never thought this would be my life. A widowed mother, living in a shack crumbling around us. The isolation is getting to me and I'm just angry. Seems I'm angry all the time at this fucking situation." Lachie looked at her, ignoring Ned's pleading eyes. She put her hands in her pockets. When Ned turned his attention to her with his stick, she shook her head.

"How could he do this to me? How could he do this to us?" Her thoughts tumbled from her mouth. "We had a plan. We had dreams together. How could he be so stupid and take the boat out in that weather? He knew the risks. No one else went out that day. He was pissed off and drunk before he even left the house!"

She wanted to stop there, but the words spilled out of her like molten lava.

"And why say such cruel things to me? They've haunted me ever since."

She'd not shared that last part with anyone. Sam confirmed he'd been drinking when the police questioned her. She remembered how embarrassed it was to reveal that. But she never shared why he was so drunk, not with anyone. No one knew about the fight they'd had the night before.

"Sam..."

"Zed forgot the anniversary of my parent's death. Twenty years. I was in bed crying all day, missing them like crazy. Zed called me a lazy, selfish bitch, and complained about having to 'babysit' Bee all day. That set me off more than forgetting about my parent's deathiversary. He was Bee's father, for fuck's sake! Parents don't babysit their own damn children."

Sam was quiet for a moment, then added with a thinly veiled fury, "After that, I told him how lucky he was to have this time with Bee. I told him how hard it was without my parents around. For some reason, I thought he knew what it was like to be without a parent. But when he looked at me with this... stupid fucking stare, I realised it was different for him. He had no clue what it was like. Not really. He was raised by Jackson and Beverlee." Her voice grew louder again with ravaged pain. "*They* were his parents. *They* raised him."

Lachie calmly regarded her with empathy, letting her vent.

"Then I told him I wanted to be more than just a fisherman's wife. That I resented him for having to give up my own dreams. Do you know what he said to me?" Her eyes brimmed with tears. Lachie shook his head.

"That maybe I was better off without him." Her voice was a hoarse whisper. "Makes you wonder, doesn't it?"

"And now? Now, it's four years later I'm left feeling angry at how much he's missed. Bee will finish school in a few weeks. Then what? She'll leave, as she should. But he's missing out on seeing her discover her world. He was so stupid to get on that fucking boat in those conditions. He was pissed at me. Why? Because I called him out on his shit.

He knew the gaping hole in my heart from my parent's death. So why put yourself at risk when you don't have to?"

Lachie waited for her to finish, his eyes never leaving hers. When she ran out of steam, he picked up the stick for Ned, who sat patiently at their feet. The moment stretched out, like he was trying to find the right words. He threw the stick down the track, watching Ned take off on his mission before he turned to her.

"He was an idiot, Sam. But he was crazy about you. He loved you so much. And Bee. He was starting to realise his responsibilities around then. Some men don't do well when shown the mirror. Beverlee spoiled him; you know that. He didn't have to face responsibility until you came along. We all make choices with the information we have at the time, right? I remember when Bee started high school. It spun him out. He told me that. He said he'd started thinking back to when you guys met. He was scared she'd make the same mistakes."

"Mistakes? So, he was thinking we were a mistake?"

"No, that's not what I meant. I remember we were at Bee's netball game one Saturday morning. He and I were standing on the sidelines together. I think Bee was about eleven or twelve. Zed said hello to every single person there. He knew everyone. He was engrained in the community. Other than your trip together, he'd never left. Melbourne was even a big trip for him. Later, he told me he was worried about Bee staying here when she got older, not having more experience in the world. He wanted to see her fly. Have wings. He just didn't know how to show her. That was his limitation, and it weighed on him."

"Wow, he didn't tell me any of that," Sam said. "I thought he was happy here. He always said how lucky we were. That we had the dream life. That when he watched people board the Maria Island ferry, he realised they were the same kinds of people we met when we travelled. And now, here they were, exploring our backyard. I had no clue he felt any other way."

"I don't think he knew how to tell you. He told me, right before he married you, that you were too smart for him. That you had plans to go to university for a degree in social work. How you wanted to work with people who'd dealt with trauma, like you had with your family.

He said he felt he was holding you back from greater things. He didn't want the same for Bee."

"I forgot about that plan. Ironic isn't it? Because look where I am. Dealing with another trauma. And now? Now I'm stuck," she said, crossing her arms across her chest.

"Not stuck. You just need to work out what's next for you."

Yeah, and what the hell was that?

BROOKE. REVELATIONS.

NOVEMBER.

Brooke rode the train from Epping to Chatswood to join her parents for dinner. They never met for dinner mid-week, so it had her on high alert. When she asked why tonight, her father said he needed to discuss something with her. At first, she thought it was a medical issue. But no, he insisted. It had to do with Marty's will. She dreaded to think what it may be. It was just one more thing to confirm her grandmother's death. At first, she thought it was odd the beach house didn't go to her parents. She assumed her father, an only child, would inherit everything. But as the executor, he stated certain things in the will were very clear. The beach house was clearly left to her.

"But there's more we need to talk about," he said.

As the train rattled along the tracks, she thought to Fergus Bay. She was glad for the house. The more time she spent in it, the more she realised how much it meant to her. Sydney felt hollow to her now. As soon as she walked back into her house in Cheltenham after her time in Tasmania, she felt an overwhelming sense of loneliness. Maybe that was just her reaction to losing Marty? It made sense. No matter how busy she was, she always spoke to her grandmother every afternoon. Now she had an enormous gap in her life.

"Hey, love. How are you?" her dad asked when he picked her up at the train station.

"Doing okay," she said, reaching for her seat belt as he pulled into traffic. They talked a little about her time in Fergus Bay as they made their way through downtown Chatswood.

"And work? How's that going?" Ray asked.

"Okay there too. Dae ran things like clockwork while I was out. So, no issues there. I just get nervous leaving him to it while I'm gone."

"He's a good man. I think he has more business sense than you give him credit for," her dad said as he navigated through peak hour traffic. She was glad he was driving. She would hate to deal with this kind of traffic every day. People never honked or cut you off on the train.

"And, you know, his idea to add more staff isn't altogether a bad idea," Ray said, finally pulling into the driveway.

"It's not that I think it's a bad idea", Brooke said, wondering when this dead horse would finally be beat. "I just think he needs his own practice. His ideas of how the practice needs to change vastly differ from mine."

"That's what you've said before," her dad said.

"As much as Dae was pushing for the changes he wants, he has said nothing since Marty's death. Knowing Dae like I do, that makes me nervous," she said. "I just wonder what's percolating in that head of his."

They went into the house through the garage, and while she headed to the kitchen, her dad deactivated the house alarm.

"Let's grab some wine and talk in my office. Your Mum won't be home for an hour, and I have the will on my desk," he said, taking his suit jacket off and flinging it over a dining room chair. Brooke knew her mother would walk in and immediately hang her father's jacket up in the closet. They had been dancing to this tune for years.

Brooke hung her handbag over one of the high stools at the kitchen counter, and her work bag on the seat, then walked to the cabinet where they kept the wine glasses. Her father walked to the butler's pantry, always fully stocked with a nice variety of wine.

"Red, white, or rosé?" he asked, looking into the wine fridge.

"Red please," and placed two red wine glasses on the counter.

"Red it is. Found this bottle at Dan Murphy's last week. It's not a bad drop." Brooke smiled, knowing her dad would drink anything the guys at Dan Murphy's recommended and not even blink at the price, contrary to the frugality in which he lived his life.

"Take a sip, then tell me how much you think I paid." He loved this game. He poured a sample in her glass. She sniffed, swirled, and sipped. It was full-bodied yet smooth, pushing the price higher in her opinion. Her dad stood next to her, sniffing his glass with a superior look. She studied his face, thought she'd start high, thirty-five dollars per bottle, but now he looked smug. She loved this game, too.

"Thirty dollars," she said, pleased with herself, taking a longer sip.

"Nope. Eleven," Ray boasted with unreserved pride, his lips curling around the edge of his glass.

"Well done. I'd buy it," Brooke said.

"I just happen to have an extra dozen. Remind me to put a box in the car before I drop you home," he said. "Now, come with me. We need to talk about this will." She took another long drink, imagining only doom and gloom.

Her father's enormous desk took up most of the room in his office. A wall of books stood behind it. Maybe she'd make Marty's room into a library? She couldn't see anyone sleeping in the room now, so maybe a library of sorts would work? Yes. Even Marty would have loved that idea.

Her dad took in a deep breath and cleared his throat. She gave him her full attention. She knew he hated this part. He'd told her that, for him, dealing with Marty's estate was like reliving her death every time. She wished she could make it easier, but there was nothing more they could do than plough through it.

"As I told you, the beach house in Fergus Bay is yours. Mum talked to me about it, and I agreed it should go to you. We love going down there, but we love our place in Queensland more. We're just not fans of the cold like you." Brooke smiled at that. She liked their place in Queensland, too. The surfing was significantly better.

"Does this mean I can never go to the Queensland house again?" she asked, although she knew the answer. She loved teasing her dad, and she really wanted to lighten the mood. He looked way too serious.

"Of course not. It's yours whenever you want. Moving on," he said, his glasses perched on his nose, his brow furrowed. He flipped over a page and shifted into business mode again. "You have money for the upkeep, but I'll skip the legalese. I'll need to transfer that money to you, so let me know which account you wish to use."

"Dad, just give me the highlights. I know this is hard for you. And you know I trust you to do what's best."

"Okay," he said, taking his glasses off. He looked directly to her, and the pained look made her want to gulp what was left in her glass. "Do you know if Sam has read the letter you gave her?"

"What letter?"

"The letter you gave Sam a couple of months ago." His tone thrummed with impatience.

"Oh. Right. Yes, I gave it to her. Sam looked at the letter, then put it in her back pocket. Said she couldn't deal with it and would read it later. She was running late for work and…" Her Dad sat back in his chair, ran his hands over his face, then picked up his wine.

"Why? Was it important?

"Yes. I can't do anything until she reads that letter," Ray said, his tone tinged with exasperation.

"About what?"

"Doesn't matter. But next time you speak with Sam, prod her, will you? Otherwise, I'll have to do it, and I'd be going against Mum's explicit instructions if I do." Brooke nodded. "I have the deed to the beach house to give to you," he said, and handed her the paperwork.

"It's officially yours once you sign it." Brooke took it, scanned the document, then looked to her father.

"Did you know someone named Gilly growing up? A relative maybe?"

"Gilly. Hmm… rings a bell," he said, looking over the rest of the paperwork in front of him. "I remember someone calling Mum that when I was really young. She went by Margaret in those days, but I think she preferred Gilly. No idea where it came from, but Dad didn't like it, so he called her Marty."

"Wait. What?!" Shocked, her voice left her. *Marty* was Gilly?

"What? Why do you ask?" He looked curiously amused.

"Do you know who Henry was?" Brooke asked, trying hard to keep the excitement from her voice.

"Henry? No. Why? Who's Henry?" her father asked.

She didn't mention the stack of letters, only that she'd found a letter from someone named Henry mixed amongst Marty's things. Clearly Marty hadn't told her dad about Henry or the letters. There had to be a reason for that. She wondered now if this was why Marty left the house to her and not her father. By doing that, Brooke would learn of her secrets if there were, in fact, secrets to be found.

"No one. Doesn't matter. What else in the will do we need to talk about?" she asked, desperate now to change the subject. Because something about this new information was niggling at her.

Over the next week, Brooke re-read every single letter, now she knew Marty was Gilly. The idea bewildered her. She scanned every letter for clues. Henry often talked about how important Gilly's work was, but it was so ambiguous that Brooke never realised it was Marty's work he was talking about. He also mentioned the beach house, calling it her sanctuary. From the deed, Brooke now knew Marty bought the beach house in July 1961. That was three years after she married her grandfather, Bert, but the same year the letters began from Henry. And the house was solely in Marty's name.

The timing was off. Something wasn't adding up.

Brooke called her father and asked him if he knew of anything that had happened with Marty around the early 1960s. He was baffled by her questions.

"First you asked who Henry was, now you have questions about Mum in the sixties? What's going on Brooke?"

"Oh, I'm just missing Marty, I guess," she said casually. "I noticed the beach house was only in Marty's name. That was unusual for back then, wasn't it? Since she was already married to Granddad?"

"It was probably because Dad hated the beach," Ray replied, as if that explained everything. Brooke knew it didn't. The what ifs were driving her crazy.

She tried calling Sam to tell her what she'd discovered, but she couldn't reach her. Instead, she got texts back at random times. The frustration mounted as she and Sam played phone tag. She tried called Merritt but couldn't reach her either. She was buried in contracts and divorce negotiations. Brooke just wanted to tell someone what she found out, and she knew she couldn't tell her dad. She didn't know why, but something nagged at her. It wasn't time to share this news with him yet.

Even work was driving her crazy. Spring fever was making the rounds, reminding Brooke that Marty's garden would be overrun by now. When she finally got on to Sam, she'd ask if there was anyone she could recommend to manage it until she got there at Christmas. No matter how busy it was in the practice, Marty was still at the forefront of her mind.

She'd spend Christmas in Fergus Bay for sure now, even though her parents had decided to go to Queensland. It was too hard, her father said, and hoped she understood. And she did. The season would be hard on all of them without Marty. The beach house was where she wanted to be, where she needed to be. Plus, there was no way she would miss Bee's eighteenth birthday.

"So, wait. You found a box of love letters written to Marty, from a man named Henry? But her name is Gilly in the letters?" Dae asked over dinner. Brooke nodded, picking up some edamame and peeling the shell away. Jase was working late, and since she was only going home to the letters, dinner with Dae sounded like a great distraction. And now she was telling Dae all about her new discovery.

"And you have no clue who Henry was?" he asked. The server placed a plate of sushi in front of them.

"Thank you," she said, smiling at the young woman before turning her attention back to Dae. "No. I don't have a clue."

"And this was when?" he asked, picking up his chopsticks.

"The letters were written between early 1961 until mid-1962," she answered.

"When did she marry your grandfather?" he asked. She was surprised by his enthusiasm. He sounded as obsessed as she was.

"1958. So, you can understand why I'm confused. I just don't know who Henry is or his importance to her. I mean, the letters looked well read. They were bound by ribbon and placed in the same box as other meaningful mementos. So, they clearly meant something to her."

Dae played with his sashimi as he pondered the information.

"And they were beautiful letters, full of such love and admiration. I mean, I'd marry him if he were my age."

"Maybe Henry was your granddad? Bert. Maybe Henry was his middle name?" Dae suggested, finally eating his forgotten tuna.

"No. I thought that too, after I learned who Gilly was. Dad mentioned she went by Gilly when she was younger, but my grandfather didn't like it. He called her Marty. That's what he always called her, according to Dad. Henry mentioned Marty's husband in one letter, but it was so veiled it was hard to figure out what he was saying. He wrote about her deciding her future, but it was right after he talked about her work and how proud he was of an award she received."

"Do you think they were having an affair?"

"That's the part I can't figure out. The language suggests an affair, but they went to events together, so they were public about their relationship. Not secretive at all. Henry wrote about people they both knew. Friends of theirs, not just his. So, I don't think it was a secret. I also thought they may have been colleagues at one point, but I don't think so. I'm truly stumped."

She picked up a slice of shaved ginger. "There's one letter that's haunting me, though."

"Oh?" He asked, picking up another piece of sashimi from the shared plate.

"Yes," she said, her chopsticks resting now. "It's not a letter from Henry. It's a letter to Henry, and the letter was unsent."

"What did it say?"

"That she was ending it. That she lost their baby, and it was too painful to be with him." Brooke's eyes filled with tears.

"Oh shit, Brooke," Dae whispered. He was quiet for a while before continuing. "But you say the letter was unsent?"

"Yes. It was unsealed and unsent," she said, sniffing back her emotions.

"You have to find him, Brooke. You have to find Henry."

"Yeah. I know."

23

SAM. HELPLESSNESS.

NOVEMBER.

Sam was not having a great morning.

"Oh, my God Mum. You're driving slower than Marty ever did. Hurry up! I'm going to be late!" It didn't help that her car was making weird sounds, or that she was almost out of petrol. Geezus, why did she drive her car, and not the 4WD this morning? But she knew the answer. Habit.

"Doing the best I can, Bee," she retorted just as they came to the footbridge. It was better to say little, rather than add to her daughter's aggravation, since Bee had been short with her all week.

Bee sprang out of the car, expletives flying. She flew across the footbridge and when she got to Jackson's car, slammed the passenger door closed with more words. Sam hadn't even turned her car off. Nothing she said was the right thing.

Bee began her exams on Monday, and she was acting like a complete bitch. Sam was too loud. There was no food in the house. She didn't have time to take Ned for a walk. Blah blah blah. It added fuel to their unspoken war.

Sam sat for a few minutes as the car ticked over. She needed to let the anger go. Her conversation with Lachie had rattled her.

She was stuck. As much as he didn't think so, she was in a bottomless hole she couldn't find her way out of. She was tired of always feeling hopeless. She was tired of being angry. She was tired of bearing the brunt of everything. She looked across at Bee fuming in Jackson's car. She needed a change, but today was yet another day of mooching off someone's generosity. Jackson's car. Mick's 4WD. Lachlan's free labour. The fridge Brooke had paid for. When was she ever going to get a handle on her damn life?

Bee honked the car horn at Sam. Geezus. Could she just chill for a bit? Sam got out, locked her car, and walked over the footbridge. Taking a deep breath, hoping the invisible armour was still intact, she got into the driver's side to find Bee with her fingers flying over her phone. Sam wished Doris Day would return. The wicked bitch of the west routine was getting old.

By noon, Sam was exhausted. She was being pulled in a million directions. Nicole worked the kitchen while Sam managed the front of the café. She just hoped Becca was still coming in to help with the lunch rush.

Sam couldn't stop thinking of her upcoming expenses. What could she jostle? Bee's eighteenth birthday loomed, and her formal was coming up as well. At least she had a dress for the formal, thanks to a shopping trip with Brooke and Merritt. But what was the weird noise coming from her car? That couldn't be good. She needed to have it checked out. Geezus. She was bleeding money.

Taking a customer's order from the kitchen, Sam pivoted too close to the counter and bumped her hand, losing her grip on the plate. It shattered, leaving food and broken ceramic littered across the wood floor.

"Fuck!" she yelled; her hands immediately flew to cover her mouth when she realised where she was. She mumbled apologies to those who turned her way, then quickly ducked into the kitchen to let Nicole know she needed a redo of the last order. Broom in hand, she walked back out to clean up her mess.

"Let us help," said a voice behind her. She turned to find Georgina's friends, Pam, and Aubrey, standing behind the counter.

"I've got it," she mumbled, her face feeling like it was on fire. She was deeply embarrassed. She didn't remember the last time she'd dropped anything in the café.

"I know you do, but you look like you're having a time of it today. We've been watching you for the last thirty minutes and you need a break. Go on, we've got this," said Pam, reaching for the broom. Aubrey asked a customer at the counter if she could take her order. Sam was mortified. Especially in front of Aubrey. Not only was Aubrey wearing a dress similar to one her mother had owned, but the Chanel No. 5 fragrance she wore was throwing Sam back in time. Today was not the day to be losing it over someone who reminded her of her mother!

"Go. We've got this," said Pam. Remembering Georgina telling her that Pam was not one to contend with, Sam took refuge in the kitchen.

"I've been kicked out of the café by Pam and Aubrey. They've taken over," said Sam to Nicole. "Sorry about the plate." Nicole flipped the fillet of fish on the grill for the replacement order.

"It's fine. Don't worry about it. I'm more concerned about you. Are you okay?" asked Nicole. Sam desperately tried to hold it together. She muttered she was fine and leaned against the counter to watch Nicole fly around the kitchen, doing ten things at once. Sam usually worked at that speed too, but today she felt like she was standing in quicksand. Nicole ordered Sam to sit and take a breath while she finished up the rush of orders.

"Hey, did you know Pam and Aubrey are serving customers at the counter?" said Becca, walking into the kitchen a few minutes later. She stopped short when she saw Sam sitting on a stool, drinking a glass of cold water.

"Everything okay, Sam?" Becca asked. Sam nodded, although she couldn't find the words to express how embarrassed she was. The three of them had been partners in crime while Georgina was in Spain.

THE DECISIONS WE MAKE

They ran a tight ship and right now, Sam felt like she was sinking that ship.

"All fine. They're just helping for a few minutes. Things got a bit nuts out there. Sam's been run off her feet all morning," Nicole said, and although it wasn't entirely true, she appreciated her friend's support. "If you can relieve Pam and Aubrey, that would be great."

Becca looked to Sam with a worried expression. She gave her an empathetic smile, put on her apron, and walked out of the kitchen.

"Let her take over the front for a while. Want something to eat?" Sam couldn't think of eating. Right now, the guilt ate at her stomach.

"Here." Nicole thrust a panini in front of her. An order she had placed only minutes before.

"I'll take it out," Sam said and got up from the stool. Nicole would have nothing of it.

"Sit. You eat it. I've got another going. You've probably just had coffee today, right?" Sam thought back. Yeah, she'd been too riled this morning to eat breakfast. She nodded guiltily. "Then eat."

"Becca's taken over, so we've come in to steal Sam for a bit," said Pam, sticking her head in the kitchen. What? Why? Nicole nodded.

"What, no. Let me just eat this and I'll be out to help her," she insisted. Pam took the plate from her.

"Becca's got things handled. Come on girly," said Pam.

Don't fuck with her, Nicole silently conveyed with her eyes. Sam grabbed her water and followed them out to their spot in the corner.

"Now. Tell us what's going on with you. We're worried," Pam said when they settled in.

"Worried? But you don't even know me," Sam said, her cheeks reddening with humiliation.

"Maybe not, but we know Georgina and she says that she's worried about you, too. She said you've been distracted lately. Watching you today, it's obvious there's a lot on your mind." Was she that transparent? Probably.

"We just want to help. If we can," said Aubrey, her tone considerably softer than Pam's. Sam stared at the woman speaking words of encouragement. The similarities she shared with her mother was unnerving - the perfume, her flowing red hair. Her skin was flawless, and Sam wondered how old she was. She carried off the boho chic thing, too. Like, really well. Sam tried to smooth out the wrinkles in the leggings she threw on that morning. They'd been scrunched up in a pile of laundry on her bedroom floor. They smelled clean, at least. Aubrey, on the other hand, looked like she'd just stepped out of a fashion magazine.

"It's okay. We just want to help," Pam prodded gently. "Trust me, between the two of us, we can most likely offer you some kind of words of wisdom."

Sam looked up and saw a gentleness in the woman's eyes, then turned her gaze back to her wrinkled lap.

"My life is a mess. I'm just at a loss," Sam whispered. The last thing she needed was for the whole town to know she was falling apart. It was hard enough admitting it out loud to two strangers.

"Georgina told us your husband died four years ago," Pam said quietly. Sam nodded, tears welling.

"Are you angry at him?" Pam asked.

Sam shot her head up and stared wide-eyed at the woman.

"Oh love, I know," Pam said softly.

"Although you're probably not angry with your husband for the reasons Pam was," Aubrey said, and smiled at the grandmotherly figure sitting next to her.

"But Jack? Isn't he…?"

"My husband? No. Jack and I are partners. My husband died a few years ago. Best thing that's ever happened to me," said Pam. Shocked, Sam looked to Aubrey, hoping for some kind of explanation.

"Yeah, you need to stop telling people that, Pam. At least until they know you better," said Aubrey. She smiled at her friend, then looked back to Sam.

"Tell us why you're angry at him," Aubrey said.

"Because he left me with a pile of debt, a house that's falling apart, and he's missed out on, well, everything."

"Georgina said something about it being an accident?" Pam asked. Sam nodded.

"It was a boating accident. He took the boat out in a horrific storm.

He'd been drinking and ..." She hesitated. No, she couldn't admit that to these women.

"Did you have a fight with him? Is that part of it?" Aubrey asked softly. Damn it. Was this woman psychic?

"How did you know?" Sam asked, horrified. She only told Lachie about that piece, and he wouldn't say anything.

"I didn't, but the guilt is written all over you," said Aubrey. "I know about guilt. My daughter committed suicide almost three years ago. We had a huge fight beforehand. Until I met Georgina and Pam, I carried that burden with me like a dark cloud. I was so angry. Angry that she left with that argument hanging. That she'd left me, left her brother, left us hanging without knowing why. But I know why, deep down. I've had to let the anger go. But it wasn't easy. I realised, later, that things are said in the moment. Sometimes they're things you wanted to say but hadn't for whatever reason. Sometimes it's to let out frustrations. And, sometimes, like with my daughter, it's to say things just to release the pain."

"I said things to my husband that were honest," Sam said. "Words I held for too long. I shouldn't have said them when he was drunk. Now, I'm trying to figure out what to do with that."

"Figuring out what to do with the anger you carry? Or with what you said to him?" asked Pam.

"Both, I suppose. He made a stupid decision because he was drunk and angry. Because of what I said to him, I pushed him to go out on to that boat. I feel..." Sam looked around. "I feel responsible. It's my fault."

"Okay. I'm stopping you there," said Aubrey. She took her hand and looked her in the eye. "You can't feel guilty, or responsible, for other people's decisions. Trust me, I carried that one myself for a long time. People make their own decisions. Take their own actions. That's not on you." Sam nodded, slowly.

"I can't change what I said. I know that. It's just I'm now stuck. I'm broke. I'm angry that he left me to deal with a house that needs so much work. To rely on friends for help. That he left me to raise our daughter alone. That he's missing out on her life. Her first serious relationship."

"Oh, that's right," said Aubrey, her smile broad. "You're Bee's mum. Oh, she's a gorgeous girl. Tom and I met her a few weeks ago when we ran into them in Hobart. We had a quick lunch together. You've done an amazing job with her." Tears spilled from Sam's eyes. Aubrey dug into her cavernous bag and pulled out a tissue.

"It sucks that your husband is missing out on your daughter's life," Pam interjected while Sam blew her nose. "I can't imagine that pain, although Aubrey knows. It's got to be hard. But no matter what shit situation you're in, there's always a way through. Always. I was in the worst marriage. My husband was abusive. It was sheer hell. I was bound to the man because of our religion. But then I realised, eventually anyway, that life isn't always helpful in showing you the right path when you need it most. Nor is it good at reminding you have choices. You just need to work out what your choices are. Then, one step at a time, figure out how to get there."

"Easier said than done," Sam sighed.

"You mentioned relying on friends," said Aubrey. "You know what? That's not a bad thing. But it's hard to ask for help, and it's just as hard to receive it. I was like that. I was an extremely stubborn woman. I wouldn't let anyone in. It took me a while to trust, and it took ages before I allowed George and Pam to help me. So I get it. It is hard to open up and let others help you, even if they are people close to you." Sam knew she was stubborn too, but there were some days she had no choice but to ask for help. Especially from Lachie.

"Georgina told us you're the one that's always there for everyone else," Aubrey continued. "That she'd never known someone so willing to help, even at your own detriment. She said you're always helping the oldies around town, always first to raise your hand to volunteer."

"The isolation that came with the bridge washing away must have been awful. When Lachlan told us about building the footbridge, he said people lined up to help," Pam said. Sam was stunned by this news. She hadn't heard about any of this.

"Tom said there were about fifty people who showed up. He said everyone wanted to pitch in," said Aubrey.

"When Jack and I were in at the council," Pam added, "some old man was railing on them about getting the bridge reopened. Lachlan told us it was your father-in-law?"

"My grandfather-in-law, Jackson," Sam laughed.

"He was saying he'd lived in the area for years," said Pam. "How his family died working for this community and it was time they did some good," said Pam. "It was amazing to watch. He was having none of the bullshit they were tossing back at him."

"Yeah. That sounds like Jackson. He's a stubborn one," smiled Sam.

"The point is: let people help. It all comes around in the end," said Pam. "As for holding on to your anger, let it go. You're right. It's easier said than done. It'll take time, but once you do, your heart will be lighter. And remember, no matter what happens in life, we still get to choose who we want to be and live the kind of life we want."

BROOKE. TRUTHS.

NOVEMBER.

Two days after her dinner with Dae, Brooke was driving down the track to Fergus Bay. She hadn't told Sam she was coming. She figured she'd drive to Marty's house – her house – and head over to Sam's later when she got home. Brooke had to jump through hoops to make it happen, but she knew it was the right decision as she navigated through the stunning Tasmanian forest.

Glad to finally get on to Merritt, her friend asked a million questions about the letters once Brooke shared with her that Marty was Gilly. Dae had revved her up. Talking with Merritt clarified things. She knew now she needed to dig deeper into Marty's past. Her mental health depended on it. The woman was a world of mystery, and the more she was discovering, the more she felt disconnected from her grandmother. She was determined to find out what the true story was. Marty must have left the letters in easy reach for a reason, right?

"Am I nuts to do this?" she'd asked Dae while she packed up her office.

"Probably the best plan you've made in years," he said, but she'd questioned her decision the entire flight down. Now she was here, it felt right.

As she turned down the track toward Fergus Bay, she heard music booming. Was Sam home? Bee was deep in exams, so it couldn't be Bee. Brooke opened the car window and quickly realised the music was not what either Sam or Bee would listen to. Was that… Lionel Richie? It couldn't be Sam. She refused to listen to Lionel Richie. She said it brought back memories of her parents. Brooke rounded the corner and slammed on the brakes when she saw Lachlan's truck parked in Sam's driveway.

That explained the music. It didn't explain why Lachlan was here in the middle of the day. Brooke got out of her 4WD rental and walked toward Sam's house. She could hear Lachlan's voice singing 'You Are', and he was horrendously off key. That song. It had been one that they played over and over during their last summer together. Shit.

"Hello?" she called. The last thing she needed was to catch him off guard wielding a nail gun.

The music stopped. She heard someone descending a ladder and the stomp of boots coming toward her. It may not be him. Let it be someone on his crew, she prayed.

"Hello?" she called again and rounding the corner was the man who still made her catch her breath.

"Oh, hey," he said. He was dressed in blue docker shorts and a grey t-shirt with Jones Custom Construction emblazoned across his broad chest. His arms were buff and tanned, and she saw the hairs on them standing, as if a chilly breeze had wafted in.

"Sam here?" she asked, ignoring the pounding in her chest.

"Nope, she's at work today. I'm just, ah, working on her sunroom," he said, waving his arms like a show host, to reveal the plastic and sawhorses behind him.

"Do you know when she'll be home?"

"She isn't expecting you?" he asked. "Figured she'd mention something this morning about it." Probably so he wouldn't be playing Lionel Richie. She hadn't been able to listen to any of his music since that long ago summer.

"She doesn't know. I flew down this morning. I'm staying until

January," she said. Why am I telling him this? "Thought I'd work on Marty's garden and do some other things while I'm here."

"Can you take that much time off work?" he asked, and promptly blushed.

"Yes, I can. I own the practice, remember?" Her tone was harsher than she meant, and she saw his eyes go cold.

"I cleaned out Marty's garden last weekend. I was doing work on the other shacks. Figured I'd do that for… Marty." Yes, except it was no longer Marty's house, she wanted to say. Moments went by. When Lachlan reached up to scratch his head, the tattoo on his forearm caught her eye.

"What's that?" she exclaimed, pointing to his arm.

"What?" He waved his arm like he had a spider crawling on it until it became apparent to him what she'd asked. He stared at his arm, then at her. Yeah, that. What the fuck was that?! Anger rose in her.

"Your tattoo, Lachlan. When did you get that tattoo?"

"Years ago, Brooke. But, as they say, getting a tattoo is stupid. Because it's on your body. Forever." And with that, he turned and returned to work, leaving her there, shaking.

"Hellooo!" called Sam, walking in the front door. Brooke cocked her head to see behind her, expecting to see Bee trailing behind.

"I left Bee at home. She's studying, but if she wasn't, you wouldn't want her here. She's a bloody nightmare lately," Sam grumbled, kicking her sandy thongs off at the door. It was a habit Marty had engrained in all of them.

"If she's not bitchy about her exams, she's silent about Declan. I have tried to talk to her about him, but apparently, I won't understand," Sam said, scoffing at that last statement. Yeah. If there was anyone who understood what it was like to be seventeen and dating a twenty-one-year-old, it was Sam. Brooke hadn't met Lachlan until she was almost nineteen.

"Hello to you, too," Brooke said, giving her friend a hug. Seeing Sam made the anger at Lachlan wash away.

"Sorry," Sam said and pulled back from the hug first.

"What are you doing back so soon?" Sam asked. "You just left."

Brooke stood with her arms crossed and smiled. Sam looked an absolute mess. She wore paint-stained overalls over one of Zed's t-shirts, and her curly red hair gathered into a haphazard bun.

"Please tell me you didn't go to work looking like that. Have you looked in the mirror today?"

Sam looked down at herself. She tugged at her overalls, then looked back to Brooke with a grin.

"What? This is what I normally look like. I clean up more when you visit. Besides, I had a shit day. Lach... crap. He, who was working on my sunroom, called me to say you were here. He told me I needed to get down to your place. Like, as soon as I got home. But, you know, I needed to change first. My work shirt stank like a rotten dairy after a kid threw a glass of milk at me first thing. Great way to start the day."

"Well, I just poured a glass of wine. Actually, it's my second glass. I've had a confronting day."

"Then pour me a glass too and tell me why you're back." Sam took a seat on one of the two bar stools while Brooke poured a glass of red wine for her.

"I have a question for you first. The tattoo on Lachlan's right forearm. Do you know what it means?" Brooke handed her the wine.

"Yeah, it means life or happiness or something. He got it when he... ugh, never mind. You don't want to know," Sam grimaced, squirming in her seat.

"Actually yes. I do want to know," said Brooke. Sam hesitated.

"He got it when he went to South Korea... I don't know... about seven years ago? He went travelling after he broke up with what's-her-name." Sam acted like she was trying to remember the woman's name, but Brooke stared her down. "Anyway, he came back with the tattoo."

"Hmm..." Brooke said, picking up the glass before placing it on the counter again. Should she tell Sam what the tattoo really meant? She had nothing to lose by it.

"The tattoo doesn't actually say that." Sam looked confused. "It doesn't mean life or happiness."

"He lied to me?" Sam asked, exasperated.

"He did," Brooke said, turning to get some cheese out of the fridge. "It says Brooke and Love."

Sam almost spat her wine out.

"What? Seriously?" she spluttered.

"Yes," Brooke said, "and I find it really interesting that he's telling people it means something else. I guess those who can't read Korean wouldn't know any better."

"Well shit, Brooke."

"Yeah, that's what I thought when I saw it today," she said, taking a knife from the butcher block to slice the cheese. Sam took another sip of wine. But Brooke noticed this time it was more of a gulp.

"What?" Brooke asked. She knew when Sam was keeping stuff to herself.

"Nothing," she said. "This is great wine." When Sam tried changing the subject, Brooke knew there was definitely more to it.

"Yeah, I know. Dad put me on to it. Portuguese wine for about eleven dollars at Dan Murphy's. Now tell me what you're not saying." Brooke reached into the pantry and pulled out a box of crackers to go with the cheese.

"Nothing. It's nothing," Sam said, but she looked guilty as hell.

"Sam, seriously?"

"Fine. So, he got the tattoo seven years ago, right? I guess I didn't share with you that he almost got married about ten years ago to a woman called Morgan."

"You alluded to something like that, back then," Brooke said. "You told me he was living with her. I don't think you told me he was getting married."

"Yeah, except he didn't. That's the point. He backed out," Sam said. "Zed and I really thought he was going to go through with it, but he called everything off about a week before the wedding. Apparently, he and Morgan got into a huge fight. She accused him of not being 'all in', or something. And he wasn't. He told Zed and I afterwards that he was still in love with you."

"But that was ten years ago. We've been over for seventeen years.

And you said he got the tattoo about seven years ago? When he went to South Korea? The timing doesn't add up."

"That's the point Brooke. The timing doesn't matter. He's still in love with you."

25

SAM. TIMING.

NOVEMBER.

"How could you not know?" Sam asked Brooke. "It's so obvious. Even if you look at how he's been lately? I mean, Marty's gone, and he spent all last weekend weeding and working in the garden. He's not doing it for Marty. He's doing it for you!"

"But I wasn't coming back for months," Brooke said, still shaking her head.

"Again, timing doesn't matter. He would have continued to do it for you until you came back." Sam loaded some cheese on a cracker. The wine was already making her feel tipsy. When had she last eaten? Crap, she needed to get home and feed the grumpy one. Ugh. No. Bee was old enough to get food for herself and there were still leftovers from last night. She'd be fine.

"I don't get it," said Brooke, hopping up onto the second bar stool. "Clearly."

"Is this why you came back down?" Sam asked, taking another cracker. "How long are you here for this time?"

"Until January," Brooke said, grabbing some cheese and a cracker for herself. "I'm here to find out more about Marty. I'm beginning to realise I didn't know my grandmother at all. That really bothers me."

"What do you mean?"

"I found out more about the letters. That's why I've been trying to call you. Turns out, Marty is Gilly. According to dad, she went by that nickname when she was younger. I just don't know where she got it."

"Seriously?! So, Henry is some beau from when she was young?"

"Yes, except the timing is off. You said the timing doesn't matter, but it does. She was still married to my grandfather if the dates in the letter are anything to go by."

"Whoa!" Sam exclaimed.

"Yeah, which is why I'm here. She married granddad in 1958, and the letters from Henry were dated from 1961. Henry's letters suggest it went on for a while. Which means there may be a question of my dad's paternity."

"Oh, shit! What did your dad say when you told him?" But Brooke's stony face held the answer. She'd hadn't told Ray. "Right. Okay. Could she really have had an affair?" But Sam realised that was probably the point of Brooke's visit.

"Your wheels are spinning now too, aren't they?" said Brooke, taking another sip of wine. Sam was dumbstruck by the information, but soon she started thinking through everything Brooke had just said. She stared into her wineglass, this time looking for the answers.

"It doesn't sit right," Sam finally said. "This doesn't seem like Marty at all."

"That's what I thought," Brooke said, then hopped off the stool and walked into her bedroom. She returned with the two bundles of letters. She put one stack aside and pulled the ribbon to untie the first stack. They were sorted with coloured tabs, which made Sam laugh. Brooke was so pedantic about her organisation methods.

"This stack is the beginning of the letters. When you read the letters again, you'll see clues that it was Marty. Henry talked of her ambition in one. The good work she was doing in another. He also mentioned her life in Hobart. But I don't think he lived in Hobart at the time. I think he lived in Sydney."

"When was your dad born?" Sam asked.

"July 1959," Brooke said.

"And the first letter is dated when?"

"January 1961?"

"Hmm…" murmured Sam, taking another sip of her wine. Should she tell her? Was it betraying Marty's trust?

"What?" Brooke asked.

"It's just…. Well, I guess I can tell you, now Marty is gone. And this may be another piece of the puzzle. Remember the gravestone in the backyard?" Sam said.

"Yes," Brooke answered quickly.

"The gravestone is for Marty's daughter. She lost her soon after birth. She told me not long after Zed died," Sam said, but Brooke didn't look as stunned as she thought she would.

"She told you? Until I found out Marty was Gilly, I thought Mae Finlayson was another woman's baby. Not Marty's." Sam was relieved. It was hard to keep that secret. The marker in the backyard was something they'd all wondered about over the years.

"I couldn't believe it when she told me," said Sam.

"You can imagine how I felt when I pieced it together. I wanted to talk to you about it, but we could never connect."

"I'm sorry. I'm just glad you know! Marty looked pained when she told me. This was something she carried heavily and had for years." Brooke pulled out the last letter, handed it to Sam, then stood to refill their empty wine glasses.

Sam opened the letter slowly, hesitant to read the actual words.

Henry, my love, I must end our relationship. I know this is a shock for you. My last letters were filled with joy and excitement, knowing that I was with child. Our child. It is with great sadness that I tell you our baby was not to be. I lost her two months ago. She came early. Too early to survive.

I know that there was an absence in my letters, and I apologise for that. The grief has been unlike anything I have ever known.

"Wow, you can feel her heart breaking," Sam said, staring down at the letter. Her mind drifted back to Ray.

"Does Henry ever mention your dad in the letters?" Sam asked when she found her voice again.

"Once or twice. Look," Brooke said, sifting through the stack to pull out another envelope. This one had a yellow post-it tab on it along with a pink post it with 'Dad' written on it.

"What do the tabs mean?" Sam teased.

"Years. It helps me work out the timeline and the pink tabs are the letters with the important information. Anyway, Henry refers to dad as 'the youngster'. I thought he was referring to someone Gilly worked with. When Dad told me Marty went by the name Gilly, he said granddad didn't like it. So he would call her Marty. Marty was a nickname her mother gave her."

"Wow. I wonder why your grandad didn't like the name Gilly?" Sam said. "The plot thickens!" They buried themselves in the letters for over an hour before coming up for air. Knowing Gilly was Marty put a whole new light on it.

"Wow, he was so in love with her, wasn't he? But there was respect, too. He loved her ambition and what she was accomplishing. I really wish my marriage had been like that," Sam mused, then regretted the words. "Not that it wasn't good…" She needed to shut up now.

"What you had with Zed was solid," Brooke said, but Sam knew better. She shook her head.

"Not all the time. There were a lot of issues. A lot. Now I'm on the outside of it, I can see there were things we should have done differently." She drained her glass with a long sip.

"Well, you're aware of it now. That's good, right?" Brooke asked.

"At least I know what a healthy relationship looks like," Sam said, holding up the letter in her hand.

"But was it?" Brooke asked, raising one eyebrow. "Now you know why I'm here."

"Or one reason why you're here," Sam mumbled under her breath.

By the time Bee made it to Brooke's house, they were unloading Brooke's suitcase from the car.

"I just can't believe Marty is Gilly," said Sam, standing off to the side while Brooke pulled her suitcase from the back of the SUV.

"And who is Henry? And is he still alive?" continued Brooke.

"How long are you staying for this time, Aunty Brooke?" Bee asked as she struggled to carry Brooke's suitcase up the front stairs and into the house.

"Couple of months," she said, following Bee to her bedroom. "Dae's running the day to day. I'll manage the backend pieces of the business from here. But only part time. Dad's still going to run the financials. So, there won't be a lot for me to do."

"What are you going to do?" Bee asked. "Won't you get bored?"

"I'm going to do some research. I've learned some stuff about Marty, and I want to know more."

"Oh? Like what?" Bee asked. Sam opened the closet door and found Jon Bon Jovi staring right at her.

"Maybe you should do some redecorating while you're here?" Sam said, but Brooke smiled and shook her head.

"Nope, that's staying right there. Anyway," she said, turning to Bee. "Remember those letters I found?" Bee nodded. "Turns out the letters were written to Marty, but she was going by the name Gilly when she was younger."

"Geezus, that's an old-fashioned name, isn't it?" Bee said. Both Sam and Brooke laughed. Beverlee wasn't a modern name either.

"Was Marty living another life or something?" asked Bee when they walked back out into the lounge room.

"We don't know what it's all about. That's why Brooke is here. Look, run home and get the lasagne out of the fridge and bring back the whisky, would you?" Sam asked. "Can you carry all that?"

Bee looked back at her mother with haughtiness when she got to the door.

"She's not a child anymore, Mum," said Brooke when Bee stomped out.

"Don't I know that! God, she's a pill lately."

The following day, Brooke drove into Hobart to dig up some information on Marty's professional career at the historical society, while Sam went to work. She was surprised to see Georgina at the café so early.

"Hi Sam. Looks like it's you and me in front today. Kyra went to Launceston for a family thing. Her dad's in hospital again."

"Oh no. That's rough. Wasn't he in only last month?" Sam asked.

"Yeah, and things don't look good, I'm afraid," said Georgina, running the steam from the coffee machine.

"And Nicole?" Sam asked, poking her head into the kitchen to grab her apron.

"Just ran to Triabunna for the fish run," said Georgina. "She'll be back in about a half hour. It's been quiet this morning."

"That's a first. It's been insanely busy lately. Business has picked up dramatically in the last month or so. Are you second guessing your decision to hand over the business to Nicole?" Sam asked, refilling the cake case with the fresh pastries Nicole made that morning.

"Nope, not at all. It's given me a lot of time to think. And work on some new stuff."

"How's Patrick? I haven't seen him in a couple of weeks. I need to thank him for arranging the 4WD for us with Mick and Beth. Their land cruiser has really been great to have on hand."

"He would have given you his own 4WD if he could," said Georgina. "He wasn't happy you were all stuck down there."

"So, things are going well with you two?" Sam asked, watching Georgina make a flat white for each of them. Georgina returned from Spain a lot more confident, surer of what she wanted in her life. To pursue her photography and prioritise herself in her marriage. She and Patrick legally separated for a few months before they reconciled, but not in the traditional sense. They still lived apart, but they were dating again. Getting to know each other as they are now. The gossip around town would have mattered to Georgina once. But after Spain, she just lived her life. Her best life, as Bee liked to put it. Sam decided she wanted to be just like Georgina when she grew up.

"Things are going well. We're going away for a dirty weekend, as Patrick likes to call it," Georgina said, but it was the smile on her friend's face that even made Sam blush.

"Good for you. Oh, what I'd give for a dirty weekend."

"Are you ready to date again?" Georgina asked, passing her the coffee.

"God, no. But I'd like to have sex again. I do miss sex. Just need to find someone... with no attachments."

"The gossip mill can be brutal around here," said Georgina. So, she did still care.

"Yeah, well, it's not happening. I'm too worried about my daughter getting pregnant by Tom and Aubrey's son."

"Declan? He's Tom's son. Aubrey's son is Simon, the architect and website wizard from Melbourne," Georgina corrected her. "Tom and Aubrey haven't been together a year yet."

"Oh, that's right. They just seem like they've been together forever," said Sam, remembering they'd met in Spain earlier in the year.

"The Camino will do that to people. You may be complete strangers. But after a day or two, you feel like they've always been in your life. It's like speed dating with depth."

"Maybe I should do that. I need to meet new people," Sam said.

"Might help you decide what's next as well," said Georgina, but Sam didn't like the seriousness of her tone.

"You mean when Bee runs off with Declan?" she said half-heartedly.

"You know she won't do that. You raised a smart girl. She won't do anything crazy. But no, I was talking about you. What do you want? Whether or not Bee stays."

"What do you mean, what do I want? I'd like to have a house that doesn't leak, and a roof that doesn't fly off in the first big wind." She would have added 'earn more money' to that list, but she knew Georgina offered all she could. It wasn't Georgina's fault that the opportunities in the area were limited.

"What I mean is," Georgina said, leaning against the counter, her hands wrapped around her large coffee mug, "the Camino may give you the headspace to think about what you truly want, Sam. Beyond the repairs and Bee leaving. The deeper stuff. It helped me with that. A lot actually."

"Yeah, you seem a lot happier since you got back. More relaxed." Georgina smiled like she was hiding a secret.

"I suppose I am. So, here's a question for you. If you could ask the Universe for anything, what would that be?" Georgina pressed. "What would that life look like?"

Sam laughed. Hell if she knew.

26

BROOKE. CONFRONTATION.

DECEMBER.

Brooke drove the forest road from Hobart for the fourth time that week. She had been back in Fergus Bay for three weeks now and she was still spinning out. While her focus was trying to learn more about Marty and Henry, seeing Lachlan's tattoo had thrown her off kilter. Why had he gotten that tattoo and why did he get it only seven years ago? They had split up almost seventeen years before. And why make the coffin? Why would he make a coffin for Marty? It still boggled her mind that he had stayed so close to her grandmother.

For the millionth time, she thought back to when he left her at the airport. For her, their relationship wasn't over. They had an arrangement. She'd focus on getting her degree and residency in Sydney, while he started his business in Tasmania. Then she'd open her own practice in Tasmania. That was the plan. Their plan.

But thinking about the airport scene, she was fuzzy. Was he flying in or out? She remembered telling him she was married. She remembered saying the words. Surely, she told him why. But why would Sam say he heard about it from Zed? Why else would Lachlan leave her like that at the airport?

No. Lachlan ditched their plans. He'd left her. She figured he was upset because she hadn't told him about getting married to Dae earlier. But Lachlan ended it between them. That she remembered clearly. It had taken six months to get over the shock of his leaving. It had broken her. Dae was there to pick up the pieces. When Brooke finally asked Sam how Lachlan was, she expected Sam to tell her he was just as confused and upset as she was. It would explain why he hadn't responded to any of her phone calls or voice mails. Instead, Sam told her he was seeing someone else, which felt like a knife cutting into her heart all over again.

What happened to their plan? What happened to the dreams they talked about? He'd moved on. He was the one that forgot their dreams. He was the one that tossed them aside. Not her.

The airport scene rushed back to her.

"You married him?" he screamed.

"Well, I don't regret it," she remembered saying. And she truly believed that. Marrying Dae kept him from... when she'd found him lying on his bed, an empty bottle of pills and a letter from his parents beside him, saying they were coming to Australia to find him a wife, she knew she had to help.

"That's fucking good to know. What about our plans, Brooke?" Lachlan raged.

"We agreed to put everything on hold until I finished my degree," she whined.

From there, her mind went blank. She remembered telling him she was married, but maybe, just maybe, he was right? She didn't remember saying why she married Dae in that conversation. Had she just told him she was married?

Her plan was always to go back to Lachlan. Just as they talked about. She only married Dae for a short time, just to help him out. And she thought she had shared that plan with Lachlan.

Driving down the track to Fergus Bay, Lachlan and his crew were still working on Sam's house. Seeing him after Marty's funeral brought up feelings she thought she'd shut down. That was all part of it. Add in his tattoo, the fact that he didn't marry that woman, custom making Marty's coffin... and thinking about the airport, brought all her feelings to the forefront.

She drove past Sam's and parked at Marty's beach house. Her beach house, she reminded herself. If she was going to be here, she needed to accept the house was hers. She also had to accept that she would see Lachlan now and again, since he would be working on Sam's house for a while. Maybe Sam was right. They needed to talk things out. Ruminating over the past was not getting her anywhere.

Brooke got out of her car and walked to Sam's house. Lachlan worked a large circular saw in the side yard. She walked toward him but stayed back so not to distract him while he cut the long piece of timber. When he noticed her, he reached down to turn the saw off.

"Hi Brooke. Sorry, Sam's not around. She's working late tonight, and I think Bee is staying at Liv's house, too." He knew more about Sam's schedule than she did.

"I'm not here for them. I need to speak with you if you have a moment?" He looked surprised, but soon gained his composure.

"Ah, yeah," Lachlan said and whistled. Declan popped his head around the side of the house.

"Back soon. Timber is cut here. Want me to pass it around?" Declan shook his head, gave the thumbs up, and disappeared again.

"Beach?" she asked. Lachlan nodded. He grabbed his water bottle and followed her across the track and down the beach path, each focused on the sandy trail. She faced him once they hit the sand.

"It wasn't real Lachlan," Brooke said, diving right in. Confusion shrouded his face. "My marriage to Dae. I only married him to help him. He was... not in a good place. His parents were hounding him about finding a wife, having children. He tried to..."

"And you thought by ditching me you could help him?" His words cut her to the core. Her mouth dropped open. "I'm sorry. I didn't mean that like it sounded," he said.

"I thought I told you that part at the airport. That my marriage with Dae wasn't a real marriage," she said, but he shook his head.

"Nope. I found out from Zed two weeks later that it was a marriage of convenience." He kicked the sand with his boot, the sand drifting away in the wind.

"Then why didn't you call me when you found out?" she said, her voice rising.

"I figured there was a reason you didn't tell me. Either you were in love with him, unrequited obviously, or it was an excuse to bow out from us. After..." He trailed off for several beats. "Figured it was the latter. When, you know, *that* happened, it threw you off balance. That we got too real for you."

She was speechless.

"I was angry. It felt like, I don't know..." He shook his head. "It didn't matter that the marriage wasn't real Brooke, it still felt like a betrayal."

"Lachlan..." She looked into those piercing blue eyes, flecked with amber, and saw... pain. He shook his head again.

"I've got to get back to the crew. Make sure they aren't screwing things up," he said, then turned back to the track. Brooke watched him walk away, just as he had the night on the beach, after Marty's funeral. Head down, lost in thought.

Lachlan had been her great love. She knew that. Henry's letters made her wonder if she let her chance at love pass by.

Marty's words - Gilly's words - floated into her mind from the last letter in the stack. The baby. A little girl. Marty left Henry because she felt it was too hard to be with him. She was grieving. She probably suffered from postpartum depression, although the vicious nature of the condition wasn't known then. No one came out of that unscathed. Something niggled at Brooke. She slowly walked back to her house, trying to pull at that thread.

Brooke was barely twenty-one when she discovered she was pregnant with Lachlan's baby. They hadn't meant for the pregnancy to happen. The timing was all wrong. She agonised over what to do, even telling Lachlan. Between throwing up all the time and keeping up with her studies, she was exhausted. When she finally called to tell him about the baby, two months into the pregnancy, there was an unending silence, and his ragged breathing at the end of the phone.

"Lachlan?" she had whispered. She needed him to say something.

"Two months. When you were here. When we were at my parent's shack. When they went to Singapore," he said. None of what he said came out as a question, but as a statement. She didn't need reminding of when it happened. They lived like newlyweds for two incredible weeks. It had been one of the best times of her life. Her mid-year holidays. And they'd been careful. Except that time when they had been surfing and had washed the salt off afterwards in the outside shower...

She wondered now why she didn't tell him right away that she was pregnant. The thought weighed on her. Instead, Brooke had called Marty. Only Marty. By then she was ready to give up everything in Sydney and move to Hobart to have the baby. But it was Marty who steered her down the path she took.

But that day, the day of the abortion, was one she'd never forget. Lachlan flew to Sydney to be with her while she terminated their baby. He'd held her hand. Held her afterwards. Rocked her. Bathed her. Let her cry in his arms while he cried with her. Even to this day, the abortion was still too painful to think about, and it was the one thing she always pushed down.

And two months after that, she told him she was married to someone else.

Lachlan thought her marriage to Dae was a response to the abortion. That she didn't want the baby. That she didn't want him. Tears welled. Oh God. No. No, that wasn't it at all. She never connected the two in her mind. Never. No wonder Lachlan was so angry and hurt.

Oh shit, what had she done?

27

SAM. BIRTHDAY.

DECEMBER.

Sam tried not to freak out. Today was not the day for that. Except it was. Tomorrow, her daughter would officially become an adult. And tonight, they would celebrate the end of her childhood. It was surreal.

"I can't believe Bee's eighteen tomorrow," Brooke said, looking out the window, watching Bee and Declan string party lights along the reconstructed fence. "Do you remember her first birthday party? I've never seen a child covered in so much cake." They were making fairy bread, upon Bee's request. White bread, slathered with butter and multi-coloured sprinkles, were piled high in triangles. They ignored the fact that it was December 23rd.

"I dug cake out of her nose and ears for days," Sam said, remembering that moment with her baby girl and trying to reconcile it with the woman she saw outside.

"Do you remember the tantrum afterwards? I remember Jackson told me he wished he had hearing aids so he could turn them off," Sam said. She wished she had them, too.

"Oh my God, I forgot about the sugar crash afterwards," said Brooke, grabbing the serving platter from the kitchen table.

"Yeah, Zed and I were ready to hand Bee over to the nearest orphanage. The screaming was at a whole other level," she chuckled. "We wouldn't have, of course, but God we were close."

"I remember Bee's first day of school. You called me freaking out," said Brooke, sprinkling 100s and 1000s on another piece of buttered bread.

"Oh right! The meltdown I had! I was pissed off because Zed was out at sea and had missed the entire thing. And Bee? She was so nonchalant about it," she smiled, rinsing her hands in the sink, thinking about her bright, shiny girl. "She was so eager for 'big school', in her brand-new school uniform. It was so big on her it reached her knees. Oh, and her spotless Dora the Explorer backpack. Didn't stay that way for long."

"You should have known then that she'd be an independent one," Brooke said. Sam nodded.

"The years have zoomed past, haven't they? One minute she's bossing Lachlan and Zed around her tea parties, and the next she's done her exams and finished high school."

"Yeah. I wish I could have skipped twelve and thirteen though. They were horrible years. And just when she was coming around at fourteen..." Brooke reached over, squeezed her shoulder.

"I know," Brooke said, but Sam knew she didn't. Not really.

The day Zed didn't come home burned in her mind. And they wouldn't know where he was or what happened for almost three more days. The waiting. The crying. The screaming. It was horrendous. And Bee... walking around in a daze, silently crying. That was the worst. And now it was her fault Bee was spending her eighteenth birthday without her father.

Georgina's question came back to her suddenly. *If you could ask the Universe for anything, what would that be? What would that life look like?* The answer was immediate: a life with Zed in it. But that was not possible. Not anymore. Somehow, she had to make this birthday an amazing one to remember.

. . .

"Hey. Do you have enough alcohol?" asked Merritt, looking at the trough overflowing with beer and wine just outside the newly built sunroom. She and Brooke had just finished filling it.

"I hope so. There are more in the eskys positioned around the back-yard. And Lachie is bringing more when he comes."

"Lachlan's coming?" asked Brooke, paling. Crap. Were they back to not speaking his name? Because Sam was so over that. She couldn't win with Brooke and her flip-flopping about Lachie. It was fine when Brooke was barely around. But Lachie was a huge part of their life.

"Yes, of course. It's Bee's birthday," said Sam. "Please be okay with it because tonight is not the night to be weird about it. It's Bee's birth-day. And he's coming for her."

"Yeah, I know, I know. It's fine. Just didn't dawn on me. That's all," Brooke said.

"Tonight is the night to put your bullshit with Lachie aside," Sam said.

"Okay," Brooke sighed, and Sam watched Brooke transition from distressed to fake happy. "Yes, you're right, it's Bee Baby's birthday. So, what else can I help with?"

Sam looked around. The shackies were walking toward her house, one household at a time. She looked down at her watch. It was just after seven. "Music. Can you put that on, please?"

"Any specific playlist?" Brooke asked.

"Yes. Bee made one for tonight. I did too, but let's start with hers. They're both on my iPod."

Sam looked around and admired her new sunroom. Gone were the old louvre windows, wood panelling and rotten pine flooring. Now, she had double-paned windows, which would help insulate against the weather, gorgeous dark-stained, recycled timber flooring, and walls painted a crisp white. She wasn't sure about the white at first, but Lachie assured her it would work. And it did. It brought sunshine in while reflecting the beachy vibe she wanted. Lachie had done an amazing job with it. She only wished the rest of the house looked as good.

Sam fidgeted nervously as the guests arrived, shuffling plates of cheese needlessly. She wanted it to be perfect. When P!nk declared it was time to 'Get The Party Started' Sam looked out the back and saw her daughter beaming. There she was. Her baby girl. Smiling. For the first time in weeks.

Ned pranced the crowd, looking for love or for scraps. The dog would be happy with either, she mused. Looking to the sky, she was thankful the weather was cooperating. But best of all, the shackies were in. Maybe she'd even get some extra income if the holiday makers needed their houses cleaned? Ah, but tonight was not the night for that. She needed to relax and enjoy the party. It was just nice to see so many show up for Bee.

Merritt was talking to Mark from number four. She was glad Merritt had joined them, not only for Bee's birthday, but also for Christmas. They agreed it was going to be Girly Time, something they were all looking forward to.

"She's happy," said Lachie from behind, startling her.

"Yeah, she is. Hi, I didn't hear your truck," she said, giving him a side hug.

"Because there were three others coming in at the same time. Some of her friends, I think. Which is surprising, since it's so close to Christmas." He looked over her shoulder and stiffened.

"Brooke. Hi," he stammered. Sam stopped herself from groaning out loud. She didn't need to be in the middle of these two. She grabbed a beer and walked over to Bee.

When the music changed to Birds of Tokyo, Bee took Sam's beer and set it down on a table. She grabbed both of her hands and pulled her to the makeshift dancefloor in the middle of their yard. Sam loved this version of Bee. It reminded her of when she was a little girl. Because that was when they were happy. Free. When they had their lives still in front of them.

2 8

BROOKE. MUSIC.

DECEMBER.

Brooke watched Lachlan approach Sam, reminding her of how close they were. Sam had supported her when she and Lachlan broke up all those years ago, but somehow, navigating it all, she balanced their friendships. When Lachlan visited Fergus Bay, he kept their yards manageable, not just Sam's. All the shacks. Brooke doubted the shackies paid him for it. Brooke guessed they paid Sam to do it, and it was another thing Lachlan helped her with. Brooke just never realised how involved he was in their lives. Being here, seeing it, was a whole other thing. It made her feel... jealous? Left out? But that was crazy. She was a shackie, just like the other homeowners who came and went.

With the sun setting, the fairy lights were switched on, lighting the backyard up like it was a fantasy land. Declan had constructed a makeshift dance floor at Bee's request, and it was just big enough for those brave enough to show off their dance moves in public. Brooke missed Marty more tonight than she thought she would. She would have loved this party. She would have been dancing with Sam and Bee, finally sitting when her feet were tired. It was a great party. People were dancing and laughing, and it was nice to see the shackies here as well.

Bee was in her element. She was glowing. Sam had been right. She had been bitchy, and Brooke knew if she hadn't seen it for herself, she would have thought Sam was just overreacting. But once Bee's exams were over and she'd received the results, it was as if the butterfly had emerged. Since then, they'd hardly seen her. Between working at the café and hanging out with Declan, she'd been absent for weeks. She knew Sam missed her girl, but it was also good to see Bee finally landing on her own two feet. Brooke noticed Bee pulling away from Sam, which made her wonder if she was doing it on purpose. Was it a protective thing? She'd have to ask Bee later. Maybe the butterfly was planning on spreading her wings further than Sam expected and she was testing the waters?

"There you are," Sam said, handing Brooke a glass of wine.

"Just watching the party. It's good to see Bee so happy," Brooke said.

"I'm just glad the year is almost over. This one has been hell," Sam said, taking a swig from her beer bottle.

"It's been a hard one, no question," she said, her eyes drifting to Lachlan in the crowd.

"Did I tell you that Declan fixed my car?" Sam asked. Brooke shook her head no. "I may have forgotten to tell you. I guess it was when you were in Hobart for a couple of days. He and Lachie came out with a new alternator and some other stuff. They fixed it. Don't know how, but it's working. No shudders. No squeals. It runs like magic."

"And have you driven it since then? Seems every time I see your car going down the track, Bee's behind the wheel," observed Brooke.

"Once. And it drives like it was ten years younger. I didn't know Declan was good with cars. I would have been more welcoming, had I known," Sam said, laughing.

"Seems things are heating up between those two," said Brooke. She'd seen Bee and Declan frolicking in the water at the beach a couple of times. They reminded her of days gone by.

"Yeah. Just hoping she won't end up like her mother," said Sam before taking another long drink of her beer.

"She's protected, don't worry. Dr Choi-Scott made sure of that. Besides, I assume you had that conversation with her when she was, I don't know, about ten?" Brooke smiled.

"Yes," said Sam. "And she told me you got her on the pill. Thanks for that. I bought them condoms last month too. She was mortified."

"I bet! But you're an amazing mother. She knows you're only looking out for her," Brooke said, but Sam was staring at Bee and Declan, who were currently full-on kissing and not caring who saw. "But it looks as if you have every reason to be worried. Feels like history repeating itself."

"Let's fucking hope not," said Sam, just as Bon Jovi rang out on the stereo.

"Come on, they're playing our song!" Sam grabbed Brooke's hand and pulled her to the dance floor. Jumping up and down, they sang Bon Jovi's 'It's My Life' at the top of their lungs. Before they knew it, Bee was beside them, singing along. The intense sadness that had been in Sam's eyes for most of the day vanished. Laughter rang out when Sam started singing with gusto, letting it all out. She looked over and saw Lachie laughing at them. Brooke smiled and found it an easy one to give.

"Looks like our little Bee has grown up," said Georgina later. She hugged Sam and then Brooke. "Sorry, we just arrived. Late night at the café with Nicole. She wanted to stay open for the travellers passing through, but she'll come along later."

"Did Patrick come with you?" Sam asked.

"Yep." Georgina nodded her head toward Patrick and Lachlan, standing at the edge of the yard, deep in conversation. "He's talking to Lachie about clearing some trees, so I thought I'd come over for more engaging conversation. It's got to be better than listening to them talking about backhoes and chainsaws. Anyway, I wasn't sure what to get Bee for her birthday, so I hope she likes what we gave her."

"You didn't have to get her anything, Georgina!" Sam exclaimed.

"Oh Sam. You know how I feel about you two. You and Bee are family," she said, reaching over to squeeze Sam's arm as Bee approached the trio with tears in her eyes. She hugged Georgina for a long time, whispering thank you, then showed Sam and Brooke the gifts Georgina had given her moments before.

"The silver bracelet is one Aubrey designed," Georgina explained.

"It's absolutely gorgeous," Brooke gasped, watching Georgina help Bee put it on her wrist. If fit perfectly.

"And the photograph is of your beach, Bee. So no matter where you are in your life, you always have a reminder of home." Brooke felt the sting of tears in her eyes and was startled when Sam quietly took her hand. She looked over to her and found Sam struggling to keep it together. She squeezed gently.

"Thank you," croaked Bee. "I love them both."

The music switched to 'She Will Be Loved' and Brooke instinctively looked for Lachlan. He was already staring at her as their song played. She usually fast-forwarded, or turned the music off altogether, but people were already slow dancing. She used to love this song, but now if felt like someone ripped open the stitches around her heart. It took her back to the night she got pregnant. Lachlan excused himself from Patrick and walked toward her. She was frozen in place.

Lachlan held out his hand for her.

"Let's dance. For old time's sake."

29

SAM. GIFTS.

DECEMBER.

"Bee! Come on!" Sam called, feeling the hangover reverberate through her head. "We're leaving in two minutes!"

They told Bee they were heading to Hobart for their last-minute Christmas shopping, but Sam, Brooke and Merritt had a surprise for Bee for her birthday. If they made it in time.

"I'm coming. Hold your damn horses," she said, hopping out of her room on one foot while trying to put on a sandal.

"You can't go dressed like that," Sam said, seeing her daughter in cut-off denim shorts and a crop top. "Go put a dress on."

"Why? We're just shopping, mum. No one is going to care what I look like today!" Bee said, although she looked about as bad as Sam felt. Once midnight hit, Bee was legal to drink and so Lachie, the one she thought she could trust, had shots of who knew what lined up for her. The poor girl didn't know what hit her this morning.

"Just put on a dress. Look nice," she said, but knew what she was wearing kind of gave the secret away. She wore her green floral sundress that she'd dug out from the back of her cupboard - and ironed it. She'd even wrangled her curls so that they looked soft and tussled. She drew the line at heels. Merritt, however, sported a strappy three-inch high pair, matched with her bronze-coloured jumpsuit.

"You guys ready? We need to go," called Brooke from the backdoor, dressed in a short blue sundress, her hair pulled high into a ponytail, and wearing minimalist makeup. Even hungover, Brooke looked fresh and young. Sam looked at Brooke's feet. Phew. She wore practical sandals as well.

"What's going on?" Bee asked, looking pointedly at her mother. "You look dressed up and …. holy shit, are you actually wearing mascara and lipstick?"

"Just put a dress on and let's go! You'll find out soon enough," Sam pushed. Bee smirked, then turned on her heel to change.

"Gig's up, mum. Should we tell her now or later?" Brooke asked.

"Later," Sam said as Bee came flying out of her room, hair up in a topknot, and wearing a short navy-blue dress that barely covered her bum. But at least she was dressed more appropriately.

"This work?" asked Bee, spinning around. Sam looked to Brooke, then Merritt. She always deferred to them for fashion advice.

"As long as you don't bend over, you'll be fine," laughed Brooke.

"She looks fabulous and flirty," added Merritt, which made Sam groan.

"Let's go," Sam said, then herded them all outside, locked the door and jumped into Brooke's new Jeep. Sam was still gobsmacked that Brooke had bought it.

"I'm in love with your new car, Brooke," said Merritt, sitting in the back seat when they started down the forest road. "Better than your old Subaru in Sydney."

"Thanks, but don't knock that car. It's been good to me. This was more of an impulse than I would have liked, but renting a 4WD over the summer was going to cost a fortune. In the long run, it works out better."

"What are you going to do with it when you're in Sydney?" asked Bee.

"Give it to your mum to use until the bridge is back open," said Brooke like it was a no-brainer.

"What? No. You can't do that!" said Sam, but her eyes wandered over the dash and wondered what it would be like to drive.

"So, you can borrow a 4WD from a stranger, but not from me? That makes no sense at all." Yeah, she knew it sounded lame.

"Well, mine is fixed now. I should be able to drive it into Hobart," Sam said.

"I wouldn't tempt it Mum. Declan told me it would be lucky to last another year. Less if it's abused. And driving this road? That counts as abuse." Well, crap. He hadn't told her that. Damn it.

With the sun shining, the outdoor restaurants were bustling at MONA, the Museum of Old and New Art. MONA was a mecca of all things eclectic. Even MONA's website claimed it couldn't describe the place if it tried. And today, surrounding the lawn at the top of the museum, a funky fibre arts festival was in progress. Brooke found it online when they were trying to work out what to do for Bee's birthday.

"We have a reservation for lunch at one, so that gives us just over an hour to look around," Brooke said after they'd parked her car and made their way to the lawn area. "If there's something you like Bee Baby, let me know. And if we can't see it all before lunch, they're here until four."

"Except it's Christmas Eve," stated Bee, knowing that her birthday wasn't the most convenient day of the year for birthday celebrations.

"Then go. It's your birthday. We're just here to make it happen," Brooke said. Sam hated Brooke was footing today's bill, but she insisted since it was her idea, and she'd missed out on the mid-year shopping spree. Sam's account was low after the party last night, although this morning, she found four hundred dollars in her whisky glass in her kitchen cupboard. She asked Brooke about it, and she swore it wasn't her. Nor was it Merritt. She called Lachie. He said it wasn't him either. The mystery remained.

"So, does this mean you don't have Christmas shopping to do?" Bee asked Sam, making their way to the first artist canopy. Brooke and Merritt trailed behind.

"Nope. Got it all finished last week," she said.

"So you lied?" Bee asked, feigning shock.

"Put me on the naughty list," Sam said, admiring the work on the table. "Look at this Bee. This is gorgeous." But Bee was already talking to the artist about stitches and wool sourcing, both subjects way over Sam's head. Sam left her daughter to it. This was Bee's mecca, not hers. Brooke had made a smart choice coming to the festival, but Sam just wished one o'clock would roll around soon. She was starving.

"Why did we drink so much? I don't think I've had this much to drink in years," said Merritt. It was Christmas morning. Barely. Gone were the five o'clock wake-up calls because Santa had been. Now it was almost noon. They were all nursing hangovers to various degrees. Still in pyjamas, Sam and Bee sat on the outdoor lounge together, their feet tucked under them, in the newly constructed sunroom. Brooke sat on the floor on a large pillow with her back against the wall, while Merritt slumped in the nearby chair. Their little Christmas tree stood proudly at one end, with presents still stacked underneath. Christmas music played quietly from the stereo speakers, and the screened open windows allowed the cool, summer sea breeze to waft in.

"I think this is the way to do Christmas," Sam said. Bee nodded, lost in her phone.

"How is Declan this morning?" Sam asked, nudging Bee with her foot, trying not to sound edgy. She was on her third cup of coffee.

"He's good. They're already done with presents and are now just sitting around talking."

"How about we get to the presents?" asked Brooke, bouncing up off the pillow and crawling over to the tree.

"How the fuck are you so perky?" Merritt asked.

"Morning surf," said Brooke. "Best hangover cure ever," she said, kneeling in front of the tree to sort through the small array of gifts.

"Oh, and I saw your dolphin this morning, Sam," Brooke said. Sam perked up.

"Really? I haven't seen him for weeks. I thought he'd gone," Sam said.

"Nope, still there. He looked about and then left quickly," Brooke said. "Now, here. Open this present. It's from Bee. Merritt, yours is from Bee too. Bee, this one is from Merritt. And for me, hmmm... I'll open mine from Bee as well."

Sam pulled out the tissue-wrapped gift from the Christmas bag and found a gorgeous dark grey merino wrap dress within the tissue folds. Sam gasped. It was exquisite.

"Oh Bee. This is beautiful. Did you find this yesterday at MONA?" Sam said, running her hands over the soft wool. Bee shook her head. She looked nervous.

"You didn't? Where'd you find it?" Sam asked, but before she got her answer, Brooke inhaled, catching her attention. She held up a short, navy-blue A-line dress. She jumped up and undressed, putting the dress on immediately. It fit like it was made for her. Merritt was running her hand over a bold red merino wrap.

"Bee, you can't afford these," Merritt said, wrapping herself in red wonder.

"I know. That's why I made them," Bee said, but she still looked nervous.

"What?" asked Sam. "When? How?"

"Marty taught me. I've been working on them for months. Mum, try your dress on. I need to know it fits. I'm glad yours does, Aunty Brooke. I was a little worried, and sorry, but I had to go into your closet to check your size."

"Seriously Bee? I don't care. This is amazing!" said Brooke.

"Marty taught you how to do this?" Sam whispered, standing to take off her pyjamas. Bee slowly nodded, still looking anxious. Sam carefully opened the tie to the dress and placed her arms through the long sleeves, then lifted the soft, buttery wool around her shoulders. Bee stood and helped tie it together for her. It hugged her curves perfectly. Every inch of the dress draped and flowed exactly right. Even the sleeves were the correct length.

"Oh Sam. That looks incredible on you!" said Merritt. "Bee, you need to go to fashion school!" Sam looked up and Bee's face told her that was exactly what she was planning to do.

"I've already applied to The University of Technology in Sydney," Bee said, but the look she gave Sam was full of pain and guilt. "I want to do a Bachelor of Design in Fashion and Textiles. The uni is ranked number thirteen in the world for fashion. I want to specialise in fine merino designs."

"Oh, that sounds incredible Bee!" Merritt said, but Sam felt like the floor had dropped out from under her. Not because she didn't want Bee to leave, but because she never noticed how talented her daughter was. She thought knitting and crocheting was a cute hobby that she and Marty did together.

Sam hugged her, whispering her thanks. She pulled back with tears in her eyes. She only hoped she masked the pain of feeling left out of Bee's decision.

Three days later, Sam sat at her kitchen table drinking coffee. The house was quiet. Bee was in Hobart with Declan, hitting the post-Christmas sales. Brooke was down the coast, surfing, and Merritt was probably still in bed at Brooke's, reading a book. Laughter from the shackies next door filtered in, and the birds nattered to each other outside the window. There was usually music playing in her house, but she couldn't listen to her stereo right now. Georgina's words were haunting her: *If you could ask the Universe for anything, what would that be? What would that life look like?*

She was still trying to work it out, and now she was one job short. When Sean told her to 'sex it up' to bring the younger patrons, Sam tossed a beer in his face. The man was a pig. Now she stared blankly at her planner. The planner Brooke had teased her about weeks ago. Brooke was right, she didn't plan and, although she knew Brooke was joking, it still stung. Her life was a mess. She was always running, always reacting.

Maybe that's what she'd like to change? To be more proactive with her life.

But Georgina had asked about her dreams. Sam couldn't remember having any. Nothing outside a life with Zed and Bee at the beach. And with Zed gone and Bee moving to Sydney, that dream was now in the past. She thought back. She wanted to go to university, just like her friends, but she'd travelled with Zed instead. That had been great, and she had planned on university when they returned. But that was put on hold when she found out she was pregnant with Bee. Not that she regretted having Bee, never, but when she thought about it, really thought about it, she'd been reacting to her life since her parents died.

The kettle squealed and as she poured boiling water into the coffee filter, she realised she'd always lived with someone. With Bee heading to Sydney, it would be the first time she'd be on her own. What then? Did she want her life to stay the same? Or did she want something different?

The phone ringing interrupted her thoughts.

"Hello?" She nestled the phone in the crook of her neck while she removed the filter.

"Sam? It's Jackson."

"Hi. Is everything alright? I'm coming into Orford a bit later today," she said, grabbing milk from the fridge.

"Yes, everything is fine. I wasn't sure if you were coming in. I wanted to ask you something pertaining to Bee."

"Oh? What's up?" Sam asked.

"Well, now Bee has finished high school, I wanted to give you something to help with university."

"What do you mean?" She was confused. Jackson had given Bee a suitcase for Christmas. It was an odd present, Sam thought, but a practical one. He'd even slipped two hundred dollars into the pocket. For her birthday too, he said.

"Beverlee and I had money set aside for Zayden. For when he went to university," he continued. Sam was surprised. Zed had never planned on university, and neither Beverlee nor Jackson had mentioned this before. Neither had Zed.

"I forgot about the money, to be honest. The bank manager called me today and asked me about it. It's not much. But it would at least help her with living expenses." Wait. First the money for Bee's birthday and now for university? What had happened to her curmudgeonly old grandfather-in-law? This was a change of tune, for sure.

"How about we stop by around five? Bee and I are both working later, so you can tell her about it after work?"

"That sounds like a plan. I'll see you then," he said and promptly hung up. Sam sat back in her chair. Bee knew financing university would be up to her primarily. There was no choice there. But Jackson's comment about forgetting about the money? My ass, she thought. This was his plan all along.

"Knock, knock," called Brooke, but before Sam could answer, Brooke was in her living room. "Just got back and I forgot to ask you this the other day, but Dad called me again last night. Have you read Marty's letter yet? Dad's been nagging me about it, but now he's getting grumpy."

"What letter?" Sam asked.

"The letter I gave you just after Marty died. Remember when I was looking for Marty's PIN? I gave you the letter the same day. You popped it into your back pocket."

"Oh," Sam said, vaguely remembering the letter. She wondered for a moment where it even was.

"Okay. Get to it soon. I really need dad off my back," said Brooke. "I'm heading home to shower. Catch you later."

A letter from Marty? That was the last thing she wanted to read. After Bee's party and Christmas, she was missing her elderly friend almost as much as she was missing Zed. What she wouldn't give for a piece of her carrot cake and a cup of her god-awful tea. But reading a letter from her? No. She couldn't deal with that right now.

30

BROOKE. DISCOVERY.

DECEMBER.

Brooke tasked herself with cleaning out Marty's bedroom with the goal of transforming it into a library. She'd finally succumbed to asking Lachlan for his help in building the bookcases. Had she done the right thing? Yes. She needed to deal with the fact he was deeply engrained into the community. But before he could measure, she had to clean out the room. She stood with her hands on her hips, formulating a plan. The bed and dresser could be put into the shed for now, until she could work out what she wanted to do with them, and the side tables she could use in another room.

Seeing her grandmother's favourite quilt at the end of the bed, the plan halted. She walked over and inhaled the scent. She could still smell Marty's lily of the valley bath soap. A lump formed in her throat. Shaking her head, she reminded herself not to get distracted by the sentimental things. She had a job to do. She folded the quilt gently and took it into her own room.

Heading back, she grabbed a box and the vacuum and returned to the bedroom. Marty's things still hung in the closet. She'd leave that for another day. None of that was going to be in Lachlan's way to measure. The bedside tables would, so she began there. After the bookshelves were in, she would put end tables beside the chairs she had her eye on in Hobart. Side tables were more fitting for a library than the bedside ones. But until she worked out what to do with the ones in the room now, she'd clean them out and put them in the spare room.

She opened the top drawer and found some hand cream, a nail file, an old bookmark, a few letters… nothing out of the ordinary. With a quick look at the letters, she realised none were from Henry, so she emptied the contents into the box and continued on with the bottom drawer. She set aside the books she found there, thinking they might be interesting reads. When the bedside table was empty, she pulled it away from the wall, finding a thick layer of dust coating the back side. Gross. Holding it as far from her body as possible, Brooke carried the table into the lounge room. She'd clean it before setting it in the spare room.

Returning to the room, Brooke slid the second bedside table out from the wall and stopped. A dusty envelope sat against the wall. She bent down to retrieve it and blew the cobwebs off as she turned it over.

Brooke.

Only her first name was written in her grandmother's beautiful handwriting. No address, so it wasn't a letter she planned to send. Brooke opened the envelope, curious to see what was inside. She found a letter, dated July 18th, 2019. So, it had been a while since the letter was written. She pulled the paper from the envelope and began reading.

Sunshine,

I have been meaning to give this letter to you for some time. I hope, by the time you are finished with it, that you will still speak to me. But I need to say these words as my heart is broken. And you, my girl, are the one who has broken it.

"Me?!" Brooke gasped. She leaned against Marty's bed and read on.

I have just spent the last two months in Lachie's company while he finished renovating my kitchen and bathroom. He and I have had some truly wonderful conversations. Deep, heartfelt conversations. He's got a heart of gold, that one. Such a good man. His heart is in the right place. Few men of his generation do. But he's an old soul. He reminds me a great deal of someone I once knew. Someone I wish you had met. Before I tell you the purpose of this letter, I'd like to tell you a story.

When I was in my late thirties, I met a man who pushed me to my limit in a loving and supportive way. He challenged me to go outside of my comfort zone. To think of different ways to achieve my goals. Goals I never realised I had until I met him.

Brooke stopped reading. Oh my God, she was talking about Henry. She was finally learning who Henry was! She kept reading.

He and I were colleagues of a sort. He was a cardiologist from Sydney. He came to Hobart to work on a study of Antarctic scientists, to see how their bodies reacted to the extreme conditions and how diet affected their health. It was fascinating work. We met at a function held by the Royal Hobart Hospital to welcome the Antarctic team home and into the study. We began meeting regularly to discuss women's health and cardiac studies for women. Over the course of those weeks, we found we had a lot in common in the way we saw the world. He had also travelled extensively, which I had also by then.

Bert and I had been married for a year by this stage. He was my second husband. My first died after the Great War. (Sadly, he died from suicide, from what they now define as post-traumatic stress disorder.) I was single for many years before I married Bert, and I found living with someone very difficult. Don't get me wrong, I loved your grandfather very much. But he had a very sheltered perspective of the world. Until I came along, he had not travelled outside of Tasmania, and had no interest in travelling outside of Australia. I thought at first it was a fear of flying. But no. It was a fear of other cultures. It was one of the biggest contentions of our marriage. His closed view, not seeing past the country's borders, was enough for me to leave him. Well, that and other issues, but I won't get into that.

When Henry Finlayson came into my life months later, my world opened. Henry was intelligent, driven, cultured, but he was also incredibly kind and empathetic. I had met no one else like him. He made me laugh - and cry - and made me question everything in my life. Everything.

My time with Henry was, without question, the highlight of my life. I had joy in my life every day. I had a purpose. I saw what I wanted and what I could achieve. And Henry was by my side the entire time. Not physically, as he still lived in Sydney and travelled extensively, and I needed to remain in Hobart. But we made it work.

Until we couldn't. What I haven't told you are two important factors.

The first is I already had a son - your father - by that time. Your father was only a baby when Henry came into my life. He would have no recollection of Henry. Why I didn't tell him all this later, I don't know. Maybe because, by then, it didn't matter. It didn't affect his life.

The other piece is that Henry and I had a daughter together.

Brooke's heart was racing. She placed her hand to her chest but kept reading.

We called her Mae. I know that is probably a shock to you, Sunshine. Getting pregnant was a jolt to me, too. But Mae was very much a wanted baby. Henry and I were over the moon, and I couldn't wait for your father to meet his sibling. We were creating a beautiful life together, with Ray and now the baby.

Mae was blonde and pale, with strong Nordic features, like Henry. But our darling Mae only lived for one day. I went into premature labour. Henry was in Sydney at the time. I spent hours saying goodbye to our baby girl. We were both devastated, and Henry was distraught he couldn't be there, as you would imagine.

You've asked me about the grave marker in the backyard many times. I told you it was an old relative, as I told everyone who asked. Everyone but Sam. I

told her about Mae after Zayden passed. But telling people it was an old relative was easier than telling the truth. It's a marker for Mae Finlayson, our
daughter.

There's another piece to this story. The beach house. Henry and I found the
beach house after a year of being together. It was our sanctuary. But eventually
it became solely mine.

You may wonder by now about Henry, and why I returned to Bert. It all came
back to Mae. After she died, I fell into a deep depression. Just looking after
your father while dealing with my grief was all I could manage. Henry wanted
me to divorce Bert and marry him. Our relationship was considered scan-
dalous in those days. Having a baby with another man while I was still technically married? Well, that was bucking societal norms! Bert knew by then of
my involvement with Henry, but he did not know how deeply I loved him. But
after Mae died, I couldn't be with Henry. He reminded me too much of Mae.
Of the hurt of losing her. Seeing his face made it too confronting. It destroyed
us. Henry came to be with me. But I sent him back to Sydney. After that, well,
that was that.

I returned to Bert in late 1964, four years after I left him. We never did
divorce. I realised that Bert was a stable force, and I needed that to aid my
career. He was also a good father, and that was also very important to me. Bert
thought the beach house was my place to escape Hobart. He hated Fergus Bay.
He visited twice, complaining that the sand was dirty, and he hated the
silence. He vowed, after the second visit, never to return. And that was fine
with me because I got to live with my memories. He didn't know the significance of Fergus Bay for me. Then, once Bert was gone, I moved to Fergus Bay
full time. Living at the beach house kept Henry close.

And so, this brings me back to you.

When Lachlan worked on the renovations, he stayed overnight a few times. I
will add that he may have been drunk when he told me, but he reminded me of
your pregnancy. I remember you begged me to allow you to stay in Fergus Bay

at that time. But I knew the entire world was waiting for you. You needed to fly, Sunshine. I saw so much of myself in you. But I also saw Henry in Lachlan and it broke my heart to send you back to Sydney to your studies. But I never thought it would end for you two. Just a pause while you finished your degree. Then you could live your life together. That's what you told me you agreed on.

I never thought that you would hurt Lachlan the way you did. Now, don't misunderstand me. I love Dae, and I completely support your decision to marry him. The boy needed help and while marrying him may not have been what I would have advised, that's the direction you took.

But you need to know how much you broke Lachlan's heart, Brooke. Stomped on it, ground your foot in it, then walked away. Marrying Dae so soon after the baby? That broke him. If I look at how I reacted to my own pain with Mae and Henry, I assume you pushed Lachlan away for the same reason. Because it was easier than dealing with the pain. But Sunshine, Lachie is still reeling. He is still very much in love with you. He's still waiting for you.

I've shared with you my story so you could understand one thing: I regret ending things with Henry, and I will regret them until the day I die - and beyond. I don't want the same for you because I know you. I know you still have feelings for Lachlan, too.

So please, do something about this before it's too late. Before you are old and wrinkly, writing a letter to your granddaughter, telling her about the biggest mistake of your life. And I hope you know this is written with your best intentions in mind. Because I love you, child.

I will love you 'til the end.

Marty

With tears streaming down her cheeks, it was the last line that caught her. Brooke had seen that expression before. Where? In another letter? Yes! She jumped up and ran to her bedroom, rifling through her work bag, until she found the letter from Gilly to Henry. The very last letter in the stack. And there, written at the end of the letter, was the same line: I will love you 'til the end. And so, she had. Except the letter was never sent to Henry.

Brooke had to find Henry.

31

SAM. FUTURE.

JANUARY.

"I'm sorry, but I don't understand what you're saying," Sam said, sitting at the kitchen table with her cold toast and coffee. Bee sat across from her, her hands shaking.

"I want to take a gap year. I don't want to go to university right away," Bee said, her voice quivering with nervousness. The weight in the room was about as heavy as the humidity outside.

"But you were so excited about the university in Sydney. Of studying fashion design. What happened with that? And Jackson just told you two weeks ago that he wants to give you money for it, and now you're saying you don't want to go? Are you crazy?" Sam was confused, and she knew her voice was rising with the level of frustration she felt. Jackson had shocked them both when he said he was holding fifty thousand dollars in an account for Bee for uni. Yeah, Jackson knew he had that kind of money stashed away.

"It's not that I don't want to go, Mum. I just don't want to go right now," she said.

"But why not? You've already applied, and you've already received early acceptance into three universities. Do you know how rare that is?" Sam could feel history slapping her in the face.

"I do. And I know you're probably mad at me, especially since…"

"Since what?! Since I didn't go? No Bee, I'm confused. And I'm pissed, to be honest. You're throwing away an excellent opportunity here."

"But Mum, you're not listening to me. I'm not throwing it away. I'm just postponing it for a year."

"And what if, in that year, something else happens? Something that makes you delay it further, or even give up on the idea altogether?"

"What? Like getting pregnant like you did?" The moment the words came out of Bee's mouth, her daughter went as white as a sheet. "I'm sorry, I didn't mean…"

"Yes, you did. And yes, that crossed my mind. I'm assuming you and Declan are sleeping together. And, if you are, then you should know that accidents happen. Even if you are careful." Ugh, this wasn't coming out right.

"Look, accidents happen. Doesn't matter if it turns out to be the best thing that ever happens in your life. But those things disrupt your plans."

"We're careful, mum. I promise."

"Keep staying careful. But I still don't understand why you want to delay going to university. Jackson's money may not be there next year."

Sam was still astonished it was even an option. She and Bee had already discussed what Bee would do. While Sam would help with the initial expenses, Bee needed to sign up for Youth Allowance and get a part-time job. If she moved to Sydney, she already had a job with Brooke's mum at the catering business, but that wouldn't be consistent. Brooke offered her a place to live, and a part-time job at her practice, but Bee didn't want either of those things. Bee insisted she wanted to do it her own way, to live independently, so she wouldn't feel she had the family watching her every move. Sam admired her independence. She would have felt the same, had she had the same opportunity. Now that was all out the window. What the hell?

"Granddad said the money is there for me whenever I need it. So,

I'll just hold off on drawing from it until I start uni. I'm sorry, Mum. I know this isn't what we talked about," said Bee. She got up to make more coffee. Sam picked up her cold mug. She hated cold coffee just as much as she hated tea. She handed her mug to Bee to refill.

"So then, what are we talking about? What are your plans for the year? I assume you want to stay here and keep working?" As a mother, it would make her happy to keep her daughter in the nest, but she feared that wasn't the case.

"Is Declan part of this plan?" Sam asked, but Bee ignored the question.

"I want to travel," Bee said, pouring coffee into the filter for them both.

Sam snorted. "Wouldn't we all? With what money? I know you have some savings. But not nearly enough to travel for a year."

"I want to go backpacking through Europe, working as I go. Declan said…"

"So, he *is* part of the plan?"

"Yes, Mum, he is. He said he'll go with me. His brother, Liam, will join us for some of it. So, I'll be protected. You said you like Declan."

"And I do, but I didn't think he'd be my son-in-law so quickly," said Sam. Declan won a lot of brownie points with her over the last few weeks, fixing her car, taking care of her lawn when he visited, shuffling Bee back and forth when he could manage it around his job with Lachlan.

"I'm not marrying him, Mum. I'm just going travelling with him," said Bee, pulling the fridge door open with more force than necessary.

"So, what about his job? With Lachie? How does Lachie feel about it?"

"He was only contracted to work with him until February. But he talked to Lachie about it. He didn't mention me, of course, and Lachie said if he wanted to come back, he'd take him on in a heartbeat. So, we thought, we'd backpack for a year and then come home. He'd go back to work with Uncle Lachie, and I'd go to university."

"Wait, so now you're going to the University of Tasmania? I thought you were going to Sydney or Melbourne?" Sam was feeling like she'd lost her daughter already. All these plans made, and she hadn't been included in any of it. Hell, she hadn't even been asked what she thought.

"I still plan on going to Sydney. And I will come home often enough that I'll still see Declan. And he can always come to see me." Sam noticed that she wasn't in any part of Bee's plan.

"If you're still together after a year of travelling together, you mean. Travelling can be stressful on a couple." Or it could be a highlight of your life, like it had been for her and Zed.

"Are you mad?" Bee asked, carrying the mugs to the table.

Sam considered it. Was she?

"Honestly, I don't know. Disappointed, maybe? Hurt that you didn't discuss any of this with me before, definitely. Jealous, for sure. But I still don't know how you're going to pay for it, Bee. I can't help you. Not with this."

"I can use my savings for the plane ticket. Then I still have enough to float me for a bit until I find work."

"But that money was supposed to be for University," she said, hating that she was always the practical one. What she wouldn't give to toss everything in the air and say, 'fuck it, I'm going to travel for a year'.

"With Granddad's help for university, I can use the money I've saved for travelling," Bee said. At that moment, Sam hated Jackson. Not only would Bee be leaving home. But now she may not see her for a year. The weight of that felt enormous.

"You and Dad backpacked, didn't you?"

"Yeah, we did," Sam admitted.

"And how is that any different? From what Dad told me, you had a great time. He said there was one story I'd have to wait until I was eighteen before I heard about it. It was too embarrassing otherwise." Bee looked at Sam expectantly.

The Bullshit story. Sam laughed.

"Okay, I'll tell you the story, but we're going to need some Tim Tams. I need food to absorb the coffee," said Sam. She rose to retrieve their travel album from her closet.

Sam took a deep breath and opened the album. The memories jumped out at her, pushing away her emotions of Bee leaving.

"Okay. We were on a freighter sailing from Madagascar to São Paulo," Sam began, pointing at a photo of herself, sitting at a poker table with a bunch of rough sailors, all looking like they hadn't showered in a month.

"Few of the sailors spoke the same language, let alone English," she said, "so we communicated via an improvised sign language. While most on board had their heads in the toilet, your dad included, I was learning how to play 'Bullshit' with the sturdiest of the crew, while we drank a bottle of whisky. Or maybe three. It was hard to remember after the first two." She laughed, remembering just how drunk they all were, as the boat rolled over the waves.

"What was the game?" Bee asked, looking down at the photo in the album.

"Bullshit," Sam said. She waited for her daughter to catch on.

"What?"

"The game. It's called 'Bullshit'. The aim is to get rid of all your cards as fast as you can, but it goes in order of suit. If you don't have that card, you put any card down. But if someone suspects it's not the right card, they call bullshit. Turned out bullshit was a word we all understood perfectly well. It's actually a really fun game."

"I remember you played this with Uncle Lachie and some guys at the marina when I was about twelve," Bee recalled, biting into her second Tim Tam.

"Probably," said Sam. "Uncle Lachie was always terrible at the game. He's too honest for his own good. But he still claims it's the best story about your dad he's ever heard."

"Why?"

"Because your dad didn't make it out of the toilet the entire time we were on that freighter. He liked to tell people it was the smell of the engine room, but it was seasickness, pure and simple," Sam explained to Bee.

"Why didn't Dad want me to hear that story?" Bee asked.

"Because it showed your dad was weak in rough waves. And he hated to admit that, considering he was a fisherman."

"Maybe that's what happened to him in the storm. Maybe he just got seasick and went overboard?" Bee mused.

"Yeah. Maybe. We'll never know." Sam told herself that for many years, but since Lachie's comment about Zed feeling out of his depth, Sam began to question if it wasn't something more troubling. But thinking back to their freighter experience, she realised seasickness and falling overboard was more likely. Zed was too much of a dreamer to fall into a depression that deep.

"Sounds like your adventures were pretty great, Mum. So why can't I have the same experience?"

"Maybe you're right, Bee. I just don't know if I'm ready for it. In Sydney, I can get to you if you get into trouble. I can't get to you if you're on a freighter in the middle of nowhere," Sam said, feeling as though her world had just shifted.

"What's the big deal?" Brooke asked when she came by an hour later. Sam was still sitting at the kitchen table. Bee had left for work. Her hands were still shaking at Bee's announcement. Either that or it was the coffee, but she suspected it was the former. Sam looked through her photos, trying to imagine her daughter playing poker in the middle of the ocean, and couldn't. She was just too young and naïve.

"It might be good for her," Brooke said, but her tone may as well have added, "to get far away from you".

All Sam could think about was everything that could go wrong. She left out the stories of when they were held at gunpoint in Turkey. And when they walked forty kilometres in the blistering summer sun, when their old campervan ran out of petrol in Italy. She only shared the fun bits. Like when they ran with the bulls in Pamplona, and how she cried when she first saw the Eiffel Tower in Paris and the Colosseum in Rome. Zed had already shared with Bee, years before, that his favourite part of their travels was watching the Wales vs. Ireland rugby game in a pub in Dublin while they drank Guinness with the locals.

"So what if she takes a gap year? It's not the end of the world. You went when you were her age. Surely she knows about your adventures."

"Some. I just wasn't expecting this. And with Declan?"

"You need to trust her, Sam. She's a good kid. She won't do anything stupid. Hell, I couldn't even get her to get a tattoo with me."

"What? When?"

"Oh, when Merritt and I took her into Hobart a few months ago. We were trying to get her to get a tattoo. I was even willing to get a matching one with her, like we did when we turned thirty. But she wouldn't budge. So, I think she'll be fine. She'll be the voice of reason between her and Declan."

"His brother is joining them," said Sam. Bee with two Irish boys. What would Zed say to that? Probably 'good on her' and offer the boys a toke.

"She'll be protected then. Look, Declan is a stand-up guy. Maybe you should talk to them both, ask them what their plans are instead of acting so scared. If it really bothers you to have Bee travel with the boys, talk to their parents. Aren't they Georgina's friends? Ask them to put the fear of God into them if anything were to go wrong." Sam thought about it. Maybe she would talk to Tom.

"You have to trust her, Sam. You've raised a strong, independent woman and I think she's brave and bold for doing this. What did you expect from her?"

"To go to bloody university like she was supposed to! Like you did, when you left Lachlan to chase you own damn dream," she said, knowing she was pushing Brooke's buttons. Why couldn't Brooke take Sam's position with this?

Wait. Why wasn't she doing that?

"Why is it you are supporting Bee doing this when you left to go to university? How can you take Bee's side? A bit like the pot calling the kettle black, isn't it? And wait. Did I see Lachlan over at your house yesterday?"

"So what?"

"So what? Because I haven't been able to talk about him to you in years! Now you're dancing with him at Bee's party and having him over? What changed?"

"Nothing's changed. Maybe I just realised it was dumb to hold on to the past. Like you are."

"What?" She did not just say that to her, did she? She lifted her hand to her cheek as if Brooke just slapped her.

"Nothing can be gained from holding on to the past. It's stupid. Like you hoping that dolphin you look for every morning will suddenly turn into Zed and walk out of the sea. Or for Bee to stay with you forever because you can't bear her leaving you. Or because you can't bear being alone. She's not abandoning you Sam. She's getting on with her life. Maybe you should take some initiative and do something too! Something which will actually improve your life! All you do is whine about how hard things are. And how you hate to rely on other people's help, yet you never say no when it's offered. For fuck's sake. Stop playing the bloody victim!"

Sam was stunned at Brooke's outburst. Geezus. She was so tempted to throw her steaming coffee at her, but that would be cruel. Just as Brooke's words were. She sunk back in her chair and stared at her so-call best friend, hating her in that moment with every fibre of her being.

"Please leave," Sam said, trying to control her voice.

"What?" Brooke's anger turned to confusion.

"Get the fuck out of my house," Sam said, slowly and deliberately. Brooke stood, the chair scraping the wooden floor, and stormed out the back door. Sam collapsed into tears as soon as she heard the rusty front gate slam.

3 2

BROOKE. REGRETS.

JANUARY.

Brooke texted Lachlan on the way back to the beach house to cancel the bookshelf build. She was going back to Sydney. Fuck this. She needed to find Henry and she sure as hell wouldn't find him from here. And she needed her bloody life back. What was she thinking, believing she could stay here? She was letting her past invade her life.

And why shouldn't Bee travel? The girl needed freedom. And when had Sam become such a fucking victim? What happened to the red-headed spitfire who told her off when they were seven? Where'd she go? Sam had become a bloody sad sack. She always seemed happy when Brooke came down to visit. Or, when she and Bee flew to Sydney. Wow. Reality with her was a lot different.

Brooke jumped on her computer and emailed Dae, then booked a return flight. Shit. Her house. She'd rented it out until the end of January. She opened another email to Dae and asked if she could stay in his granny flat for a few weeks until her house was available. But she paused before she hit send. Was she running away from the problem or returning to her life? Shaking her head, she hit send.

She pulled her suitcase from the closet and tossed it on the bed. Ripping clothes from the hangers and emptying out the chest of drawers, she threw all she had into her suitcase. Her mind whizzed at what she would do once she returned to Sydney. She'd go back to work. Wait. She had no work clothes with her, and she couldn't get back into her house for a few weeks. Screw it. She needed new suits for work, anyway. She'd hit the post-Christmas sales when she got back. Yes. She missed David Jones and the variety of shops in Sydney. Suddenly, she was excited to return to her city.

Her phone dinged. Lachlan.

Hi Brooke. No worries about the build. Just let me know when you'd like to reschedule. L

Reschedule? She laughed. Unlikely. It was just too... what? Marty's letter came to mind. No. She was not going there. She tossed the phone on the bed and headed to the bathroom to collect her toiletries.

Her email dinged this time. Dae.

Hey B. Yeah, not a problem. We probably need to talk about the practice, anyway. Ping me when you arrive. Looking forward to seeing you. Dae. x

That was more like it. Normalcy. Her practice. Her friends. Her life. Yes, it was time to go back to Sydney.

By the time she reached Sydney's Central Station, the train platform was packed with commuters. She navigated her way to the Northern Line train and squeezed in right before the doors closed. Grabbing a handle when the train jolted forward, she felt her phone ping in her jean's pocket. She pulled it out, expecting a message from Dae.

You left?!

A message from Sam. Took her long enough to realise. Yes, she left. She didn't want to respond to the message, but habit propelled her.

Yes. I needed to return to Sydney. That's what I came to tell you.

Sam's reply was quick.

But decided to be a bitch instead. Got it. See ya.

Brooke put her phone away. A bitch, was she? At least she wasn't an overbearing mother who couldn't let go of her dead husband! The vicious thoughts swirled. She didn't mean any of it, but Marty's letters had thrown her for a loop. She didn't know how she would have responded if Marty had given her the letter while she was alive.

The train pulled into North Sydney. She was relieved to see Dae waiting by his car as she exited the station. She walked toward him, feeling the weight of the day on her shoulders, then hugged him, finding it difficult to let go.

"Whoa. Are you okay?" he asked. He pulled away, watching her. When she nodded, he leaned over to take her suitcase, then lifted it into the back of his Audi Q5.

"Yeah, just tired. Glad to be back," she said.

"I expected you back sooner," he said as they buckled their seatbelts. "Wasn't sure you'd be able to hack the remoteness for that long." She didn't mind that piece. She missed the conveniences Sydney offered, but she loved the quiet.

"I came back to find Henry. I have more information," she said.

"So, you're staying?" he asked, pulling out into the bumper-to-bumper traffic, heading toward Mosman.

"I haven't thought about it. Probably. My life is here. I did what I needed to do down there." But had she? She wasn't so sure. She was coming back to Sydney to check in on the business and find Henry. That she knew. But she hadn't considered whether she was staying or going back. The fight with Sam threw her.

"I said some awful things to Sam this morning. I needed space," she added.

"Oh? What happened?" he asked, glancing at her with concern.

"I'll tell you later over copious amounts of wine. Tell me about work," she said, hoping business would calm her. She was sick of talking about her personal life for now. And so, he filled her in on the details until they arrived at his house. Jase's car was in the carport.

"Jase is home already? Isn't it early for him?" she asked, stepping out.

"Yeah, he took off this week. Post-holiday crash," he said. "Your Mum is off next week. She didn't tell you?"

"No, but I haven't spoken to them for a couple of weeks. My dad kept bugging me about getting Sam to read a bloody letter from Marty. It was driving me nuts, so I stopped answering."

"Sounds like you had a lot going on. Don't worry, Jase will have the wine open. I'll take your stuff out to the granny flat." They got out of the car and walked to the boot to get her suitcase.

"Thanks, Dae. And thanks for letting me stay. I completely forgot I'd rented my house for the summer holidays. Wasn't thinking when I booked my flight to come back."

"Yeah, I wondered about that. But you know you're welcome anytime. Your surfboard is waiting for you." She was glad that she'd bought a second one last summer. Her other board was locked up in her shed in Cheltenham.

"Great. Oh, can you drop me off at my house in the morning so I can get my car from the garage? I texted the renters while I was waiting for my flight to let them know I needed my car."

"Yeah, no worries. You're on the way to the office anyway," he said. "Oh, and just so you know, Jase and I are heading down the coast for a few days over the long weekend. We've had it booked for months."

"Oh, lovely. I can manage the office if you need me to?"

"Nope. Got it covered already," he said, but he wasn't making eye contact.

"What did you do?" she asked. She'd left running the practice completely to him, but any permanent changes still had to be passed through her.

"I hired a doctor on contract. He's covering over the summer holidays. He's…"

"Oh, did you?" she said, crossing her arms.

"You said no permanent changes. This is a contract position, and he's great. Very flexible. Speaks fluent Korean, which the patients love. You'll like him a lot," he said, locking the car and walking toward the back gate with her suitcase. She entered the house via the side door.

"Jase? It's me," she called, leaving her shoes and bag near the console table that was littered with mail, keys, and whatever else they still needed to put away. It reminded her of Sam's house. Still upset about Sam's text, she pushed the idea aside.

"Hey, B! It's great to see you!" Jase hugged her, and she clung to his warmth. She could almost forget the awful day she was having.

"Just opened the wine. Dinner is in the oven. Hope you're feeling adventurous because I'm trying out a new recipe," he said, walking back into the kitchen.

"Aren't you on holidays?" Brooke asked, following him. "That usually means you don't cook, if memory serves."

"Usually yes, but we tried a new restaurant last week and I'm inspired." She loved their life. They were always trying fresh places and finding inspiration in food or art. "How was Tassie?"

"Cool, but quiet. It was a shock to return to peak hour. Didn't plan that very well," she said, accepting the glass of wine as Dae walked in the back door.

"Hey, love. Great, wine is open!" Dae said and walked over to kiss Jase. Brooke turned away. Their personal displays of affection would make most blush. She ached for that kind of intimacy.

"Long day?" Jase asked.

"Not too insane, I'm happy to say. The new doctor is…"

"Here we go," said Brooke. "I haven't been in the door for five minutes and you're already on that." She smiled. She found comfort in returning to the familiar. It helped numb the chaos swimming in her head. Attacking Sam like that left her with an awful feeling in her gut.

"What the hell did you do?" asked Merritt hotly. It was barely nine in the morning, and she'd missed five calls from Merritt while she was out surfing.

"What do you mean?" Brooke asked, struggling to get out of her wetsuit while juggling the phone.

"I just got off the phone with Bee. Sam is one pissed off woman. I called to wish them a belated happy new year, and I got Bee, who was beside herself. She didn't know what happened. She said Sam called you a bitch and demanded she delete you from her phone. Bee said she tried calling you." Oh shit. She was so caught up in the logistics of getting back that she forgot to return Bee's call. God, she hated to leave Bee hanging like that.

"We had a fight a few days ago," Brooke said.

"Must have been a doozy," said Merritt. "But why didn't you call Bee? She was telling me about Europe and Declan and then she just lost it. Now she says she's not going to Europe, not going to uni, and that she can't leave her mother alone. She's seriously worried about Sam. So am I!"

"We had a fight. That's all. I said some things that I probably shouldn't have. But I was spinning too. Marty left me a letter. She said things in it that really upset me and, well, I guess I took it out on Sam."

"What did the letter say?"

"It doesn't matter. Sam pushed. So, I pushed back." She finally wiggled out of the wetsuit and flung it over the railing. Her hair clung to her neck like a piece of seaweed.

"Sounds to me like you both had some weight behind the pushing."

"Probably. So, what's going on with you?" she asked, changing the subject. She'd call Bee when she got back to Dae's.

"Just got out of a meeting with my solicitor. I'm officially on the divorce track."

"Oh. Well, is it congratulations?" Brooke asked, hoping she was saying the right thing. God knew she was on a roll lately.

"Yes. I'm glad to be free of him. There was a lot more going on than I knew. Looks like I dodged a bullet there." She sounded as exhausted as Brooke felt. Sam's reaction to their fight didn't help.

"Then, good. I'm happy for you," Brooke said, eyeing the shower. Her skin itched from the salt water.

"Thanks. Sam told me that the homeowner in number six is selling their house."

"They are?" She hadn't heard that, nor had they mentioned that to Brooke at Bee's party. It was the house next door to hers. It wasn't a terrible house, but it needed some work.

"Yes. And they already have a buyer, apparently."

"Who? Not you?" Brooke laughed, swatting a fly away.

"No, not me."

"Is it someone we know?" There was a long silence at the end of the line.

"Yep. Lachlan."

33

SAM. QUESTIONS.

JANUARY.

The morning light hit Sam square in the eye. Georgina's question lingered in the back of her mind when she went to bed. Now, with Brooke's nasty comments, the question pounded on her brain like a ball pein hammer. Problem was, she still didn't know the answer. What did she want from her life? The only thing she could come up with was to not be in this situation. Even if she won a million dollars in the lottery, she would be in the same position. But at least then she'd be able to repair the house and get a new car. But then what?

Ugh. She had no clue.

She listened for the low hum of the fishing trawlers as they puttered out to open waters. It was her sign to get up, but all was quiet. That meant it was way before six. Sleep wasn't returning, so she got up and dressed. Ned waited patiently at the back door, looking like he'd slept just fine. Typical.

When she reached the water's edge, the sky was ablaze in pink and peach. At one end, mist hugged the cliffs. The waves were flat and methodical in their rhythm. The soft breeze kept things cool enough that Sam kicked herself for not grabbing a jumper, or at the very least, her yellow jacket by the back door. Too tired to walk back to the house, she resolved to suck it up and just walk faster. Ned pranced beside her with a prideful grin. He carried a log the size of a felled tree between his teeth. He'd scored big this morning.

"No Ned. You need something small, mate. I can't throw that." Ned dropped the log and gave her a crestfallen look. Sam looked around, found a smaller stick near the sea grass, and held it up. Ned looked down at the log, then up at the stick and wagged his tail.

"Ready?" The tail wagged faster. Sam threw it as far as she could and watched Ned bolt after it.

Soon it would be just her and the dog. Bee was leaving. While she acknowledged the fact, the reality of it scared her more than she wanted to admit. Without expressly telling Bee, her daughter was already heading down the same path as Sam. Feeling the trauma of losing a parent? Check. Losing more family members soon after? Check. Finding a boyfriend who distracts you from said traumas? Check. Backpacking plans? Check. Check. Check. She didn't want Bee to continue down that path. To return to her after a year (or when the money ran out) and fall pregnant within weeks, as had happened to her.

She wanted Bee to pursue her dreams. She was so damn talented with her craft. How did she miss that? If Sam had anything to do with it, Bee *was* going to study in Sydney. Find a place off campus with Liv. *That* was the plan.

But wait. Bee hadn't mentioned Liv in weeks. Did they have a falling out over Declan? She and Brooke were strained for a while until Brooke began dating Lachie. Had Brooke been jealous of Zed? Sam couldn't remember. God. How could Brooke say those things? She was still pissed but she couldn't think about Brooke, or the things she'd said. She needed to focus on helping Bee.

What could she do to convince her daughter that she was following the same path she did? Would Bee repeat history? She knew Bee. She knew she was smart and logical. But Sam also knew when a guy was involved, all that went out the window. Either way, Bee was leaving. To uni or travelling with Declan.

A shooting pain seized her chest. The anxiety attack always came around when she felt stressed. But it was more than anxiety this time. Sam felt lost and suddenly alone. Everyone had left her. Her brother, Paul. Her parents. Zayden. Marty. Brooke with her cruel words. Now, Bee was leaving her too, in her own way. She'd be on her own. The pain intensified. It was too much. She couldn't bear to lose her baby girl. She was all she had in the world.

Sam sank down to the sand and placed her face into her hands, feeling the sobs build. Ned pranced over to her, dropped his stick at her feet, sniffed at her face, then licked her arm. She looked up, and he tilted his head, as if to check on her to see what was wrong. She reached out and stroked his head. He took it as a positive sign and picked up the stick again. She shook her head, so he dropped the stick and lay down in front of her, resting his head on his front paws, and looked up at her worriedly.

Sobs engulfed her. She put her head down to her knees, wrapping her arms around her head. She felt helpless against the pain. Her breath caught and emotion crushed her like a tsunami. Her nose dripped and her tears plunked into the sand. Ned got up quietly and nuzzled up under her arms. He licked at her tears. It caught her unaware, snapping her out of her misery. She pulled back and embraced him.

"I don't deserve you, Ned," she whispered, then kissed his head. He nuzzled his head into her lap. With her fingers feeling quite numb in the morning cold, she put her hand down to pat the dog. For all the rejection she was feeling in her life, it was nice to know that the dog would always need her. She was thankful for that, at least.

The sun shone upon her. The day was beginning like any other, and that was the problem. Her life had become one big routine she could do blindfolded. She didn't want to be this person anymore. She was done playing the victim. Brooke was right. She was living in the past. She'd been stuck since Zed died, vainly wishing for life to rewind. And she knew it couldn't. She *knew* that.

She missed Marty. She missed her company, her advice, her kindness. What she wouldn't give for a chat and a damn cup of tea. She could almost taste the bitter brew on her tongue. Marty's words came back to her again. "Come on Sweet Pea, time to get up". Maybe it was time to stand up and finally face the world. Hadn't Brooke mentioned a letter Marty had written her? Something about Ray nagging her. Maybe that's what she needed: to read Marty's words.

"Come on Ned, let's go find that letter," she said.

Buried in a pile of bills on her chest of drawers, tears welled when Sam saw 'Sweet Pea' written in Marty's beautiful cursive handwriting on the centre of the envelope.

Coffee. She needed coffee for this. She returned to the kitchen to make a cup.

Sweet Pea. Marty's voice rang loud and clear in her mind. When had she written it? And why was Ray so pushy with Brooke to get her to read it? That was weird. She sat at the table with her coffee and started reading.

Sweet Pea,

It brings me great sadness knowing you will read this letter after I'm gone. But I want you to know how much joy you and Bee brought to my life. Yes, I have a granddaughter, and because of circumstances beyond anyone's control, I was fortunate to inherit another. And the bonus? A great-granddaughter!

Because you and Bee are that to me, Sweet Pea. You are my family. Part of my heart, as much as my blood relatives are.

Sam inhaled a deep breath, forcing the lump in her throat down. Tears dribbled down her cheeks. She reached over and grabbed a tissue from the box at the end of the table, blew her nose, then kept reading.

When you and Zayden told me you wanted to buy the Fischer's house in Fergus Bay, my heart burst open. I was so relieved when they listened to my pleading. When you moved in, I was excited to share my sanctuary with two beautiful souls who loved it as much as I did. Bee was the bonus. But I felt your pain too. Having a baby without your mother around, I knew you felt her absence. I am just so thrilled you allowed me to fill the void and embrace you both as my own. It's brought me nothing but happiness to teach you both over the years. You with gardening. And Bee with sewing, crocheting, even cooking. Oh, but if only her mother had learned those skills too! It would have brought her some relaxation from the manic life she leads. I say this in jest, of course.

I know it hasn't been the easiest time for you, especially keeping up with everything since Zayden died, but having you and Bee close to me helped me heal from his passing, too. I hope I've helped ease the pain a little for you. I know what it's like losing someone you love so desperately. It's an excruciating pain that's hard to describe, especially to those who have not lived it.

But now it's time for me to help ease your burdens. Had I done this while I was alive, you would never have accepted the help. In fact, I forecast you will resist and possibly even oppose. Because that's who you are. Independent, strong, and fierce.

Once you read this letter, you need to reach out to Ray. He has some details to share with you regarding how I'd like to help. I asked him not to contact you until after you read this letter. But don't wait. He'll be eager to discuss it with you.

There is one piece of advice I want to give you before I end this letter, and it is this: Let Zayden go, Sweet Pea. It's time. You experienced the best parts of your life with him: a beautiful wedding surrounded by those who love you both. Hours spent dreaming and planning your lives together. Then, bringing an amazing human being into the world. And what an incredible woman she has become. And that is because of you.

But Sam, your life continues beyond your role of Zayden's wife and Bee's mother. If I know you, you have a glorious future ahead. I know it's difficult. It's taken me many years to let go of the love of my life. And letting go of your child as they enter adulthood, that's something no one really tells you about. But until you let go of both Zayden and allow Bee to find her own way, you won't find happiness again. That's all I want for you. To be happy. Find something that lights you up. Something which makes you eager to get out of bed in the morning. Release your pain and untether yourself from what is holding you back.

I can hear your mind churning, asking: But how do I do that?

Dig deep and find what nourishes your soul. Then accept my help in making it happen.

I love you Sweet Pea, and I love our Bee. Please know you were loved immensely by this old woman down the track. And I hope you always keep me in your hearts, as you'll forever be in mine.

Marty

Sam sensed Marty's presence, as if she was sitting there with her, holding her hand, speaking directly to her. She dabbed her eyes with another tissue and blew her nose. Marty's letter was written exactly as she spoke. It was comforting. Had she known of the love expressed in this letter, she would have read it when Brooke first gave it to her. But when was that? Sam couldn't remember exactly, but Brooke had pestered her for months.

What did Marty mean, that she wanted to help? That was crazy. Marty helped them tremendously over the years. They ate at her house at least twice a week. She was the one that kept them in baked goods, for goodness' sake. Sam hadn't needed to buy bread or eggs for years. How was it she was going to help them now?

Let them go, Marty said. She was slowly getting there with Zed. Now, she had to let her daughter go. Let her fly, have wings. Isn't that what Lachlan said Zayden wanted? Brooke told her Bee was brave to make this choice for herself. They were right. Of course they were. But the idea of losing her daughter to the world was hard. But she had to give Bee credit. Deciding to go on an adventure like that at eighteen was brave. Sam had been almost relieved to fall into a life with Zed after her parents died only a few years before. He offered her safety, but she hadn't felt safe since he died.

But now, she had to find her own way. She clung to busyness like an addict clings to their fix. Find something that lights you up, Marty said. Georgina said that too. Find something that makes you want to get out of bed in the morning. She had no clue what that was. Life got her up. But something was brewing in the back of her mind. A thought from long ago.

She had a phone call to make. She needed to follow through with the instructions from Marty's letter.

3 4

BROOKE. LOVE.

JANUARY.

Brooke stood at the entryway of Henry Finlayson's room in the Castle Hill Nursing Home, wondering if she'd made a mistake. He suffered from dementia. The nurse said it was unlikely he'd remember Marty or Gilly at all. But she had to try.

"Henry. You have a visitor," said the nurse.

"I do? Oh, that's terrific! I don't get visitors very often," he said, his eyes bright, his smile broad and his voice clear.

"Hello Henry. My name is Brooke. I'm Gilly's granddaughter," she said. The nurse advised that it was risky to mention her grandmother so quickly, but today was a good day so far.

"Gilly. Oh, now there's a memory!" he exclaimed. "She was a spitfire, that girl." Brooke laughed. She was, and she was relieved he remembered her. The nurse smiled and pulled a chair closer to the bed for Brooke before excusing herself.

"She had some stories about you, too," Brooke said.

"And how is she? It's been a long time since I thought about her. But then, the mind isn't quite as it once was," Henry said, chuckling.

"So I understand. I'm sorry to say, but Marty, Gilly, passed away recently." His face shadowed with sadness.

"No. Gilly? Really?" His voice cracked. She reached for his hand and gently squeezed, a gesture she often did with her own patients when delivering bad news.

"Yes. She was, as you say, a spitfire until the end. She died peacefully in her sleep at the beach house."

"Fergus Bay? She kept the house?" Oh my God, he remembered.

"Yes, she did. She also kept your letters. She kept them in a beautiful wooden box."

"I made that box for her. It was a Christmas present to keep all her treasures in," he said, his voice wistful.

"Clearly she treasured your letters. I hope you don't mind, but I read them. They were beautiful. It was obvious how you felt about her." He nodded.

"How's the boy? Ray? He must be a grown man now." He smiled a gentle smile now. He remembered.

"My father. He's doing fine. He lives here in Sydney, in Chatswood. He's an accountant."

"Oh, that's marvellous. I'm sure Gilly taught him money smarts. She was a frugal one. We were going to buy the beach house together, but Gilly already had the deposit saved and she insisted it be in her name only. I was rather upset about that, to be frank. But it was best, given the times." She nodded.

"How did she get the name Gilly? Do you know?" Brooke asked. It was one piece that she couldn't figure out.

"Gillyflowers. They were her favourite. I think they're also called stocks. Gilly loved them. She planted them everywhere and filled vases and vases with them. I used to tease her about her obsession. That's how the name stuck. Golly. I remember the scent of those flowers like it was yesterday." Brooke smiled. It explained why Marty wanted those flowers at her funeral.

"And what's to come of the house now?" he asked.

"She left it to me. I love it down there. It's peaceful and calming. Like a…"

"Sanctuary," he finished. "She called it that. Her sanctuary. She was so busy in Hobart, always going, making great strides in her career. The beach house was the place where she became whole again. Except for…" He paused when emotions took over.

"Mae," she said, and he looked straight at her.

"You know about Mae?" he whispered.

"Yes, she told me. Your daughter. The grave marker remains in the backyard. I will take care of it. I promise." Tears rolled down his cheeks.

"Oh, it was a horrible time. I don't blame her for what happened between us. We just couldn't recover. I heard, through the grapevine, that she went back to Bert a while later."

"Yes, she did. She wrote a letter to me where she called him safe." Brooke almost felt disloyal to the grandfather she didn't know. But after reading Henry's letters, she felt she knew Henry more than she knew of Bert. "And you? Did you ever marry?"

"I did. But it didn't last. I shouldn't have married the girl. We were only together for three years. Turns out, I only loved one woman in my life. No one came close to the bar Gilly set." He was quiet for some time after that, living through his memories.

Moments later, Henry looked back up, his tears dry now. Brooke knew the memories were gone. He wouldn't remember any more today.

"Are you okay?" Dae asked later when they were cleaning up the kitchen after another epic dinner. She was seriously thinking of re-joining the gym. She'd never eaten such copious amounts of food in her life, as she had over the last two weeks.

"Yeah, just a lot on my mind," she said, rinsing the dish soap from a glass bowl.

"Was it Henry at the nursing home?" Dae asked, taking the bowl from her.

"It was," she said.

"When I got back today, I just felt overwhelmingly sad," she said. "He never forgot her. And she never forgot him. They missed out on something amazing. She clearly had depression after Mae's birth, but it doesn't sound like she had any help to cope with it."

"I'm surprised he didn't stick around, insist he stay with her," Dae said.

"He probably tried, but you knew Marty. She would have dug her heels in. When she was in pain, or angry, she pushed people away."

"Sounds like the apple doesn't fall far from the tree there," he said, placing the bowl in the lower cupboard.

"What? What do you mean?" She turned and stared at him, suds dripping off her hands and on to the floor.

"You're back here when you weren't scheduled to return for another six weeks. It wasn't just to find Henry. If it was, you would have scheduled that because you're a planner, Brooke. Turning up at the last minute is not something you do. So, this fight with Sam has left you hurt and angry, and you've pushed her away. You do this. This is your way of coping. When you and I fight, I don't hear from you for days." Brooke looked at him, then grabbed a baking dish and started scrubbing it furiously.

"So? We had a huge fight," she finally said.

"Have you ever had a fight with Sam?" Dae asked, his voice now soft and calm. "And please stop taking your frustration out on our bakeware."

She blinked, eased off the scrubbing.

"Twice. Years ago. Once when she started dating Zed and totally ignored me. And then when I moved back to Sydney after I broke up with Lachlan."

"At least you're saying his name now," he said.

"We talked. Kind of. Lachlan is…" she hesitated, "angry I married you and not him."

"Of course he is. You didn't think he would be? You were in love with him, Brooke. I knew that. Shit, everyone knew that!"

"I thought he'd wait for me. The plan was to pause on our relationship until I finished med school and he got his business started. Then we'd build a life together in Tasmania. Helping you was just a side path. I thought he knew that." Dae shook his head.

"What?"

"It remains, to this day, the stupidest plan I've ever heard," Dae said.

"Why? Why is it a stupid plan? It made sense at the time!"

"Not if he was the love of your life," he answered. "Which he is. You've been pining for Lachlan this whole time. No one you have ever dated has come close to the bar Lachlan Jones set."

Brooke stopped scrubbing the pan, remembering Henry's words about Marty, then scrubbed harder. Water splashed everywhere.

"Stop. You're going to owe Jase a set of pans the way you're going. Brooke, look at me. I love you, you know that, but it seems like you had all these conversations in your head," Dae said. She huffed in frustration. "What was the fight with Sam about?"

"I said some things to her I shouldn't have. Basically, I told her she was holding on to the past. Told her she was afraid to let go of Bee for fear of losing her, like she did with Zed. Even said something stupid about expecting this dolphin she's convinced is Zed reincarnated, to come to life and walk out of the water."

"Geezus, B. That's harsh. It's got to have been hard for her."

"I know," she whined. "I fucked up."

Her phone rang behind her. Great. Probably Merritt calling again to tell her what an idiot she was. She'd already called her three times, but now Brooke ignored her. She didn't need the reminder.

"Can you check that, please? See who it is?" Her hands were pruny from the dishwater.

"Your dad," he said, checking the caller id.

"Can you get it? It's weird he's calling now. It's almost ten."

"Hello Ray, it's Dae. Brooke's just washing up at the moment... I know, he's horrendous... Yeah, I think it's a chef thing." He laughed at something her dad said.

"What does he want?" she mouthed. He held his hand up to her, listening to Ray.

"Do you want her to call you back? She's almost done... Yep, no problem... Okay.... Will do... Great, thanks. Byeee." He pressed end.

"He called to let you know Sam has finally read the letter, and he needs you to give her the documents. They're heading to Queensland early tomorrow morning for a week. Apparently, she needs to sign some forms?"

"Fuck," she said, drying her wrinkled fingers. "Can't he just express mail them to her?"

"No idea. What letter is he talking about?" he asked, putting away the last of the dishes.

"A letter that Marty wrote to Sam. Dad's been waiting for her to read it for months," she said, slathering her hands with lotion they kept on the kitchen windowsill. Brooke thought back to when she gave the letter to Sam. It was months ago. And now Sam decides to read the damn thing? Shit.

"Why do I have to deliver the documents?" she asked him, expecting him to know the answer. "Did Dad say? Why can't it wait until after they get back?"

"He didn't say."

"I need to call him back. I need to know if Sam knows what they are. Maybe I can send them to her?" Shit. Shit. Shit.

"I'll be in the lounge room with the rest of the wine when you're done," he said, and retreated from the kitchen.

She hit her dad's number on her phone and waited.

"I knew you'd call back. I was going to bed since we have an early flight, but I just got through talking to Sam a little while ago. I thought you were in Fergus Bay?"

"No, I came back last week. Had some stuff to sort out."

"Sam said you two had a huge fight," he said. Great, thanks Sam. Thanks for sharing with her father that she'd been a total bitch. She heard her father take a sip of something, probably scotch at this hour. She picked up her glass and took a gulp of wine.

"You okay, Brooke?" Her father asked when she didn't respond.

"Yeah. But it's my fault. I said some things I shouldn't have. I was just reeling. I found a letter from Marty addressed to me, and it threw me off. So, I took it out on Sam."

"What did the letter say?" Should she share the information about Henry with her dad? No. Marty hadn't, so Brooke would take her lead.

"Just that I needed to give Lachlan a chance," she said.

"Well, she's right," her dad said. "The fact that he handcrafted

Marty's coffin says a lot. He really loved her, and she loved him. I'm surprised she didn't leave him anything when she died, to be honest."

"Hmm," she said. She didn't need her dad ganging up on her, too.

"Look, I won't keep you, but I've talked to Sam. She's aware Marty left her something in her will, but she doesn't know the details. I would go down myself, but your mum and I really need this time away."

"And it can't wait until you get back?" Brooke said, hoping he would say yes.

"No. Can't now. She needs to sign the documents so we can get the process started. Marty left her some money, and I'd like to get it to her sooner than later."

"How much are we talking about? Enough to make some repairs to the house, or something that will help her long term?"

"For Sam, we're talking about life-changing money," he said. "There's money for Bee too."

"Holy crap. Sam won't accept that."

"I'm aware. So was Marty. And I know this is bad timing, but I wondered if you could be there when I call and tell her the details. You can witness her signing the paperwork. I was going to express mail it, but if you could pick the documents up and take them to her, I think that would be best."

"Yes. I will be there," she said, after a few moments. "But she won't be happy about that either. But, knowing how this is going to affect them, I want to be in the room when Sam hears the details."

"You know what Marty left you was significant too, right? She was very strategic with what she left everyone. Marty left you the beach house for a reason. She knew that's what mattered to you. And because she knew that your income was significant enough to sustain you."

"Oh yeah, I'm fine with it. I'm happy with the house. It's the only thing I would have wanted. But for you and Mum?" she asked. She was excited for Sam and Bee, but this was still her father's mum they were talking about.

"We are happy with what she left us. We inherited some of her investments. She was quite the clever investor, it turns out. She bought a significant amount of Apple stock back when it was about six dollars a share."

"Whoa. That's got to be worth a lot more now!" she exclaimed, relieved they were happy.

"Yes, and the shares have split several times since then. So, we're okay. Sam gets some of that stock as well. So does Bee, which I think will make her happy."

"Considering she has her head in her iPhone most of the time, probably." Her dad filled her in on more of the details, preparing her for what was to come. Sam was going to freak, so Brooke knew now that she had to be there.

"I'll book my flight as soon as we're off the phone."

"Good. Look, I'll leave the paperwork in an envelope on my desk. Call me when you have both Bee and Sam with you, and we'll get this done. I've been waiting for months to get this last piece closed. I was ready to go down there and tell her to just read the damn letter myself!"

"Sorry Dad. Had I known the significance, I would have been more aggressive."

"I'm just glad we're almost there. And thank you for helping me."

"No problem," she said and picked up her wine, not looking forward to the apology she'd have to make before the will could even be discussed.

"Oh, and I heard you're about to have a new neighbour. Number six sold. But Sam didn't say who it was. Any ideas?" God, she'd forgotten about that. Her head was totally focused on Henry.

"Yes. Lachlan," she said, her voice deadpan.

"Well. That's going to be interesting, isn't it?"

3 5

SAM. BELIEVE.

JANUARY.

"Hey, Mum," Bee said, throwing her backpack near the back door. She was surprised to see Bee at this late hour. The spotlights from the trawlers had already been past, highlighting the shoreline as they made their way over to Triabunna. So it had to be past eleven.

Should she tell her about Marty's will? No. Not yet. Not until she knew more. With her luck, it was probably only a few hundred dollars. Nothing to get Bee excited about, although even that much would be helpful. At least it would be enough to get the new leak in the bathroom repaired.

"Hi love. I was waiting on a text from you, telling me you were staying the night with Declan. Are you hungry? I made pasta earlier," she said, trying to sound casual. Her heart was still racing after her conversation with Ray.

"No thanks. I ate a late lunch in town. I might grab some ice cream, though. Any left?"

"I think there is a scoop or two," Sam said. Bee walked to the freezer and took out the ice cream and a spoon. She skipped the bowl altogether, Sam noticed, when she sat on the couch next to her.

"Feels like I haven't seen you in days," Sam said, realising it came out more like a whine than a statement. "I mean, I know you're busy and everything. Just miss you, that's all."

"Yeah, I know. I miss you too. And I know it's been hard since the fight with Aunty Brooke. Feels like we've been on overdrive since Marmy died. I think I need a day just to chill at home."

"You're off tomorrow, right?" Bee nodded.

"Declan is working a two-day job with Uncle Lachie out in National Park starting tomorrow. Are you working?"

"No. I'm off tomorrow too. I have a ton of stuff to do here. Washing for one. Ned is becoming like the Princess and the Pea sleeping on my dirty pile."

"Same."

"Georgina told me you were asking about her trip to France and Spain last year." Bee looked up, surprised. It had stung to hear Bee's plans from her friend. She would have preferred to hear them from Bee directly. Please Bee, she begged silently. I hate this. I hate being the last to know. This is not like us. What happened to us telling each other everything?

"Yeah. I was going to cancel the trip, because of, you know, your fight with Aunty Brooke. But I really want to go," Bee said, hesitating, then scraping up another spoonful of ice cream.

Hearing Bee's words felt like a knife slicing her open. Guilt flushed through her. She heard Marty's words: Let her go.

"Do you want to tell me about your plans?" Sam asked. She hoped it was interest masking her face and not the anxiety she was still feeling.

"Are you sure you want to know? I mean, the last time we talked, you were still angry and telling me to go to uni," Bee said.

"Well, I think your mind is made up. So, let me support you," Sam said, trying to keep her tone in check.

"Thank God, because I've been dying to tell you," Bee said giddily, her face completely lighting up. "We're going to start with a road trip through New Zealand. We can do some work through WWOOF, or Workaway. From there, we'll head to America. Declan and Liam want to drive as much of Route 66 as they can. We'll start in L.A., then stop in Vegas, the Grand Canyon, and then pick up on Route 66 from there. We can only be in the U.S. for three months and, since we can't work while we're there, it'll just be the road trip. Then we'll head to Ireland, stay with their mum for a couple of weeks. Pick up some more work there. Then we'll drive up to Scotland for a bit, hit London for a week or so, then take the ferry from England over to France. From there, we're still planning."

"Wow! Sounds exciting. The Vegas part worries me, but…"

"I'll be fine. Liam and I are underage by U.S. standards, so we can't get into too much trouble." She smiled, like it was an inside joke, except Sam wasn't sure she wanted to know what kind of trouble they were planning for the places they were legal.

"And you have the money for this?" she asked instead.

"I have enough for the round the world airline ticket, which has some restrictions we need to work around. Plus, there's enough for my share of the campervan in New Zealand. Declan has a friend in Christchurch we'll stay with initially. It's picking season when we arrive, and his friend said we can get work around the Marlborough area easily. There are a couple of trails the guys want to hike down south, the Kepler and Milford Track. So, we'll do that. Then we'll rent a campervan in Queenstown and head north."

"And what if you run out of money?" Sam asked.

"As you taught me, there's always a job to be found. I am planning on working while we travel, except for the U.S. part. Don't worry." She scooped the last of the ice cream.

"You know I can't afford to bail you out if you get stuck, right?" She hated to say it, but it was true. "What happens if you get into an accident?"

"Declan said I need to get travel insurance. He has it now. So does Liam. Tom told me he used World Nomads when he went to Spain. Which is funny since that's what we'll be! World nomads!" Bee was brimming with excitement. And why wouldn't she be? The trip sounded amazing. She wouldn't mind tagging along herself, but

Lachie's words echoed in her head—let her fly, fly, fly. She had to let her go.

"When do you leave?" The dreaded question. The question Sam really didn't want the answer to.

"In three weeks," Bee said, sheepishly. Sam nodded, then carried the empty pasta bowl to the sink, hoping to hide her dismay. Fuck. Three weeks?!

"I'm sorry, Mum. I wanted to say something earlier. It didn't seem right to talk to you about it at work. And every time I'm home, you're working." It was true. She was always working.

"Talk to me, please," Bee begged. "Tell me what you think."

Sam turned on the water, letting her thoughts settle. She wanted to cry. She was losing her daughter, not to university, but to the world. What if she fell in love with Paris, or Rome or even St. Petersburg, and didn't come home? She'd be halfway across the world. And what if something happened to her? What if she couldn't get to her? She scrubbed the bowl, letting the task fill the silence then left the dish to drip dry on the rack. She had to say something now.

"It sounds exciting and adventurous," Sam said, wiping her hands.

"But?" Bee asked. "I know you have a 'but' in there. You always have a but in there." She folded her arms, as if putting on her armour, waiting for her mother to pick apart her dreams. Marty's voice sang loudly in her mind. Let her go.

"It's sound like an amazing adventure. I will worry about you. I'm your mum and that's what we do. But" she said, smiling, "despite that, I give you my blessing to see the world. Try new things, have fun. The only thing I ask is that you send me lots of postcards. And emails, and FaceTime every week so I can see your beautiful face." She swallowed her tears. Don't cry. Don't cry. A piece of her heart seared off just a little. She had to do this for Bee. Sam couldn't be the reason she stayed behind.

"Really? You mean it? You're not just saying that?"

"I mean it. Just tell me where you're going, when you're going, so I know where you are. Okay? I won't worry as much. And I get to lecture Declan and Liam about taking care of you. They are not to abandon you in the middle of a desert somewhere."

"Uncle Lachie already did with that with Declan, and Tom did that with both of them," she said with a smile. "But yes, no problem." Of course Lachie did that..

"Thanks, Mum. I'm so excited, but I'm also so relieved you're okay for me to go," Bee said, enveloping her in a hug. Sam accepted the hug but wouldn't go so far as saying she was happy about the plan. But she'd accepted the reality of it.

It was time for Bee to spread those wings.

Late the following afternoon, Sam folded laundry while Bee scoured the internet, pouring over travel blogs or something. Music played on the stereo, and memories of her own travels swirled in her head. Lost in the past, she dismissed the sound of a car outside. Probably some lost tourist. No one would visit for months with the shackies gone.

Thirty minutes later, Sam heard female voices outside while she chopped veggies for dinner. She washed her hands and checked her phone. Almost six o'clock. Bee was taking the last of the laundry off the line, so clearly she was talking to someone. Ned hadn't barked either. Sam walked to the backdoor and stopped with her hand on the knob.

Great. Just great. She was having a decent day. Until now. The bitch was back. And probably back to turn the knife in if she knew about Bee's plans.

Brooke turned her head, saw her through the screen. Shit.

"Hi Sam," she said, her voice soft. Brooke squeezed Bee's hand, then began walking toward her.

"You're back," she said. She was still hurt, and fury pumped through her. Brooke slowed as she reached the back door.

"May I come in?" Sam turned and walked away. The onions needed attending. Brooke idled nervously at the door.

"For fuck's sake. Yes. Come in," she yelled. She rinsed the knife but kept it in her hand.

"Look. I came to say sorry, but I guess I didn't realise the fight was this bad," she said, pointing to the knife.

"What?" Sam looked down at the knife still in her hand. "No. I was chopping onions for dinner." She placed the knife back on the chopping board, then headed to the fridge for the cheese.

"Oh, thank God," Brooke said. "Look, I am sorry. I said some really stupid things. I didn't mean any of it. Things I don't even believe. You are an amazing mum. You were an incredible wife and what I said was cruel. I'm so, so sorry."

"So why did you say them?" Sam demanded.

"Because I was unhinged?" Sam smiled knowingly. "More than usual. I found a letter Marty wrote to me when I was cleaning out her bedroom. She told me I'd broken her heart."

"How?" The letters were a thing then.

"Marty said that I should have told Lachlan the truth, and that I broke his heart. All the things you've been telling me for years."

"Because it's easier to push him away than to be hurt," Sam said plainly.

"Which was essentially what Marty told me in her letter. And we both ended up hurt anyway," Brooke said, taking a seat at the table. Sam grabbed a pair of glasses and a bottle of wine from the cupboard.

"Meh. I've done the same thing. It's easier to push people away, so it doesn't hurt as much when they leave you." Silence filled the room.

"But you were dumb to let him go. He's been in love with you forever and he still is. Hell, he even bought the house next door to you. Did you hear about that? He told me he was going to flip it, but I think he has an ulterior motive."

"Merritt told me," Brooke said.

"Seems Marty dished out the truths through her letters. She said some bold things to me in mine. She told me I had to let Zed go. And Bee. Same thing you said to me. And Lachie, if you want to know. She also told me I need to find something that lights me up. I'm still puzzled with that one."

"Why didn't she say this stuff to us while she was alive?" Brooke asked as Bee came in the back door. Bee looked at them as if they were stupid.

"She did tell you while she was alive. You just didn't listen," Bee said, putting the basket down on the couch.

"What?" Sam asked.

"Sorry, but I heard you from the sunroom. Marmy has been saying this stuff to you both for the last two years at least. She told you both to move forward. She said the same thing to me. Seems like I'm the only one who listened. Do you think it was easy being a fourteen-year-old who lost her dad? Nope. Do you think it's easy watching your mother work herself into the ground, knowing she's doing it just to keep a roof over our heads? Nope. Do you think it was easy telling her I'm leaving when I know everyone in her life has left her? Big nope. But Marmy taught me that life is short, and you have to take advantage of every opportunity."

"Listen to this grown up," said Brooke, smiling over her wineglass.

"And this grown up is getting some wine," Bee said, pulling a glass down for herself. "Because I'm raising my glass that you two are talking again. It's been freakin' torture the last two weeks."

Sam smiled over at Brooke and tapped her glass against hers.

"Right, dinner. I'm trying to make risotto. I don't know how it will go, but Jase sent me a recipe and I've been dying to try it."

"We're going to starve," declared Bee, coming over to scan the recipe. "I'll help. Otherwise, we'll be eating at midnight, especially if you two get talking."

"Did you find Henry?" Sam asked, ignoring Bee's sass.

"I did," said Brooke and filled her in on the latest news.

BROOKE. RESET.

JANUARY.

"There is another reason I came back," said Brooke, placing the envelope on the table. "Dad asked if I'd come down to deliver this to you, since they were traveling to Queensland." Sam looked so worried Brooke nearly laughed out loud.

"Dinner is ready," said Bee, coming in from the kitchen.

"Shall we sit at the table?" asked Brooke.

"Shit, now I'm really worried," said Sam. "I can't remember the last time we sat at the table to eat."

Brooke refilled their wine. Tonight, they were celebrating. Sam and Bee just didn't know it yet. Bee brought in two plates piled high with Jase's lemon risotto. Sam followed with the third plate and the salad bowl.

Sam sat but couldn't peel her eyes away from the envelope.

"What's wrong, Sam?" asked Brooke, knowing full well she was anxious at what was coming.

"I don't know what's in that, and it's freaking me out," said Sam, nodding to the envelope.

"What's going on?" asked Bee.

"I didn't tell Bee about it. I wasn't sure what it meant," said Sam, looking to Brooke for reassurance.

"First, both of you take a sip of the wine," instructed Brooke. Sam glared at her suspiciously over the rim of her glass.

"Spill it, Brooke. What's going on?" said Sam. Brooke saw Sam's hand shaking. God, how bad did she think this was?

"What did Dad tell you?" Brooke asked.

"Just that Marty left us a bit of money. But I don't know what that means. And I'm afraid to know. Because no matter what, I'll still be pissed with Marty that she did this."

"Dad is officially the one who needs to tell you the details. I'm just the courier and witness on the documents. So, we're going to call him. Okay?" Brooke picked up her phone, dialled her father's number, hit speaker, and placed the phone in the middle of the table.

"Hello? Brooke?"

"Hey Dad. I'm here with Sam and Bee," she said. "You're on speaker."

"Hello my girls. How are you all doing?" her dad said, his voice upbeat. Brooke smiled in anticipation.

"Fine. Just sitting down to dinner. We're, um, calling you about Marty's will?"

"Yep, and I asked Brooke to be there. She's going to witness your signatures once I've walked you through it." Sam looked nervously at Brooke again.

"What does that mean?" Bee asked.

"Everyone was left something in Marty's will," Ray said quickly. Brooke and Marty had both warned him about Sam's likely resistance. "Brooke got the house, and some money for upkeep, which she assures me is all she wanted. We were left some things as well. Things we're very happy with. And Marty bequeathed you both too."

"What does that mean? She left us something..." Bee asked. Brooke laughed when Bee's eyes lit up. She probably imagined she inherited Marty's favourite crochet hooks or something, which Brooke planned on giving her anyway. She made a mental note to do it later. Brooke looked to Sam. Relax, she mentally transported. This is a good thing. She smiled at her and watched Sam's face relax a little.

"Of course, Bee. You were part of her family," Ray said. "She left you some money."

"Really?" Bee whispered. Sam sat quietly, as Brooke knew she would.

"Really. Let's start with you, Bee," Ray continued. "Marty set up a trust for you, which means you won't get the money all at once. You'll get some on your... wait, let me make sure I get this right," he said. "I have a copy of it here." The shuffle of papers made Sam's jaw clench.

"You'll get some on your eighteenth birthday, which has just passed, so I need to get that to you immediately. Then another instalment on your twenty-first, again on your twenty-fifth and then the last amount on your thirtieth birthday."

"How much did she put in the trust?" Sam shrieked. She caught on fast. You rarely got money over time, unless it was a lot.

"Two hundred and fifty thousand dollars," Ray said.

"What?!" Sam yelped. "Are you kidding me? Bee's getting a quarter of a million dollars?"

"Yes," Ray said calmly, "in a trust." Brooke smiled at Bee, who sat completely stunned. Bee reached over, picked up her glass and took a long, deep drink of her wine. There it was. The shock hitting her.

"No," whispered Sam. "That can't be right."

"It is. I have the paperwork here. Now, let's talk about you, Sam," he continued.

"There's more?" Bee said in disbelief.

"Yes. For Sam, she's left..." he paused, as if scanning the document. "Seven hundred and fifty thousand dollars. Right now, it's tied up in investments. So, I need to talk to you about that, Sam. And soon."

Sam slammed back in her chair, speechless. Yeah, Brooke thought that would shock her. Sam stood abruptly and stumbled to the kitchen. She filled a tumbler with whisky and downed half of the glass in one go. Brooke and Bee both laughed. She filled the glass again and returned to the table.

"Are you telling me..."

"That Marty left you three quarters of a million dollars? Yes. Yes, she did." Ray laughed.

"Here," Brooke said. She pulled the document out of the envelope and passed it to Sam. Sam scanned the document, trying to make sense of it.

"But that's not right," said Sam. Her face was pale. Bee looked over her shoulder, reading along with her.

"How did we not know that Marmy was rich?" whispered Bee. Ah, Bee's naiveté still surprised Brooke at times.

"Oh, I figured. She was a doctor, Bee, and those renovations on her cottage weren't cheap," said Sam in a shaky voice.

"But she was so... frugal," said Bee.

"That's how the rich keep their money," said Brooke. "By investing well and not being frivolous with it." She took a sip of her wine, watching them both absorb the news.

"Look, I know this is a lot to take in. So, I'm going to let this settle for tonight, but I'll call you tomorrow, Sam. Okay? And Bee? Will you be around? I'll need to talk to you as well," Ray said.

"We'll be here," Sam said.

"Okay, I'll call you at nine tomorrow morning. Make sure you have coffee first. I'll need you awake for the next part." Brooke doubted either of them would sleep after this.

"Okay," said Sam, her eyes glazing over. "But Ray? Are you sure this is right?"

"Yes, Sam. It's right. This was what Mum wanted, and to be honest, I could not think of two people who deserve it more. I just wished you'd read the letter sooner!" Brooke raised her glass and looked pointedly at Sam.

"They're in shock, Dad. But I've got it from here. Love you. Send Mum our love."

"Will do. Chat later. Byeee."

"Why? Why did she leave us money? And so much?" Sam picked up her wineglass but opted for a long pull from her whisky glass instead.

"Because she loved you. You were her family," Brooke said.

"We loved her too," said Sam, but couldn't hold back the flood of tears any longer as the shock of the news settled. Brooke stood and walked to Sam to hug her. Bee sat watching them, stunned, but Brooke pulled her in. Within moments, all three were crying.

"I miss her so much. I swear she's been talking to me lately. I thought I was losing my mind," she said as snot ran from her nose. Bee handed her a tissue.

"You lost that a long time ago," Brooke teased. Both Bee and Sam laughed.

"You're probably right," Sam said.

Brooke knew this amount of money would change their lives. Doors long closed would open again.

Two days later, Brooke was cleaning the baseboards in Marty's old bedroom. The room was cleaned out. All that was left was a pile of books in the corner, awaiting the custom-made bookcases.

"Hey Brooke, it's me. Lachie is here," called Sam. "I just needed to borrow some milk. We're out."

Brooke took a deep breath, wiped her hands on her shorts, and walked to the living room. Lachlan was dressed in his usual blue work pants and grey t-shirt, but with socked feet.

He noticed her looking at his feet oddly. "I always take my boots off inside Marty's. They were the rules. Besides, they're full of mud and dust," he explained, then added, "hi."

"Hi Lachlan," Sam looked at the two of them like she was expecting them to fall into each other's arms or something. Brooke shot her a look that screamed 'go away'.

"Right, I'll just grab some milk from the fridge and, ah, go home. Make sure Bee and Declan aren't having sex on my couch. I'll be home if anyone needs me," and she left without another word.

"Coffee? Tea? Water?" Brooke asked, walking to the kitchen.

"Coffee would be great." She pulled out a packet of Georgina's roasted coffee from the pantry and turned the espresso maker on.

"This is a lot fancier than I used to get with Marty. Thank God for that! Her instant was crap," he said, leaning his hip against the island, watching her.

"She hid the coffee machine in her pantry," Brooke said, tapping the coffee grinds down into the espresso arm, then twisting it on to the machine, flipping the switch for it to brew. "She's had it for years. Mum and Dad bought it for her, but she never used it. Flat white, okay? Or do you want something else? Espresso?"

"Double espresso would be great if that's not a bother," he stammered. "I, ah, wanted to let you know firsthand that I bought the house next door. Although now I think of it, I'm sure you've heard that already."

"Yeah, Merritt and Sam both told me," she said, pouring milk into the stainless-steel milk jug, ready to steam for her own flat white.

"Yeah, sorry about that. Things moved really fast. I'm, ah, going to flip the house," he said. "Hold on to it for a little while, at least a year or two. I've been waiting for a house to come on the market down here for ages."

"So, an investment property for you, then?" she asked, frothing the milk.

"Yep." He was mesmerized watching the skill she displayed.

"Do you have any others?" she asked, wiping the nozzle with a damp cloth when she was done.

"Other what?" He seemed lost at the proximity of her.

"Investment properties," she said, pouring the steamed milk over her own.

"Ah, yeah. A house in Huonville that I finished up last year, a unit in Sandy Bay, another house in St. Helens, although that's more of a holiday house. I rent it through Airbnb the rest of the time." It was weird talking with him, like they were old friends, catching up. But they were, right? Old friends?

"I've got Pam and Jack's house to build out this way, and I figure I'll stay here instead of Mum and Dad's shack in Orford. That way, I can fix up next door at the same time. I hope it won't freak you out that I'll be so close."

So, he'd be here all the time. For months. Well, that was fine. She was returning to Sydney soon.

"Yeah, it's okay. I don't live here all the time, so...," she said, handing him his coffee. Her hand was shaking. He brushed her hand when he took the mug from her, muttering a thanks, his eyes not leaving hers.

"And if you did? Would it be an issue?" he asked.

"No," she whispered.

"I," she said, although not sure where to begin. He kept looking at her with those intense blue eyes.

"I have been thinking about, well, what happened with us back then. And... I was wrong," she said, her eyes not leaving his. "I thought I was doing the right thing by helping him, but..."

"It's okay. I know why you did it. I can't say it didn't hurt."

"I'm really sorry," she said, picking up her coffee. She put the cup back down.

"There's one thing I don't understand," he said. "Why didn't you tell me?"

She stayed silent for a long while.

"It wasn't until these last few months that I recognized what I did. I didn't realise the timing of it. And, if I'm honest with myself, it's because I was scared. I was scared it wouldn't work out. The long-distance thing. I was scared that I would give up being a doctor and come back to you. And I really wanted to become a doctor," she said.

"I know you did, Brooke. It's why I agreed to pause for a while. So you could focus. It was an opportunity for me too, to set up my business, get the training I needed behind me, without distraction. We had a plan," he said, placing his cup on the counter.

"It was a really stupid plan," she said, repeating Dae's words.

"Why was it stupid? I thought we were smart to do it," he said. His eyes bored into hers. It was now or never. She took a deep breath and plunged into the depths of the scariest place she'd ever gone.

"Because you don't do that with the love of your life. You don't marry someone else and not tell them why because you're scared. You find a way to be together. You fight for what you want. And Lachlan, it's probably too late, but I want to fight for what I want," she said.

SAM. PLANS.

JANUARY.

Sam sat on her bed with her notebook in her lap. She'd spoken to Ray several times already, talking about plans for the house, what to keep in investments, and what to sell now. She trusted Ray more than anyone with money and had hired him as her accountant straight away. It was too much money to fathom. She'd lived her entire life from paycheque to paycheque. Zed's insurance had been a help, but the amount had trickled in since his death, and even then, it barely covered the mortgage every month.

Now, the amount of money she had from Marty, seemed ridiculous.

Staring at the blank page, she thought of Ray's suggestion: Make a list of needs and wants. She started her list with needs.

1. Fix the leak in the bathroom. 2. Replace the roof. She wondered how much it would cost to renovate her entire kitchen, like Marty had done. She loved Marty's kitchen. But then she felt greedy, and guilt took over. Keep it real, she thought. Is a new car a need or a want? She put it in the middle.

"Mum," Bee said, standing at her door. "Ray told me to write a list. But I don't even know where to start."

"I'm working on that, too. Come on, sit by me. We'll work on our lists together," Sam said.

"It's just weird. I had a plan already. This just throws everything, I don't know, off," Bee said.

"You know you don't have to touch the money, right? Just because you have it doesn't mean you have to spend it," she said, hoping her daughter was listening.

"Yeah, that's what Ray said. But I think I want some as my emergency fund while I'm travelling. And a little for fun stuff. He said I needed to include some fun stuff. What's on your list?"

"Fix the bathroom and replace the roof," she said dryly.

"No fun stuff?" She looked at Sam's notepad. "You've got a car on your list. That's exciting. You could buy a fun little convertible," said Bee, giddily.

"With our dirt road? No thanks," she said. She had no clue what type of vehicle to even consider. That would come later.

"Yeah, good point. Be sure you take Uncle Lachie with you when you buy something. I've heard those dealerships can be slick when selling to women," Bee said, then scribbled something on her list.

"That was probably the case twenty years ago. Doubt they would get away with that stuff now. Who told you that, anyway?"

"Granddad," they said in unison, smiling.

"What did you just write?" Sam asked.

"A new laptop. Mine is overheating," Bee said. "I have to restart it, like, five times a day."

"Ugh, okay. Well, it may not make sense to buy one before you travel. Maybe wait until you get back?"

"Yeah, Declan is taking his. He said I could use his while we're away. I'll have my phone, but I may upgrade it so I can do that dual SIM thing," she said, writing that down. Sam had no clue what she was even talking about. She was still using an iPhone 6s.

"Maybe you should buy a new phone?" Bee suggested. "Yours is cracked and I don't think you can even update it anymore."

"Good idea," Sam said, and wrote it down.

"Knock, knock," Brooke called from the back door.

"In here," Sam shouted.

"What are you guys doing? It looks serious!" Brooke said, sitting on the corner of the bed.

"Your dad told us to make lists. Wants and needs," Sam said.

"Ooh, fun. What's on your list, Bee?" Sam listened as Bee waffled on about her list.

"A new computer for later. A new phone. But the money is throwing me off," Bee told Brooke.

"You'll figure it out. Just remember, spend a little, save a lot. That's always been my motto. I mean, do the fun stuff, but keep as much as you can in case of an emergency. Oh! And plan for your retirement. Which, now I'm saying that out loud to an eighteen-year-old seems weird. But trust me, time zooms past and suddenly you are thirty-eight, wondering where the years went. What's on your list, Sam?"

"Boring stuff," said Bee. "Although I just made her put a new iPhone on her list."

"Definitely on the need side," agreed Brooke. Sam stuck out her tongue.

"I have the bathroom to fix, and the roof to replace. And I put a car in the middle. I wasn't sure if that's a need or a want since Declan and Lachie fixed it."

"Fixed it, just in time to sell it," said Lachlan, coming in the door. "Hey Ginge. Hey Bee. Sorry, I knocked, but I guess you didn't hear me."

"Come on in, join the party," Sam said, suddenly embarrassed. Her bedroom was an absolute disaster zone. "Excuse the mess. I wasn't expecting company in here."

Lachie leaned against the end of the bed, right by Brooke, looking very relaxed. Brooke looked up at him and Sam noticed the faint blush spread across Lachie's face. Something weird was going on.

"Taking in the look on Sam's face, you've said nothing yet?" Lachie asked Brooke.

"Nope. They were just telling me what they're going to do with all the money Marty left them," replied Brooke, smiling at him.

"It's such great news. It's going to make life so much easier for you guys. And I can't wait to talk to you about what to do with this house," he said, looking around the room. "Ideas have been swirling for years. Family rate, of course. Now you have money, you can afford to pay me." Lachie laughed. Sam looked at him suspiciously.

"Are you shaking me down Lachlan Jones?" Sam asked, semi-seriously.

"Ha! Nah, I'm kidding. Same deal as always." Lachie looked at Brooke and… was that a wink?

"What the hell is going on with you two?" asked Sam. Bee was even staring at them.

"Did you sleep together?" Bee asked.

"Bee!" Sam slapped her arm.

"What? Look at them!" she exclaimed, pointing at Brooke and Lachie. She had to admit, they looked… smitten. And Bee was right. They looked like they just had sex.

"Let's just say the band is getting back together," said Brooke. Sam's jaw dropped.

"Holy shit! Seriously?"

"Really? You are? Wow! You can't buy this kind of excitement!" Bee exclaimed and lunged for Lachie, the brass railing stopping him from falling over on impact. Sam hugged Brooke.

"About fucking time!" Sam exclaimed.

"So does that mean you're moving to Fergus Bay?" Bee asked Brooke.

"We're still working out the details. For now, I'm going to travel back and forth," said Brooke, looking to Lachie.

"Guess the plan to buy the house next door worked," said Sam, watching the blush grow under Lachie's beard.

"I knew it! I knew you weren't going to flip that house!" she laughed, pointing at him.

"Oh, I may still. I'm not putting the cart before the horse. We're going to take it one step at a time. We've got some catching up to do first," he said, but the blush remained.

"They totally slept together," said Bee. "Look at them."

"You'd know," said Lachie, and soon Bee wore a matching blush.

Sam laughed unreservedly, something she hadn't done in a long time. There was light at the end of the long, dark tunnel. Georgina's question popped into her head: *If you could ask the Universe for anything, what would that be?* She had what she wanted initially. A way to fix the house. Money to get a new car. It seemed the Universe had delivered her answer, although it probably wasn't the answer Georgina was going for when she asked the question.

Now Sam had a way out of the hole she was in, she felt free. Maybe for the first time. She was curious about who she was without Zed and Bee. Suddenly, the thought didn't feel so daunting.

EPILOGUE

THREE MONTHS LATER.

"Hello Lovelies," said Georgina, sitting at the corner table in the café, with Pam and Aubrey. "It's great to see you. Brooke, I saw Lachlan earlier. I don't think I've seen him so happy."

"He won't stop humming that Maroon 5 song over at the house," said Pam with a smile, clearly teasing. She began humming the tune. "It's driving me crazy! I'll be glad when he's done building, so I won't have to hear it anymore!" She winked wickedly at Brooke.

"'She Will Be Loved'," commented Sam, nudging Brooke. Brooke blushed.

"And Sam, I heard the bridge work is starting next month. That must be a relief," Georgina said.

"Yes! No more juggling cars at the bridge!" Sam said, beaming at the news.

"Why don't you join us?" Pam said, scooting her chair aside. "Aubrey was just telling us about Bee's adventures with the boys." Nodding, Sam brought a couple of chairs from another table.

"Pam, you can't keep calling them boys. They're adult men," said Aubrey, shaking her head.

"She'll never change Aubrey, you know how she is," said Georgina. "She's been doing it since we met her. Can you believe it's not even a year since we met?"

"Feels like we've known each other forever!" said Pam.

"So? Where are the adventurous trio now?" Georgina asked Sam. "Last I heard, they were heading for America?"

"They're almost done there. I think they have another three weeks?" Aubrey said. Sam confirmed with a nod.

"Right now, they're in Austin, Texas. Bee Facetime'd last night. They ditched the rest of the plan for Route 66. They're leaving today and heading east to New Orleans, then going north. They'll be in New York by mid-April."

"Oh, we should call Ben! He'd probably even put them up," said Georgina.

"Already done," said Aubrey. "All I had to say was they were Tom's sons, and they opened the doors for them," said Aubrey, smiling at Sam. The two women talked a long while, the night the trio left. Aubrey admitted to Sam that she been avoiding her, as she looked too much like her daughter. Sam admitted she'd done the same thing, for the very same reason. Aubrey had even stopped wearing Chanel No.5 around Sam. Ever since, they touched base at least once a week, catching up on how the travellers were getting on.

"How do you all know Ben?" Brooke asked Georgina.

"Camino," Georgina, Pam and Aubrey replied in unison.

"Every time I speak with you, it's 'call this person, call that person'," Sam said.

"The Camino is like that. You form a family from all over the world," said Aubrey.

"Bee fell in love with Lee in Santa Fe, by the way," Sam said to Aubrey, smiling. "She got to paint with her while the guys checked out Albuquerque. She said it reminded her a little of her days with Marty."

Georgina nodded. "I can see that."

"Lean and Mean," chuckled Pam. "Who would have guessed she'd be a sweetheart?" Sam and Brooke both looked confused, while Aubrey and Georgina laughed at her joke.

"The first time we met Lee, she was swearing up a storm. She was bent out of shape about getting run over by bikers on the trail," said Georgina.

"I was the first to meet her and she scared the shit out of me!" laughed Aubrey. "We were walking down this steep part of the trail, so I let her go past me. She was nipping at my heels, spewing obscenities. By the time I got to the café where Pam and Georgina were, Lee was sitting inside, looking like she'd just enjoyed a visit with the Queen."

"But Bee said she was lovely," Sam said, still confused.

"And she is! Once you get to know her, she's a gorgeous soul. Just don't piss her off!" said Aubrey.

"Sounds like us," Sam said to Brooke, nudging her.

"The Camino is great for sorting out your angst," Pam mused.

"And learning who you are and what you're made of," said Aubrey. Georgina and Pam smiled at her, like they shared a secret.

"You know, you two should walk the Camino," said Georgina. "Put that on your fun list, Sam." The whole town had been giving Sam suggestions of what to put on her list. Someone had suggested buying a campervan and travelling. Someone else suggested spending a day at the spa.

"Well, I can't say it'll be all fun, and you'll come back either loving us or hating us. Either way, it's a life-changing experience," said Pam. Brooke looked to Sam with one eyebrow raised.

"What do you think?" asked Sam later that afternoon. They were relaxing on Brooke's front porch, enjoying the late summer breeze, and listening to the waves crashing on the other side of the sand dunes. It would most likely be the last of any warm weather they'd have for months.

"About what?" asked Brooke. Ned sat between their chairs, happy after his long beach run with Brooke earlier.

"Walking the Camino," said Sam, setting the glass down to put her feet up on the rattan ottoman.

"Are you serious? You know it's eight hundred kilometres, right? That's like walking from Sydney to Melbourne," said Brooke.

"I know. I was here when Georgina got back. She spent weeks talking about it," said Sam. "Besides, look at Pam. She looks like a tiny little grandmother, and she walked it."

"That woman seems like the little engine that could," said Brooke.

"Exactly! And if she can do it, so can we," nudged Sam.

"I don't know. I'm not sure I can leave the practice for that long," Brooke said, fidgeting with the hem of her shirt.

"The practice? Or Lachie?" Sam teased.

"I was actually thinking about the practice. Lachlan will be fine without me," said Brooke, although she looked unsure.

"Not like he hasn't gone without you before," Sam said, but looked instantly regretful at the words. "Low blow. Sorry! It may be a good way to get away from the noise. Clear our heads." Brooke went quiet.

"For a long time now, this one thought has been spinning in my head: Is this all there is?" Sam said, eventually. "I love it here, don't get me wrong, but I want more from my life. I just don't know what that is. Maybe this is a way to figure out what's next."

"It may be what I need to sort out what to do, too," Brooke admitted finally. "I love Lachlan, but we seem to be in the same place we were seventeen years ago. I'm in Sydney and he's here. I don't know how to make this work with us." They sipped lemonade, while the sounds of the waves lulled them into a meditative state.

"So? What do you think?" Sam asked. Brooke looked to her, eyes locking.

"I think we should walk the Camino," said Brooke.

"Should we ask Merritt if she wants to join us? Every time I talk to her lately, she's spinning in circles. Seems she needs time away to gain clarity, too," Sam suggested.

"I think she may need to walk the Camino more than we do," said Brooke. "Let's ask her."

ACKNOWLEDGMENTS

After three books, I've realised that publishing is like childbirth for me. So far, a book joins this beautiful world about every nine months. Except for this latest one. She has been a stubborn thing.

Writing *The Decisions We Make* was a way of bringing my world to you. While Fergus Bay is fictional, the villages of Orford and Triabunna are not. These places are in my 'backyard'. And yes, the Antarctic winds *are* brutal.

When deciding what story I wanted to write next, I debated whether to continue Aubrey's story from *Camino Wandering*. I felt compelled to write a story about rediscovered letters, of grief, and the struggles of being isolated and losing all sense of control. And wouldn't it make sense for us to see what life was like for the Lovelies, *post* Camino? Because, in reality, the Camino does not end when you reach Santiago de Compostela. It continues (sometimes more deeply) once you return home. And we saw that with the Lovelies, as they helped Sam through her struggles. Somehow, I found a way to combine all of those elements.

Writing has become an obsession for me. The stories swirl day and night. Characters are constantly vying for my attention. To be honest, I feel sorry for my husband since he puts up with my crazy addiction. But without his support and encouragement, I could not dedicate myself to this passion. Thank you love, for all you do.

To Angela Garwood, who lives halfway across the world, yet always seems to always be there when I need her most. Thank you Ang. The books are better for your edits, suggestions, and perspective. And I am a better person for your friendship. You were with me for one baby and stayed for the rest.

I am enormously fortunate to have my own group of 'Lovelies'. They are all incredible. Not only do these beautiful women give me space in their lives, but they provide insightful, honest, and encouraging feedback and reviews - and so much in between. One even offered me money if I would use a certain name for the 'dickhead publican'! I was happy to do that for her. No payment necessary there! I simply could not write my novels without this amazing group. Thank you Kim McDaniel, Shari Hamilton, Natalie Cooke, Trish Weiner, Vickie Waters, Maree Norris, Judy Anshaw, Laura Bauermeister, Meredith Atkinson, and Tiffany McConnell. I am truly humbled by your support, thoughtfulness, and friendship.

Somehow, I have reached my fifties and found myself surrounded by an incredible group of friends. This hasn't been an easy year for me in many respects, but without Melissa, Nicole, Sue, Trish, Ang, Kim, Shane, Lynell, Sharon, Jerry, Helen, Amanda, Meredith, Pauline, Georgie, and Danielle in my life, it would have been a hell of a lot harder. Thank you all.

To the Tasmanian Indie Author group: What a wonderful writing community to be a part of! I hope I have done you proud with my Aussie vernacular! And yes, I used 'thongs'.

Thank you to the Orford community. The Orford Hub who has always offered great support to me as a local writer. The café has been the place I go for write-ins (and get inspiration for Georgina's Café!). The library - and more specifically, our amazing librarian Clare – continues to teach me so much about this area. Thank you to Christopher Izzard for his explanation of how emergency situations are managed here on the east coast, and to Heidi Nicholl, who shared her insight into house renovations in the Orford area...and the battles therein.

In August 2021, I was approached by a friend on the board of an amazing charity called MPower Alliance, based in San Francisco, California. MPower Alliance are dedicated to supporting birthmothers after they place a child for adoption. Because of COVID, charities like this struggled to find donations.

On the 3rd of October 2021, two character names from *The Decisions We Make* were auctioned off at the MPower Alliance Annual Gala, raising $800 for the charity. Ami Sheth Sagel provided "Beverlee", in honour of her mother-in-law, Beverlee Sagel. Christina Ogburn-Chow provided the name "Zayden", in honour of her son. As excited as I was to use these names, we Australians like our nicknames, and Ami and Christina were happy for me to make some slight modifications to suit the story. Bee seemed like a great fit for my 17-year-old character, 'spreading love wherever she goes', and Zed was a good match for the 'always late, always last' Zayden Taylor.

Thank you for asking me to help such a worthwhile charity!

To learn more, visit https://www.mpoweralliance.org/.

I drew from my own 'empty nest' experience when writing of Sam's angst about losing Bee. My daughter Natalie is strong and independent, and the thought of her not being in my life is sometimes too unbearable to comprehend. Thankfully, she looks past my weird questions and 'motherisms', and still wants to speak with me every day, no matter where we are in the world. For that, I'm grateful and happy.

And finally, to my readers. The love, support, and encouragement you offer allows me to be exactly who I am. I am an odd duck, I know, but no matter what, your kind words and positive comments inspire me to keep writing. I can only hope you continue to enjoy my stories.

ABOUT THE AUTHOR

Tara Marlow is an Australian author of suspense and women's fiction. Tara was born in Sydney, and spent twenty of her early adult years living in the United States. In 2011, Tara ditched the corporate desk, emptied her nest in 2017 and travelled the world, full time for three years, working as a travel writer and photographer. Today, Tara lives in Tasmania, where she has pivoted her writing focus to fiction, writing about women overcoming seemingly insurmountable challenges, revealing who they are and what they're made of.

Mantra in life: She believed she could, so she did.

Sign up for Tara's newsletter for updates on her writing, promos and more!

https://www.thecrackpotwriter.com/newsletter/

ALSO BY TARA MARLOW

If you enjoyed *The Decisions We Make* you'll love these moving stories, also by Tara Marlow.

Camino Wandering

"This is a book every Camino traveller will want to have not just read, but as woman and a Camino walker, one we want to own and proudly have in our personal book collection, taking pride of place."

- Agnes Allen, Amazon Review

Beneath the Surface

"Heartbreaking...heartwarming...sad...joyful...overwhelming! I can't say enough about this book. I would give it six stars if I could."

- Vickie Waters, Goodreads Review

Available where books are sold.

www.ingramcontent.com/pod-product-compliance
Lightning Source LLC
Chambersburg PA
CBHW070551120726
47909CB00007B/2310